LYLA

SEAN DIETRICH

ISBN: 1506120261
ISBN-13: 978-1506120263

DEDICATION

I'd like to dedicate this book to the people of North Florida, because it is about them. I hereby submit this work to the gnarled Floridian family tree that I find myself a part of.

ACKNOWLEDGMENTS

First I'd like to acknowledge the many that read my first novel and overwhelmed me with their kindness. Also, my wife for being supportive in the development of this novel, and for having a sense of humor. I also want to thank my editor Amanda, who's contribution, both to this book, and to myself personally, cannot be measured in words. Lastly, I'd like to acknowledge the myriads of dysfunctional families that find a way to march forward, through the muck and mire.

1.

Sunset is the most fidgety time of the day. It's when the bay erupts with life upon life, and everything feeds on each other. Trout and mullet can't sit still; they jump right out of the water. If you have a cane pole handy, you can catch all the fish you could ever want at sundown. The pelicans know this too, and they don't need cane poles like we do. They fly above the water, close enough for their beaks to touch the surface, until they find supper. And they always find it.

At dusk, no fish is safe.

It was the perfect time of day for an argument.

"I need to know the truth," Daddy said. "Yes, or no?"

Mother waved her hand at him. "I swear, I didn't do anything with that man."

Daddy stood on a fat log that poked out of the water. His long legs made him look like an egret that high steps through the marshlands. He gazed across the water at the horizon, the shrimp trawlers were already out. They were heading out for the night to rake in mountains of squirming brown shrimp. The boats had metal armatures that spread outward, just like the wings of the pelicans.

Daddy listened to Mother, but his body was tense. He only believed her because he wanted to believe her. That's the way things worked sometimes.

"It's a rumor, Dale," Mother said. "Nothing more."

Daddy looked away from her.

Rumors. Our town had a way of birthing vicious rumors. It didn't take much doing, either. One person said something to another, and in that instant a rumor was born. The vile thing would plop onto the floor. It would be wet, crying, and unable to crawl, until someone came along and fed it. Before long, it was prancing in dusty streets, looking for left over scraps like a feral cat. Mother watched Daddy's back while he stared out at the bay water.

"I'd never step out on you, Dale," she said. "Never."

Daddy turned and looked at her with drooping eyes. He could look like a bloodhound when he wanted to.

"Never, Dale."

He gave no answer.

Mother stood poised with her hands on her round hips, her hair like wisps of honey-colored wheat swirling around her forehead. The smooth muscles in her face strained when she spoke. And she spoke a lot.

"Alright." Daddy sighed and looked back at the water. "Let's just forget about it, then."

There was no chance of that. She half liked the attention.

My mother was a woman who got too much attention for her own good. It wasn't that she asked for it, at least not on purpose, though she sometimes did that, too. It was that the attention seemed to find her.

Male attention.

Daddy was no fool; he knew that the men in town appreciated her. He knew how they smiled at her and wagged their tails whenever they saw her walk by. She even caught the eyes of clergymen and old codgers.

"Dale, I don't care what people are talking about, I wouldn't touch Phillip Sams with a hundred-foot pole. He's hideous."

Daddy shifted his weight from one hip to the other. "It's not about.... I don't care what the man looks like."

Mother sat down on the porch and drew her knees up to her chest. The two of them silent, looking out across the bay instead of at each other.

I suppose it was more comfortable to look away.

Each of them took turns exhaling big breaths until they could think of something else to say. But nothing came to them.

She knew Daddy had her beat when it came to arguing; she was still young, much too young to argue well. You have to know a lot about living to put up a good fight. Her only hope was to close her mouth.

Easier said than done.

"I swear," she said. "I never did anything to encourage Phillip

Sams. Nothing whatsoever. He just...."

My daddy glanced at her again. "I thought we were going to stop talking about it."

"We are."

"Good."

Mother was quiet for a moment, but she wasn't finished. "Dale, I ain't no wanderer, I just ain't."

"Lyla, I don't want to talk about it anymore."

"But I'm trying to tell you the God's-honest-truth."

"I said no more." His voice sounded firm.

"I'm a grown woman; you can't talk to me like that. I ain't no child."

But she was a child.

Daddy was older than her, with little room in his person for fibs or jokes. Life had hardened him; he would not tolerate such things. Especially not from his own damn family.

"Lyla," he said, in a calmer voice. But it was all that he could say because he loved her. Mother was the beloved pebble in his shoe, she dug into his flesh. His weakness for her was like the weakness some men have for drink. She was tranquilizing, disarming, at times inflaming, but she was easy to love.

Mother looked over at me. I stood behind the screen door, watching them fuss.

"Quinn," Daddy said to me. "Go back inside, son."

I stared at him, paralyzed with a slack-jawed snoopiness. I didn't know what they talked about, but it seemed important.

"Boy, you do as I say."

And I did.

Because I was a child, too.

~

Gathering oysters is an ancient thing. Ancient man learned how to eat oysters before he learned how to cook with fire. The Apalachee boys used to dive for them out in our bay, and lug them back to shore by the sack-full. But that was several hundreds of years ago. Before the tribes of them disappeared.

The blue collar stiffs were the ones who gathered oysters in our world. Men like my daddy. They were men with lots of little hungry mouths waiting back home. Most of them lean and humble fellas who acted cocky around each other—humble around women. Men with an affinity for unfiltered cigarettes, strong drink, and the Bible.

"The pickings are slim today," Daddy said. He scissored the tongs in the brown bay water, chewing on his pipe.

He swore again under his breath. It made a little puff of smoke shoot out of his pipe bowl. "Dammit," he said again.

My daddy smoked a pipe all his life. When he was a young man, it had been a blonde pipe, a crude one; he'd carved it himself, from a pine knot. But I never saw that one, as he'd retired it before I was born. It sat on the mantle in case of emergency. I'd only seen him use the one Mother gave him one Christmas. The pipe was cherry wood, with a straight shaft and a blood-colored bowl. It was pretty as you please, and it suited him.

Daddy brought the tongs up again and opened them. Out spilled a dozen rock oysters onto the deck of his boat.

Daddy surveyed the heap of stone-like creatures. "Hellfire. Ain't enough here to say grace over. I gotta good mind to call it quits for the day."

I knew he didn't mean a word of it.

The idea of Daddy calling it "quits" was ludicrous. He worked like a forty-mule team, come rain, shine, or two-day hangover.

He stabbed the tongs into the water and brought them up again. The tongs, themselves, weren't heavy. Not until you pulled them in with a load of oysters, then they weighed an elephantine ton.

"Jeezus, George, and Joe," he said, tapping his pipe against the side of the low rimmed boat. "Someone's been pulling from our beds. People get killed for that around here. Jeezus." He let out a sigh. "I reckon it's time to eat."

"Sir?" I pointed my good ear toward Daddy.

"I said let's have us some *lunch*."

Lunch was my favorite task of the day.

His too.

Daddy sat down and nudged the bucket of oysters toward me, tossing me a glove at the same time. We popped the cement tops off them, their slimy gray hearts, slippery and ripe.

He was a lightning-fast shucker, faster than I was, because he had a few decades on me. He could turn over ten faster than your mother could unbutton her overalls.

Daddy spread out a white towel on an overturned bucket and set his knife down. He reached underneath his seat and brought out a tin of white crackers and a jar of salt. We never salted good oysters, only puny ones that needed it. You could ruin a good oyster with too much salt.

The two of us slurped the craggy things then tossed the empty shells overboard like skipping stones. He could throw them a mile further than me.

Not everyone liked oysters, which was something I couldn't quite understand. Once, some yankee folks visiting from Michigan bought a bushel from Daddy. Michigan, Daddy had explained to me, was a long way off. Somewhere between Russia and Texas he said. The man got excited about trying the oysters, but the next morning, the yankee man told Daddy he had no idea how to eat the things. When Daddy showed him how to break the oysters open, the yankee was so disgusted he vomited right on the dock. Or, so the story goes.

Daddy laughed about it, but we weren't sure if it was entirely true or not.

"Quinn," Daddy said. "You ever think about what happens when we die?"

I turned my good ear toward him. "Sir?"

"When we *die*, do you ever wonder?"

"No."

Back then, I never thought of such things. I was too young to even know how they made honey. At the time, I still thought babies came from the United States Postal Service.

"Well, I think about it," he said. "I wonder about the animals in the woods. Wonder if they used to be human a long time ago. Apalachee, maybe."

"Indian animals?"

"Why not? It's how the Apalachee believed, in animal spirits." Daddy slurped from a shell. "The Indians knew more than we gave them credit for. Them Apalachee were smart as whips."

He lobbed the craggy thing into the water, and said, "There would've been thousands of them in these parts. Before the Spanish killed'em all. Think of that, thousands of campfires around this bay at night."

I took a gander at the bay and imagined such a sight. It would've looked like millions of fireflies from where we floated, so far from shore. Like yellow dots.

"Maybe the Indians were right," he said. "Maybe animals are at peace, you know, being animals instead of people."

Animals never seemed at peace to me. They were always working, gathering food. That is, except for the lazy feral cats who nosed around our garbage can. Those do-nothings could go full days without moving a muscle.

Daddy reached under his seat and removed a bag of oranges. He, like many other fishermen, liked to carry oranges on his boat. I was never sure why.

"You know." He peeled the orange with his pocket knife. "I reckon I'd want to come back as a heron. Walking all over the bay, fishing whenever I's hungry. Sleeping whenever I's tired."

He tossed me an orange.

"What about you, Quinn?"

I thought for a moment. Out of all the choices in the animal kingdom, it was impossible to choose my favorite. I was partial to rabbits, possums, also squirrels.

"A rabbit, maybe," I said. "Or a squirrel."

"A squirrel?"

"Yessir."

Daddy wore a bewildered look on his face.

"What'n the hell's wrong with you boy?"

Well.

I wasn't quite the poetic thinker my daddy was.

~

Daddy and I rode home in silence; neither of us had much to say. Both of us sat, baked from hours spent in the broiling sun, drifting on the slick bay.

I sat in the passenger seat, feeling a pleasant soreness settle in my shoulders. It was a fatigue from too much work. My muscles were young and tender. So was my skin. I wasn't tan like Daddy yet, and my joints didn't have the same strength.

Our brick and plank town whizzed past the truck windows at fifteen miles per hour. Past the city was nothing but woods. The pines of our forest towered over the road like old men with bushy eyebrows. Long, dark shadows flitting over the truck.

I glanced through the window behind me at the fish I'd caught earlier that day. There in the bed of was a basketful of trout. They flopped against the wicker clinging to life. Their speckled colors shimmered beneath their slimy membranes, their golden eyes open, perpetually shocked.

"You hooked some good looking 'specks," Daddy said. "They'll eat good tonight."

"Can I be the one who cleans them?"

A little smile ran across his face. "You feel comfortable doing it on your own?"

"Yessir."

He smiled bigger.

We were poor—bone-poor. But in our world, being poor didn't affect the supper table much. We were hunters and fishers, with enough gall to get out and find our food. You could harvest an entire supper near the bay, during any season, or any time of day. That is, if you didn't mind eating ladyfish, poke salad, or an occasional possum.

There was a Depression going around. Everyone talked about it. But, according to Daddy, it wasn't that big of a problem, not for us. It didn't make oystering any harder than it already was.

Daddy liked to say that the Depression only depressed rich people up north—Godless yankees. To him, the Depression wasn't bad enough to affect poor folks like us. "You can't depress an already depressed man," he'd often say.

And he was about right.

I can't imagine having had any less. And I didn't know what it meant to feel depressed. Not then.

Daddy drove the truck in silence. His bird-like face was dark against the bright window. Those long, knobby arms of his rested on the steering wheel like pine branches.

He looked at me and said something. I could see him moving his mouth, but I couldn't hear him, I only saw his lips form the words.

"Sir?" I turned my good ear to him.

"I was only saying," Daddy said, speaking louder. "You'll want to sharpen the boning knife before you gut them trout. It's dull."

"Yessir."

"You might as well sharpen the others too, while you're at it."

"Yessir."

He said something else thereafter, but I wasn't able to hear it. I just nodded and smiled. I'd gotten good at pretending like I could hear, even when I couldn't.

I was as deaf as a stump in my left ear. It was only my left--I was as fit as a fiddle in my right. A series of terrible infections during infancy robbed me of that my left ear forever. All I could hear was a ringing noise that sounded like a choir of crickets.

Still, being partially deaf wasn't all that bad. And as long as people talked loud, I could hear them in my right side.

My family accommodated me by shouting things to me. Aunt Patricia called us the Screaming Applewhites because my parents had gotten in the habit of speaking everything with booming voices. We could be heard from across the bay with no trouble at all. As a result, I spoke loud, too.

We neared our small house, which had been white once, but now it was the faintest mossy green. But that's how everything is down here. Humidity paints our entire world with moldy green dust. It covers everything sooner or later.

Ours was a small shotgun house, positioned on the edge of the longleaf forest, on the shore of the bay. Above it, the sunlight poked through the canopy of trees. Light scattered on our roof within a maze of shadows that crossed one another.

Through the windshield, we saw Mother sitting on the porch. She held Emma Claire, watching the truck bob up the driveway. It bounced with each bump in the path, rattling our bones loose.

"That mother of yours." Daddy wagged his head. "She suffers incurable boredom." He laughed, but it wasn't the funny kind, it was the reflective kind. The kind that had something behind it.

"Good Lord," he said. "I swear, it'll be the death of her."

~

The three of us sat around the wooden table, staring at our empty plates. They were heavy plates, enameled white, stained with years of use. My plate was as clean as it could be, except for a few discarded pin bones here and there.

Mother leaned back and ran her fingers through her shoulder-length hair. She yawned and let out a faint moan that suggested fatigue. Creamed potatoes had a way of making everyone a little sleepy after supper.

"What's the name of that man who sells his squash and strawberries in town?" Mother asked.

"Bill Anderson," Daddy said.

"Yep, him. I heard that he's leaving town and going to visit Ireland."

"Where's that?"

"Practically on the other side of the world."

Daddy was silent, packing his pipe with ribbons of black leaves from a small pouch.

"Yep," she said. "It's somewhere near England."

Daddy frowned. "England."

"Oh, Dale, I want to go there, I want to visit Ireland."

Daddy lit his pipe, his face enveloped in a fresh swirl of smoke. He crossed his legs and counted the water stains up on the ceiling. Daddy had never been anywhere noteworthy unless you count Wewahitchka or Tallahassee. He'd always been himself, there, with us, unmoving. He never made any fuss about it, either. Daddy was born a boring, old, settled-down man.

"Ireland," he said like a turtle.

"Oh, there're mountains, oceans, and lots of green."

"Ire-land," he drew out the vowels.

"You know, my ancestors from my mother's side are from Ireland."

Daddy let out a chuckle. "I don't know where my ancestors are from."

"Not at all?"

"I reckon that makes us just a family of common crackers."

"Hush, Dale, we're most certainly not crackers. Don't say that in front of Quinn."

"Why? It's true."

"I don't want Quinn thinking that we're poor crackers."

Too late.

I already believed we were crackers. I'd heard my daddy say it at least a million times before. Don't get me wrong, we weren't as hopeless as the Chaplain boys down the road, mind you. *They* were the crackerest of crackers. Sometimes those idiots didn't even wear pants. But there was no doubt; we had cracker in us.

"Well," Daddy laughed. "If we ain't crackers, we're at least a day-old bag of bread."

Whatever we were, we were people who made our own Christmas gifts out of wood scraps and twine. We saved tin cans and glass jars and used them for tableware. We didn't dare throw away curdled milk, but used it to make stink cheese. We ate every part of a coon, and used the bones for carving.

"Okay, we ain't crackers," Daddy said.

It might've made mother feel better to hear him say it. But it didn't change anything. Daddy saved leftover chicken parts to bait his pinfish traps. Then, he'd use leftover pinfish to feed the chickens. Round and round it went.

"You know," Mother said. "My great granddaddy got seasick when they left Ireland. Granny said that he puked over the side of the steamer."

"I ain't never been seasick," Daddy answered.

"I have. Once. In Uncle Dilsey's boat. Thought I was going to die."

"An orange would've cured that."

Mother furrowed her brows. "Oranges?"

"Yep, if Dilsey was worth his salt, he'd've known that. Old seaman's trick. Good luck."

"Well anyway, I don't want to talk about Dilsey." Mother adjusted herself in her seat. "He was a horrid man."

"But you gotta eat the rind of the orange, too. You gotta eat the skin for it to work right."

"I ain't eating orange rind."

Daddy took the pipe out of his mouth. "They ain't all that bad."

My mother did not want to talk about orange rinds. She wanted

Daddy to suggest a family vacation to Neverland.

She closed her eyes and smiled.

"Ireland, they drink coffee with whiskey in it. They got good whiskey over there too, it's dark. Not that clear shine, like you drink. That stuff makes my head hurt just to look at it."

Her last thought made Daddy smile.

"Dale," she said. "You think the sun looks different on the other side of the world?"

"Naw, the sun looks the same everywhere."

"How do you know?"

"The sun's the sun."

"But how can the backside of the sun look the same as the front side?"

Daddy thought about that for a second.

"You ever seen snow?" Mother asked.

"Once, only about a bucketful, in Quincy; awful stuff."

"It looks so beautiful in pictures, white like powdered sugar."

"Maybe." Daddy pointed at her with the stem of his pipe. "But it's cold as hell, and it'll make your fingers fall right off. I heard about frost bite. John Whitaker took work up North and lost these two fingers." He pointed to his ring-finer and pinky.

Mother looked down at her fingers, sliding the aluminum band off and on again. Back and forth.

"Oh, who am I fooling?" she said. "This is foolish talk."

Mother stood up and gathered up the plates from the table. "People like us ain't lucky enough to see snow. We don't go to exotic places, or drink Irish whiskey. People like us don't go any-damn-where. We eat pinto beans and 'taters until we die, poor and sorry. And then they bury us in cheap, pinewood boxes."

Daddy looked back at her. "Would you rather be buried in a *birch* wood box?"

"Don't tease me, Dale. I mean it."

"Lyla, now, calm down. It ain't foolish talk, not to me."

"It's stupid."

Mother lit the stove and put the dishwater on to boil. She threw her old, tan rags into the big pot and slammed the lid on top with a crashing noise. Her excitement had given way to her darkness, and her face had flattened. She screeched the fork on the metal plate, scraping the tiny fish bones into the waste can.

My daddy stood up, extending his heron legs, reaching his hands toward the ceiling. "I don't think it's stupid, not at all."

The muscles underneath his arms were tight and stoved up. He needed to be stretched, but not lengthened. He was long enough as it was.

Daddy's denim shirt was several shades lighter than it had been years before, more gray than it was blue. The dog days were like that. The sun turned his brown hair blonde, and his dark eyes gray. Even so, to him, it was better than being stuck in the goddam snow.

He let out a yawn.

Daddy looked tired and sun beaten. The skin on the backs of his hands was brown like shoe leather. Wormy veins ran along his forearms, crawling up his knuckles, burrowing between his fingers.

"Come on now, Lyla," he said softly. Then, he walked to Mother over at the sink and put his big paw on her shoulder.

"The other side of the world," he said. "Why, if you ask me, I think it's a fine idea. I reckon I'd like to see old Arr-land someday."

"You damn cracker," she said, swatting him with her dishtowel. "It's *Ire*-land."

2.

The smooth surface of the bay reflected the evening light. It turned the world a pinkish orange. Everything looked better under that kind of light, even our old clapboard house, which sat like a fat rabbit, guarding its warren of babies.

On the back porch, Daddy sat on a wood bench with a sock slid over his hand. He weaved a sewing needle in and out of the sock, careful not to stick himself with it. He wasn't good at darning, but for an unknown reason he preferred to darn his socks and patch his clothes himself. In fact, Daddy wouldn't let Mother touch anything of his. Even though Mother was a better seamstress than him. It didn't matter, he wanted to do it.

The truth was, Daddy preferred to do most everything himself. That's just how he was. If he couldn't do it himself, well then, to hell with it.

"Show me how to throw a baseball, Quinn." Mother stepped off the porch. "I want to learn how."

"Baseball?" I looked at her. "You wanna learn baseball?"

For the majority of my life, my mother was my peer, not at all like a parent. I don't think she ever grew up, not completely. Mother was fifteen years old when she had me. And fifteen-year-old girls aren't old enough to be good at motherhood yet. Neither are they old enough to be afraid of it. They're more suited to be peers with their children.

"Yeah, I want to learn baseball," Mother said.

"But you're a girl."

"So what?"

"Girls don't play baseball."

Daddy had been her only lover; he was five years older than her.

And, most of the time, it seemed like Daddy was her parent instead of husband. He made all the decisions that needed making. He was more burnished with experience than she was, and so she let him steer the boat. He was a flexible captain.

As long as everything went how he wanted it to go.

"Sure they can." She smacked my shoulder. "I can do anything a boy can do. I'm strong."

I handed her my leather mitt, she took it and slid it over her small hand.

"Not that hand, the other one."

"Like this?"

She looked ridiculous wearing that mitt.

Long ago, the wheat-haired fifteen-year-old said goodbye to summer kisses, and outdoor lovemaking. She traded such things in for breastfeeding and diapers. Diapers that needed changing every half hour. Her adolescence had vanished with my birth, like a cloud on a hot day. But it didn't make an adult out of her, not in the least.

She was as much a baby as I was.

Mother lobbed the ball, and it bounced off the side of the shed.

"No, you have to use your shoulder," I said, guiding her right arm backward. "See, like this."

Mother picked up the ball and threw it again. She flopped her arm like an overcooked noodle.

I laughed under my breath. This woman was no ball player.

She grinned. "How was that?"

"Try again."

She did. "How about that one?"

"Keep trying."

None of my other friends had mothers like her. None of the other mothers cared for baseball. Much less about learning to pitch. The mothers of my friends were older women, indifferent to matters of boyhood. They were ancient, wiry-haired spinsters, who used weird-smelling soap. Most of them talked to us boys as though we still wore diapers.

My mother was nothing like them. If anything, she was the object of adolescent fantasy.

The ball smacked the shed.

"How was that throw?" Mother asked, brushing a strand of hair from her face.

"Ma'am?" I asked, turning my good ear toward her.

"I *said*, how was that throw?"

"Not bad," I lied. "But don't hold your wrist so loose next time."

Mother looked back at Daddy. "Did you see that throw, Dale?"

He didn't look up from his sock. He held his mouth sideways while he sewed, squinting through the haze of moonshine clouding his eyes. Daddy liked to claim that moonshine made chores fun. Even darning socks. Except, that he stuck himself over and over again.

He did most of the chores in our house. My mother didn't do many. Except laundry. Mother didn't cook. And I used to wonder why my mother never cooked supper. I never wondered about it long; she was terrible at the stove. The only thing Mother could do in the kitchen was make sweet tea. Even a blind man could make sweet tea–with both hands tied behind his back.

Mother wasn't lazy, that wasn't it. She could be a downright hard worker whenever she wanted to be. The fact was, Mother had never cooked a thing in her life when she met Daddy. A fifteen-year-old bride is too much a baby to be good with a skillet. So, my father took control of the kitchen. He was glad to. He could cook anything that crawled, flew, slithered, swam, or grew in dirt. And that's exactly what he did.

A terrible cook like Mother never stood a chance against him.

She pitched the ball again. It thudded against the wall.

"How'd I do that time?" she asked.

"Better," I fibbed.

"Did you see that, Dale?" She turned back to look at Daddy again, but he had already walked inside. "Oh, I guess he's already starting on supper."

Every night we watched Daddy barefoot at the stove, sipping a jar of shine, preparing something in the iron pan. Without his oyster stew or skillet cornbread, we would have surely starved to death. Each night was the same: he fed us, he fed her, and then he ate. Always in that same order. He didn't complain about it, either, because he liked it that way.

Mother tried cooking now and then. Once, she attempted to make fried chicken. It took her a whole damn day. When Daddy got home that evening she greeted him with a mess of black chicken legs, topped in a gravy that tasted like water and flour.

Because that's what it was.

Mother would up for the pitch. Even though she couldn't pitch worth a cuss, she looked a little like a dancer. The long lines of her figure were slender, full around her hips.

"I did it that time?"

"Yeah."

I ran to get the ball.

"See?" She jumped. "I'm not that bad."

I picked up the baseball and threw it back to her.

"I wish your father would've seen that last throw."

"Naw, he doesn't like baseball, he thinks it's a waste of time."

"That's absurd. It's fun."

I heartily agreed.

Fun. That's all my mother was after. But motherhood wasn't fun, and neither was marriage. Often, I wondered if Mother liked marriage. I don't know if she did. There were moments where marriage seemed to suit her well. Other moments, it seemed to bind her like a cheap dress, riding up into all the creases of the body.

Don't get me wrong, she loved Daddy, there was no doubt about that. She idolized him. He was a savior of sorts to her. He'd rescued her from a life of grave poverty in Carrabelle and replaced it with a new life of mild poverty. She went from being a cracker on the bottom of the heap, to a cracker in the middle of the pile. But her love for Daddy was a different kind of love. It wasn't the thrilling kind, it was tamer than that, more solemn.

She tossed the ball back to me. It plopped into my glove with a dull sound.

"You know, pitching's not so hard," she said. "Not once you get the hang of it."

She said it like it was a concrete fact.

None of my friends had a mother like mine.

~

The sun hadn't risen yet. The dark of morning covered the forest with a damp quietness. Even the crickets were asleep.

Daddy sat on our front steps, sipping on his pipe, holding a hot tin mug. He was enshrined in a cloud of leather smelling smoke that circled him. I watched his glowing, red embers in the darkness, warm and fragrant.

He smoked all day long, every day, but never did he love it more than in the mornings. I wasn't sure why.

Years later, I finally understood that smoking in the mornings is euphoric. Even better than eating a whole pecan pie, or making love.

Or both.

A beat up truck pulled into our driveway. The headlights beamed in our faces, and we squinted our eyes. The vehicle was an ugly thing. The years of red dust and gravel-sized pock marks had been unkind to it. It looked like old strawberry on wheels.

Mounted on the hood of the truck was an alligator head. It grinned at me from its perch above the bright headlights. A horrific hood ornament that I could not take my eyes off of. I wondered how on earth such a thing found its way onto the hood of a truck.

Mullet jumped out of the driver's side and stretched his short arms up to the sky, yawning. Dollar romped out of the cab behind him; she headed straight for me in the darkness. Her collar jingled like a collection of Christmas bells. Dollar must've liked my smell. She pressed her wet nose against my pockets and sniffed beneath my arms. Then she bathed my face with her tongue, covering me in her foul breath and frothy slobber.

"Dollar," I laughed. "Stop it."

"Dollar." Mullet snapped his fingers. "Get back in the truck, girl."

Dollar darted away from me and leapt back into Mullet's dark truck. She watched us from behind the windshield, sitting erect and poised. Dollar was a hunter. The old girl coiled with raw energy, ready to comb the woods with her tail held high and nose down. And God-willing, she would tree a coon.

Daddy stood up, and his haze of smoke stood with him like a wispy friend. He placed his hat on his bleached hair and then yawned. His flag pole legs stretched to their full length.

The tote sack slung over his bony shoulder contained everything he needed for hunting. His muddy boots were firm shoes, meant for clomping through the brush. He could step on a pine cone and not feel it in those thick things.

"How ya been, Old Timer?" Mullet asked me.

"Good."

Mullet leaned closer. "What's that you got there?"

"Me? I ain't got nothing."

"Sure you do, right there. I can see it."

"Where?"

"There. Behind your ear."

I touched my ear, but there wasn't anything.

He was crazy.

"Right there," he said. Then Mullet showed me his empty hands and rolled his shirt sleeves up. He reached behind my bad ear and plucked out an orange.

Damned if it wasn't real.

I flicked my bad ear to see if I could make it happen again, but I had no luck. I suspected I had lots of oranges floating around inside that bad ear of mine. As a matter of fact, that might've explained why I couldn't hear out of it.

"How'd you do that?" I patted the side of my head.

"Never you mind. You do good, now, while your daddy's away." Mullet shook his finger at me. "Don't do nothing I wouldn't do."

"I won't."

Mullet winked and patted my head.

Daddy tossed his rifle in the bed of Mullet's truck and then crawled inside.

"I'll be back tonight, Quinn," said Daddy. "You help your mother do her errands in town today. I'll have us a few coons for supper tonight."

Mullet fired up his engine.

I marveled at their confidence. The two of them knew they would not return empty handed.

Things like that just didn't happen to crackers

~

I looked up at the empty sky; it was wide open and blue. The bright, round sun was high, showering the sidewalk with warmth. I don't know how people live in places without seeing the sun. Hellish places where there's nothing but snow and ice. It sounds God-awful, if you ask me.

I held Emma Claire in my arms while we walked along the hot sidewalk. Emma spoke gibberish into my bad ear, mumbling like an old woman. Her syrupy drool dripped on my neck, forming a blotch on my shoulder. Mother walked beside me.

Whenever we went into town, men tipped their hats to Mother. They hoped that she would notice them, but she didn't even turn her head. She just looked forward like they were invisible.

She was no fool.

She knew they were there.

"Quinn, what do you think caviar's like?" Mother asked.

"I don't know what that is," I said.

"Little fish eggs. You eat them. They're supposed to be very high class."

"High class?" I wrinkled my nose. "How can fish eggs be high class?"

Fish eggs seemed only a few steps away from fish poop.

"I don't know, but caviar is very high class." Mother swung her purse as she walked, the tail of her dress trailed behind like a flag. "It's what all the picture-stars eat."

"Picture-stars?"

"From the talkies."

"What are those?"

"You know. The movies."

"What do you mean?"

"The pictures. Hollywood pictures."

"Like the photographs we have of Granny?"

"No, not those, these pictures talk and move."

"Granny's eyes look strange in those photographs."

"I'm talking about the movies, silly. These pictures are big, on a huge wall in a dark room."

"I don't like those photos. Granny looks like a ghost."

"She does not." Mother smacked my shoulder. "One day we'll go to the movies."

I had little idea of what she was talking about, but it sounded like a grand idea just the same.

"I've seen a movie once," Mother said. "A lady played the piano along with it."

"The piano?"

"Cost us a nickel to get in."

"Just to look at a picture?"

"It costs more nowadays; the movies aren't silent, you get to witness the whole caboodle. Sound and all."

Emma Claire became restless in my arms. She screamed and flung her figurine behind me as far as she could throw it. The figurine bounced on the sidewalk several feet away from us. It landed in front of a group of men who were loafing near an open door. All the men wore overalls, bleached and muddy from work. None of them bothered to fetch the toy. They were too busy nursing Mason jars of hooch, laughing.

"Emma Claire," Mother scolded. "Don't throw your toy like that, it'll get all dirty."

Emma Claire made a grunt.

That little girl did whatever she wanted.

Mother walked over to the toy and bent over at the waist to pick it up. The group of men eyed her like a doe in the woods.

"Lyla, baby," a husky voice said behind her. "You're pretty enough to stop a man's heart."

Sitting on a bench with his legs crossed was Clarence Allgood. He was shirtless beneath his bib overalls. His face glistened with sweat, running down his neck. He was a powerful, broad young man.

Much younger than Daddy.

"Hi, Cheeter," Mother said.

She put the toy in her purse and stood up. Mother could've walked away from Clarence right then–but she didn't.

"Won't you join us for a nip?" Clarence asked.

"It's a little early in the day for a drink."

"You could drink a soda, or ginger ale, even. I know how you like ginger ale."

It was true, Mother loved ginger ale.

"No, thank you," she said.

Clarence stood up and set his glass down on the ground. His jar of hooch was sweating as bad as he was.

"Please sit down, visit with us for a spell."

"I'm sorry, Cheeter, but I have things to do."

Clarence sidestepped in front of Mother.

He rubbed his chin. "No one's called me Cheeter since I was a kid."

Mother sighed. "Well, aren't you sentimental today?"

He folded his arms and focused his gaze below her neck. "Reckon I am."

Clarence looked at me, and spoke, but I could not hear him.

"Sir?" I aimed my good ear at him.

"I said, your momma and I used to be more than friends," he shouted at me. "Back before I was a full grown gentleman."

"You don't have to shout at him," Mother said. "And you ain't no gentleman."

The men in the group laughed.

Clarence grinned showing his big teeth.

"Good day to you, Cheeter," Mother said. "Come on, Quinn."

Mother began to walk forward.

Clarence stepped in front of her. His thick body blocked the sidewalk like a caboose.

"Cheeter," she said, "quit playing games with me."

"Aw, I'm only fooling, Lyla, it was just a joke. I meant no disrespect to the little guy. I know he can't hear worth a shit."

Mother's face became angry.

"Watch your mouth, Clarence."

Clarence touched his lips and smiled again. "Sorry."

Mother paid him no mind and started to walk past him again.

"Now hang on a minute." He pressed his palm into her chest, pushing her backward. "You ain't going nowhere just yet, I say."

Mother was silent.

Clarence ran his finger up her shoulder, and along her neck. She turned her head away from him, but he gripped her chin and turned it to face himself. Then he lifted a strand of her wheat hair up to his nose and smelled it.

"Like flowers," he said. "Just like I remember. Like honeysuckles."

Emma Claire started to fuss and squirm in my arms like she'd had enough. She bellowed, screeching and writhing in my arms.

"Lyla," Clarence said. "Ain't we still friends?"

"Friends?"

"Yeah. What'd I do to you to make you hate me like you do?"

"I don't hate you."

"Well you sure as hell don't like me." He let out a laugh. "Why is that? What ever happened to us?"

"If you have to ask, then you already have the answer."

Mother was too smart for old Clarence.

And he didn't like it one bit.

Or maybe he did.

"Aw, Lyla, all I want is the same thing you gave Phillip Sams. What's that joker got that I ain't got?"

"I don't know what you're talking about." Mother looked away from Clarence.

"The hell you don't." Clarence took Mother's hand and kissed it. "I's a lot more fun that Phillip Sams is. You know that."

Clarence released her hand and stepped aside.

Mother nodded her head at him. "Good day to you, Cheeter."

She kept her gaze forward. Clarence watched her walk passed him. He cocked his arm back, high up in the air and then slapped Mother's rear with a loud snap. Mother stumbled forward, almost toppling her off her feet.

"Don't look back at them, Quinn," she said, regaining her balance. "Just keep walking."

And that's exactly what I did.

Clarence and his pack of friends howled with laughter behind us.

3.

Daddy was silent as he stood at the stove. His thin white cotton shirt was stained with red smudges and brown streaks. His long jeans were blotched with coon blood and dirt, hanging loose around his calf.

Daddy stood barefoot on the kitchen floor. He shifted his weight from one leg to the other while he worked behind the skillet. The same fibrous muscles that heaved oyster tongs into the bay now wielded a wooden spatula.

Mother stood in the kitchen doorway, watching him cook. She knew the division of labor wasn't fair in our household. Still, there wasn't anything she could do about it. She was only allowed to do dishes and make her sweet tea.

She sighed, looking at the back of Daddy's head.

"Dale, something happened this afternoon," Mother said, twirling her hair around her fingers.

Daddy was quiet. He wiped his hand on a dishtowel slung over his shoulder, then sipped from his jar of shine.

"Clarence Allgood," Mother said. "He was...."

Daddy listened.

"Lewd," she finished.

That was a strange word for Daddy.

"Lewd?" he asked.

"Wanton."

"Speak English, honey."

"Clarence was indecent."

Daddy knew that word.

To a Southerner, it was the worst word there was.

Emma Claire crawled along the shiny wood floor. She chased the marble I rolled in front of her like a baby lizard.

"Clarence was indecent in front of the children," Mother said. "You see, Clarence. Well, he...."

Mother grew silent and looked up at the hanging light in the kitchen. Its warm glow turned the kitchen yellow.

"He what?" Daddy asked.

"He slapped me."

"Slapped." Daddy stirred the stew. The steam rose from the black iron belly of the pot and curled around his face. "Where?"

"Right outside the Norma's. He was drunk as hell. I think he was trying to impress his friends."

"No, Lyla. I mean, where on your person did he slap you?"

Mother tapped her fingers on the door jamb, like she was playing a march on a snare drum. She looked at Daddy with scrunched up eyebrows, but all she could get was the back of his head.

"Well, the truth is," she said. "He spanked me. He almost knocked me down, too."

Daddy lifted his head but did not look at her.

"He gave me a bruise." Mother rubbed her hip. "That's how hard he swatted me."

Daddy's fist clenched—indecently.

Emma Claire crawled toward Daddy, looking upward. She scuffed along the smooth floor, finally grabbing hold of his trouser leg.

"Hey, girl," Daddy said. He bent low and rubbed her bald head.

Emma Claire made a gurgling noise. We all smiled whenever she did that.

Mother waited for Daddy to respond, but he did not.

Emma Claire had his attention now.

Daddy dipped his spoon into the stew. He blew on it, and squatted low, extending it to Emma Claire. Emma Claire put her whole mouth over the thing like she was trying to swallow it whole. She smacked her two palms together like a circus seal.

Everyone liked Daddy's coon stew.

Except for the coons.

Daddy wiped the slobber from Emma Claire's chest with his hand.

"Well?" Mother asked. "Did you hear what I just told you, Dale?"

Daddy flashed his dark eyes at Mother.

"Oh, I heard you," he said.

And you can bet damn well he did.

~

A bag of oysters weighs more than you think. Lifting one is like lifting a sack of rocks, or iron chains. Daddy could lift two oyster bags, one with each arm, both at the same time. Years of labor had built his muscles into tough limbs, capable of tremendous power. He could even throw the heavy bags if need be. Sometimes he did.

It amazed me to see such displays of strength. The heaviest thing I ever cared to lift was a drumstick of fried chicken.

But my daddy was a hard worker. Like many oystermen, Daddy was initiated into the craft when he was a boy. And like the other leathernecks, he worked long hours on the water until parched.

Many of the oystermen tonged for oysters all day long, sunrise to sundown. After they finished, they went shrimping at nighttime. Usually with jars of corn liquor in their hands. Daddy worked with these men all his life, he was one of them. He had the same habits they did. Though, he was temperate when it came to drinking and smoking. Daddy only partook of such things when the sun shining—and when it wasn't.

Daddy walked light on his feet carrying the heavy bags. His dry rotted leather gloves dark with sweat. His denim shirt stained with bottom muck from the bay

Clarence Allgood worked in his docked boat. He sat hunched over, beating the barnacles from the little mollusks with a culling iron. He was strong and squatty, covered in dirt and salt. Clarence wore the grayish-blue uniform of an impoverished oysterman. And he held the jelly jar of clear hooch to complete the outfit.

Daddy dropped his bags; they clacked on the ground, almost spilling open. He walked up to Clarence, his boots digging in the sand.

"Hey," Daddy called out in a deep voice. "Clarence Allgood, I'm talking to you."

Daddy eased his weight onto one hip and shot his dark eyes at Clarence like throwing spears.

Clarence looked at Daddy standing there, and waved him off with his dirty hand. Clarence was probably already drunk--if not drunk, he was at least a little tight.

"You'll step out of that damn boat if you're a man," Daddy said.

That did it.

Such phrases were time-tested words for starting trouble.

Clarence stood up and poked out his chest, like a dumb ape. He leapt off his boat and walked on the slushy shore toward Daddy. His leather boots made deep imprints in the soft ground, deeper than Daddy's made. Old Clarence had forty pounds on Daddy.

"Is that right?" Clarence sneered. "What would you know about being a man? Your old woman grinds her corn against any fool who'll have her," then he laughed. "It don't sound like she's got much of a real man back home. Sounds like all she's got waiting on her is a limp pecker and a few gray hairs."

Daddy was quiet.

His hair was anything but gray.

He was about to prove it.

Clarence walked closer to Daddy like a hound charging a coon. His gait was arrogant, his legs were thick.

Daddy's eyes locked on the tool in Clarence's hand. "Drop your culling iron, Cheeter."

"Why?"

"Because if you don't, you'll be wearing it."

Clarence looked at the small iron tool, smiled, and threw it down. It sank halfway into the sandy mud.

"What's the meaning of this, Dale?" Clarence said. "This about yeste—"

Daddy slugged him.

Before the man could figure out what happened, Daddy hit him again. He slammed his leather fist into the man's cheek with a crack. Clarence's jaw snapped sideways, and he fell backward.

Daddy sat down on him, right on top of his chest. Daddy removed his pocket knife and clicked it open. He held it to Clarence's Adam's apple and let the point dig in a little.

My daddy didn't waste any time cutting to the heart of the matter.

"You touch Lyla again, I'll carve your face off and feed it to the shrimp." He leaned in closer to Clarence. "You understand me, Cheeter?"

Clarence looked up at Daddy, a trickle of blood running down his lower lip. Clarence's eyes opened as wide as they could. He stared at the maniac sitting on top of his chest.

"I asked you a question, Cheeter." Daddy clicked his knife shut. "Do you understand what I just said to you, or do you need me to write it on your chest with this, here, knife?"

Daddy removed his sweaty, leather glove, exposing his hand. Then, he brought his arm back like a big league pitcher and slapped Clarence with enough force to knock his teeth out and make him go cross-eyed. He laid three licks on Clarence, one for each of Daddy's initials.

Every gawking oysterman nearby winced. They watched Daddy serve Clarence a big plate of what he had coming, and thanked God that it wasn't them.

"You want to act like a hog," Daddy stood up, and wiped his

sweaty face. "I'll slap you like a damn hog."

Clarence lay on the sand holding his jaw, rocking back and forth. All he could do was moan.

"And then I'll string you up and bleed you like one, too," Daddy said. "And don't you forget it."

He didn't.

~

"Dale, did you hurt him?" Mother asked.

Daddy did not answer.

"What happened? Please tell me."

But Daddy didn't talk about those kinds of things.

High-minded morality was Daddy's addiction. He used it like drunks used booze. His personal creed was what lubricated him. It made him calm and assured of himself. It acquainted him with right and wrong, and it kept him from the den of dishonesty. But most important, it kept him from laziness.

Laziness was the blackest of sins.

He lived life by cracker rules, not by Baptist ones. He would begin each day with a sip of moonshine and a handful of tobacco. Then, he'd work like a dog in the sun until he was dizzy. He'd save his earned money like a packrat, and he'd cuss about it like a fisherman. And at the end of each day, with a jelly jar in his hand, he'd mull over a memorized proverb from the good book.

Memorized because he didn't know how to read.

"You hit him?" Mother asked, bouncing Emma Claire on her knee.

Daddy grunted a response, then brought his hammer downward onto the tall wooden stake.

"You hit him hard?"

Daddy ignored the question.

"Did anyone see you do it?"

Daddy paid her no mind; it was indecent to boast about fighting. Especially not around women folk.

Fighting, chewing, smoking, drinking, swearing, and gambling, were not discussed in front of women. That is, unless a mess of women happened to be standing nearby. These were the kinds of morals he'd learned from his father. All Granddaddy's folksy parables about doing good were part of Daddy's creed. Daddy wouldn't cheat a squirrel out of an acorn. Only if thought it right, or if the squirrel had it coming.

"What'd he do after you hit him?" Mother asked.

Daddy's lean arm swung the hammer. He pounded the tall, wooden post into the tender ground one inch at a time.

"Did he hit you back?"

Daddy gave her nothing.

We arranged the wooden stakes in a square pattern. While Daddy drove stakes with the hammer, I worked inside the square area with a hoe. I thrashed the green grass, exposing the gray sandy soil underneath.

"I took care of him." Daddy itched his nose with his glove and sniffed. "That's all you need to know."

"What does that mean?"

"I just told you, Lyla."

"Aren't you going to give me any details?"

Daddy unbuttoned his denim shirt, removed it, and hung it on one of the wooden stakes. His lean, sinewy torso was pale, his forearms were as tan as hide. The muscles of his shoulders were thin slabs of tough meat slapped on bone.

"All you need to know is that I did what needed doing," Daddy said. "Now I don't want to speak any more about it. It's not decent."

Mother slumped her shoulders.

"Can you at least tell me where you hit him?"

"Lyla, I said drop it."

She did.

Mother smiled at Emma Claire and rocked her side to side. She smiled, imagining all the horrible things Daddy inflicted on Clarence Allgood for her benefit.

Mother knew that Daddy's fury was terrible. Though she'd never actually seen it in person, few women had. Neither was his anger something that turned inward on his kin. It was an anger that was only meant for intruders and cheats; his morals would have never permitted him to use such a weapon on his own kind.

Such a thing would've been indecent.

Daddy pounded the last stake into the ground. He mopped his brow with his forearm, wiping the humidity away. He jammed his wooden pipe between his teeth and lit it with a match.

It was time to reward himself with a smoke.

"Well, I'm glad to hear that you took care of it," Mother tested him, probing further. "Cheeter deserved what was coming to him. Which I imagine was terrible."

Daddy ignored her.

He began unrolling a spool of chicken wire and began fastening it to the posts.

"What in heaven's name are y'all building?" Mother rested her chin on top of Emma Claire's head.

"Can't you tell?" Daddy puffed his pipe and a blue cloud rose above his iron black hair. "It's a garden."

"Oh, I love gardens," Mother said. "My Granny had one when I was a girl. I used to help her tend it every summer. We had tomatoes, turnip greens, and the best snap peas you ever tasted."

"I know. You've told me a million times."

"Well, I loved it."

Never before did it occur to Mother that Daddy would take up gardening. But then, she never would've thought a grown man would do all the cooking and sock darning either.

At least she was still allowed to make her sweet tea.

Mother stretched her legs out and observed her toes. Her tiny feet looked like porcelain compared to the fat brown feet that I had.

Mother told me that the biggest parts on my body when I was born were my big toes. I found that hard to believe, since my ears were also large.

Daddy stood up straight. He removed the pipe from his mouth and watched Mother on the porch with Emma Claire.

"Dale." She looked at him. "I didn't know you knew anything about gardening. Do you think I could help you sometimes garden?"

Daddy put the pipe back in his mouth and smiled.

"Help?"

Mother shrugged. "I only meant sometimes."

"Lyla, I couldn't tell you the first thing about growing greens or picking potatoes." Daddy smiled again. "I'm building this garden for you."

Mother liked to have fallen right off the porch.

~

The birds perched themselves in the trees above our house. They screamed to one another across the woods in shrill chirps. Their accumulated voices could be deafening, but never annoying. The birds were our friends, and everyone regarded them as such.

Mother knelt in the soil, her wide-brimmed sunhat drooping over her face. She clawed her small hands into the earth, staining her nails with gray and red dirt. This patch of ground that we'd dug for her was the biggest thing she'd ever owned, and she intended to use it.

Mother and I dug rows into the garden. We sprinkled the seeds into the shallow trenches and then buried them.

The paper seed packets from the hardware store had pictures of vegetables printed on them, they looked like comic book illustrations. I'd never seen a tomato as big and round as the one on the packet, but it stirred my imagination. It looked like a little, red blimp with green leaves.

"Quinn?" she asked me. "Do you like anyone?"

"Sure, I like most everybody, except for Muffin Sanders, he's a little snot."

She smacked my shoulder. "No, that's not what I mean. I mean girls."

"Girls?"

"Don't play deaf, I can see your good ear facing me."

Mother picked a rock out of the soil and tossed it as far as she could toward the bay. It plopped into the water with a small splash.

"Come on, I know there's got to be someone," she probed. "A pretty girl? Someone who you wish goodnight on the North Star?"

"Huh?"

"You know, someone who you think about all day long."

Boys did not talk about girls with their mothers. It just wasn't done. If ever something was indecent, talking about girls with your mother was. I doubted the Apalachee boys spoke with their squaw mothers about such things either.

So I remained quiet.

Mother stopped digging and sat up straight. She wore a devious grin on her face.

"Oh my Lord, you do have a girl, you're in love."

"I am not."

"You are."

"I'm not."

"Yes you are."

She watched me to see if the truth would come leaking out of my nose.

I stared at her with my best poker face. A face I'd learned while playing cards behind the shed with my friends. I was the worst poker player in three counties.

"You can't hide it," she said. "You're blushing like a radish. Tell me, what color is her hair?"

I ignored Mother, shaking the seed package over the dirt row of the garden.

"Quinn, you have to tell me, I'm your Mother."

"Ma'am?"

"You can hear me."

"Ma'am?"

"Quinn, if you don't tell me, I'll make you sorry," she threatened me with the shovel. "I'll quit washing your underpants."

"Her hair is brown."

My mother's success at loosening my stiff tongue made her giddy. She clapped her dirty hands together, scattering bits of soil into the air.

"What's her name?"

It was pointless to resist Mother.

"It's Tara Lowery," I said.

"Tara?" She stabbed her spade into the dirt. "Little Tara Lowery? Bill's daughter? Oh, I can understand that, Tara's pretty."

She was more than pretty.

She was a poem.

Mother sat up straight and thought for a moment, looking out at the bay. She adjusted her hat on her head and wiped sweat from her face.

"Alright, Quinn, listen," she cleared her throat. "I'm going to give you some advice."

I wished we could've talked about something else instead.

"If you want Tara Lowery to go crazy for you, you can't let on how you feel about her. That'll ruin the whole thing."

I furrowed my eyebrows.

"Just hear me out; I know it seems backward, but it's the truth. She won't care a thing for you if she thinks that you like her. It's just the way girls are, we only want what we can't have."

I wrinkled my face. "I don't understand. I'm supposed to be a jerk?"

"Oh no, you still need to be charming. But the trick is not to give her the upper-hand. Girls don't want the upper-hand, it makes them bored. We don't ever want to get bored." She wagged her finger at me. "Don't you ever forget that."

Check.

Mother dug into the ground with both her hands as if she were digging holes on the beach. This woman was someone who I'd never understand. Not all the way.

"Being in love is fun," she said. "But it's also a big responsibility."

"How do you mean?"

"What I mean is that love ties you down to something big and heavy, like a piece of thick tough rope."

Sounds loads of fun to me.

"You think you can walk away from love any time you choose, but you can't. Then, one day, when the fun is over, you find that you're stuck, and that's just the way it goes."

She removed her hat and fanned her face with it.

I wondered why anyone would ever want to be in love if what she was suggesting was true. Maybe this was why the Apalachee boys didn't talk about girls with their mothers.

"Well." I shrugged. "It doesn't matter anyway. I don't even know how to talk to Tara. I get choked up whenever I'm around her, and I can't say a word."

Mother laughed.

"Oh, good God Almighty. You are just like your father."

And I was.

Quiet. With big ears, and even bigger feet.

4.

The bottoms of Daddy's feet were tough as turtles. Sometimes he'd poke safety pins in his feet to amuse my friends. He'd shove a pin into his thick, tan-colored pads and hold the stillest face you ever saw. We were always enthralled when he did that. Even more than when Mister Snicker swallowed his tongue and coughed it back up. I was certain Mister Snicker would accidentally kill himself doing that one day. And I intended to be there when he did.

Daddy's bare feet looked like big boats plodding through the grass in our yard. He hated shoes. He never wore them when he was at home. Not ever.

That day, Daddy was not wearing his work denim, but his baggy cotton clothes. His green shirt looked brand new and clean. It was a rare sight to see Daddy out of his work costume, looking almost lazy. It seemed downright sinful for him to dress like that.

"Lyla, who's this letter from?" Daddy asked her.

Mother bent over the tin bucket of suds and water, scrubbing the clothes on the washboard. If you closed your eyes, it sounded like Mother was sawing a log in half.

She liked doing laundry; it was one of the few chores she did.

"It says it's from your Aunt June," Mother said, glancing at the letter.

Mother could read like a hawk, any word you cared to throw at her. She was the only person in our home who knew the difference between the letter T, and the drink served over ice. Her granny had been a school teacher.

"From Aunt June?" Daddy said. "I wonder what it's about."

Daddy sliced the envelope open with his pocket knife. He unfolded a piece of paper and then held it up to Mother. "What's it say?"

Mother stopped washing and mopped her face with the back of her wrist, then scanned the letter. "Um, June says hello, and...." she paused. All the muscles in her face tensed.

"What is it?"

"It says...." She drew in a breath.

"What Lyla, what's it say?"

Mother was silent. Her eyes darted back and forth along the cursive text on the paper.

"It's not good?" he asked.

Mother shook her head.

"Tell me honey, what's Aunt June say?"

Mother looked at Daddy, tightening her lips. She pursed her face together, and her eyes became moist. "It's about your Daddy."

Daddy didn't blink. "What about him?"

"June says he's...." Mother covered her mouth. "Oh, Dale, I'm so sorry."

"Dead?"

Mother nodded, and a tear rolled down her cheek.

Daddy didn't breathe, neither did he move his head. He stood bone-still, looking at Mother.

Daddy had no brothers, no sisters, and his mother had passed away when he was a boy. He only heard stories about her. His daddy had raised him singlehanded, and they were tight as cotton weave.

But he was an orphan now.

He folded the letter up and slid it into his pocket.

Mother watched him. His gaunt figure drooped as he walked away. The wet laundry lay in her lap, saturating her skirt.

Daddy cleared his throat and turned to look at her. "Did the letter say how old he was?"

"They think he was going to be seventy in the fall."

"Seventy?"

"In the fall."

Daddy looked down. "Seventy."

He walked toward the edge of the bay. The twisted live oaks near the water made craggy dark shapes. Their branches spiraled toward the clouds, unable to catch whatever the hell they wanted.

The bay water lapped up onto the shore in a slurping rhythm. It made that familiar sound we heard in our sleep. The water was murky, like scallops of brown topped with frothy white foam.

I knew Daddy's daddy had shown him how to be a man. How to skin a coon, drink shine, build a house, and wage a good bet. All the things I was learning myself. Things that passed down from Granddaddy. In fact, the soil we stood on was land my granddaddy had won in a bet.

"The sheep are in the pasture." Daddy stared toward the frothy white capped waves in the bay. "That's what your granddaddy used to say whenever a storm was coming."

"A storm?" I asked him.

"A big storm."

"Are we fixing to get hit by a storm?"

"Yep, folks in town say it's a bad one, on its way up to us, one that's already hit the islands." Daddy turned to look at our house. "Folks are already boarding up windows in town. We need to do the same."

Daddy shoved his hands into his pockets and took in the looming gray sky above. I knew he wasn't thinking about the storm at all.

"Goddamn," Daddy said. "Seventy. That's pretty old."

It was more than old.

It was ancient.

~

Mother's pink floral dress was one that she'd made herself. She loved to make her own clothes; she'd spend hours on them, like an artist on a painting. Mother would draw her patterns on a big sheet of tissue paper bought from Mister Corn in town. She outlined her flourished concepts with a pencil, then cut her patterns out with scissors and pinned them together. In an afternoon or two, she'd make a dress that looked like it came straight out of a magazine. My mother was a hopeless dreamer. All her ideas came from magazines—even her ideas about life.

Mother laid in the den, reading a magazine, with her legs propped up on the arm of the sofa. She circled the illustrations that she liked best with a red crayon.

Mother's favorite designs were the wide-skirted dresses. She liked them to be made from striped or floral print bolts of fabric. They were the kind of dresses that women wore with pearls and a handbag. She also liked the illustrations of the angular women in the magazines. Their thick eyelashes and slender necks were unreal. The illustrations were of tall women wearing heels tall enough you could drive a Ford under them.

Mother lifted her glass of iced tea to her mouth, craning her neck to sip from it while lying on her back. Her white feet bounced on the arm of the sofa to an unheard rhythm even though the radio wasn't on.

Emma Claire walked around in circles, exploring the den. She touched every piece of furniture that was in the room, playing her own games with herself. She was learning to use her legs better each day. She marched like a clumsy soldier from one piece of furniture to the other. I kept an eye on Emma Claire while Mother read her magazine.

My job was to prevent Emma from drowning in a potted plant.

A very possible scenario.

All of a sudden, Daddy appeared in the doorway, holding a brown grocery bag under his arm. His face tired and drained.

"Hurricane's supposed to hit tomorrow," he said.

Mother sat up straight.

"Tomorrow? So soon?"

"Yep. Just heard it from Miss Taylor at the hardware store."

"Oh my heavens."

He shook his head once. "It's a big one too."

"Big? How big?"

"Hard to say, but folks say the biggest in a long time."

My eyes widened, and my thirteen-year-old imagination played cruel tricks on me. I envisioned the roofline of our town skinned clean by high winds, our shingles spinning above China, which I reckoned was somewhere near Idaho. I imagined our water tower floating in the Nile River like a popping cork.

"Supposed to be big enough to wipe out the islands down south," Daddy said.

"Heaven help us." Mother gathered her loose papers together and set her magazine down. "What'll we do?"

"Nothing we can do. Quinn and I'll nail a few boards over the windows, and we'll sit it out. Like always."

I was hoping for a better plan than that.

A plan involving moving to Idaho.

"Quinn," Daddy said to me. "I reckon we'll get started boarding up after supper."

Emma Claire walked up to Daddy and tilted her head back, looking up at him. He must've looked a hundred and ten feet tall. She grunted at him. It was her way of saying hello. Daddy scooped her up with one arm, smiled, and walked into the kitchen. His boots clomped on the creaky wooden floorboards.

Mother's lips moved, but I heard nothing.

"Ma'am?" I tilted my ear toward her.

"I said I just love hurricanes." Mother chewed on an ice cube.

"Love?"

Love was an awfully strong word.

"When I was your age, a hurricane took our house. Lots of people died. It flooded everything."

"And you love hurricanes?"

"Mmm hmm, love them. It left seven feet of water in Carrabelle. It was a bad one. We had to live with Granny for a year after that while Daddy and my brothers rebuilt our house."

"Seven feet of water, that's almost all the way up to our ceiling."

She smoothed her dress on her thighs. "Oh relax, it only sounds bad."

I was pretty sure that seven feet didn't just sound bad, but that it was, in fact, bad.

I thought about the cyclone in the sky, headed straight for our town. I'd seen bad storms before, but never anything as bad as what Mother described. I imagined myself sucked out of our house by a gale force wind. And the wind would carry me through the air and drop me all the way over in Carrabelle. They would find me hanging from a branch by my underpants.

Mother slapped my shoulder. "Oh don't be afraid, Mister Jack Rabbit, there ain't nothing to be afraid of. It'll probably end up being a little, tiny storm."

She couldn't have been more wrong.

~

The wind hissed and howled outside. It tried to find its way inside our house. It whistled through the cracks of our rickety home, like an evil spirit. The sheets of rain slapped our walls, vicious smacks cracking against the clapboards like an ox whip.

It was loud, loud enough so that even I could hear it.

The wind gave way to heavy pouring. The torrent picked up force until it was good and hopping mad. It dished out a mean walloping on us. The storm pummeled our tender roof with its fists, demanding that we let it inside.

"Dale, what about your truck?" Mother said. "Will it be okay?"

Daddy didn't answer her. He listened to the thrashing booms that struck the house and sipped his jar of shine.

We sat huddled in our pantry, surrounded by the grits and the flour. The candles on the shelves shot golden flames straight up into the dark stuffy air. They gave us just enough light to see one another's anxious faces before we all died horrible deaths.

Emma Claire wandered from person to person in the small space. It was a game of tag she played with herself, oblivious to our peril. Her chubby, uncoordinated legs marched up and down as she walked in a tight circle.

A bolt of lightning crashed outside. The gap underneath the pantry door flickered electric blue in the darkness. The thunder sounded like gunshots, only louder. I wondered if the world was ending right then and there. I wondered if we would drown in seven feet of water. I wondered if I would wake up dangling by my underpants from a pine limb.

Daddy looked upward in the darkness. It was as if he were looking straight through the ceiling at the storm with x-ray vision. He shook his head after every rumble with a grave face.

"That didn't sound good." He sipped from his jar again. "Sounded like a damn boulder hit the roof."

Emma Claire collapsed into Daddy's lap and touched his chest with her fleshy hand. He looked down at her and rubbed her back. She hummed in delight like a sleepy bullfrog.

"Emma Claire ain't scared," Daddy said smiling at her.

Emma cooed back at him with grin.

Something smashed against the roof again.

The sounds of the wind became stronger and more threatening. I closed my eyes. I imagined the wind blowing our house loose from its foundation, tumbling it end over end, plopping right it into the bay.

"Calm down, Quinn." Mother rested her hand on my trembling shoulder. "No one's going to die, try to relax."

But I couldn't relax, I had to pee. I closed my eyes tighter and plugged my good ear. I didn't want to hear the God-awful sounds that violated the world outside. It was no use, I heard every thunderous clap.

The lightning crashed like a cymbal.

It crashed again, vibrating the food on the shelves.

Emma Claire grinned again, stood up and wandered over to me. She laid her moist hand on my face and stared at my mouth.

"Hi, Emma Claire." I said.

Her eyes lit up.

I tried to ignore my full bladder. I tried to think about something cheerful–like surviving.

Emma Claire focused her eyes on my lips. Her intense gaze made her look like a cross-eyed donkey. She watched me in the candlelight with her dark eyes, keeping her head still. She blinked and touched my lips with her fingers, mushing my mouth together like biscuit dough.

"Hi, Kinn," she said.

They were her first words.

5.

Our clapboard house looked like someone scuffed over it with a cheese grater. A few long clapboards were missing, and the roof was almost skinned clean. But other than that, the house my granddaddy built with his own two hands still stood. We were one of the lucky families that year.

Mullet and Daddy stood, looking at the house with their hands on their hips.

"It's a mess." Mullet stroked his long beard. "But it ain't all that bad; you ought to see some of the houses up in town. Like a battlefield up there...."

"I heard Harold McCull's house didn't fare," Daddy said.

"Yep. Poor, old Harold. Little shit owes me nearly two hundred dollars."

"I heard Bill Teddy's house is gone, too. I heard there ain't nothing left but his shed in his backyard."

"I don't know about that." Mullet chewed his chaw. "But I owe old Bill nearly five hundred dollars."

"Well, cheer up," Daddy said. "You owe me more than that."

"Now don't you worry about that, Dale, I've included you in my living will. You'll get paid when I die."

"But I'm older than you are."

"Well, that ain't my fault."

"Mullet, did you see the big old tree on the other side of the bridge? The wind ripped it out by the roots." Daddy held out his hands like he was measuring a fish.

"Is that right?"

"Yessir, by the very roots. Oh, and what about the Smithers' house? I heard they got it bad too."

"Well, I saw the Smithers' house on the way over; it looked fine."

"It did?"

"Not a scratch on it."

"No, can't be."

"Hand to God." Mullet spit. "Of course, the house was seven streets over from where it used to be. But without a scratch, nonetheless."

The two men crawled up onto our ravaged roof and assessed what they saw. I couldn't quite hear them from all the way up there, but they seemed eager. These were men who liked to bust ass, to sweat until the sun dried them up. It was a sentiment that I didn't understand at that age.

Loving hard work.

When given the choice between work and rest, I preferred eating.

Daddy and Mullet tossed a big wet branch from the roof. It sailed through the air, and crashed on the ground below, busting in to a pieces. Then they looked around our property. The storm had littered our land with fallen trees. The trees looked like dead soldiers on the battlefield. They had trunks as big around as washtubs.

I touched one of the pines and wondered if the trees had souls like the animals. The fallen longleafs had done their best to defend themselves against the terrible storm.

They'd failed.

But at least I wasn't dangling in one of them, suspended by my underpants.

"Good Lord," Mullet called out from the rooftop. "It looks like someone spilled a box of pencils all over this land." He pointed across the horizon. "I ain't never seen such a mess."

I climbed onto the trunk of a fallen tree and stood on it. I looked out at the forest. I could smell the sticky sap from the destruction. It smelled strong enough to take my breath away, like pure turpentine.

"Reckon we got plenty of material for shingles," Mullet said. "Enough shingles to cover our whole damn county, ten times over."

Daddy put his hands on his belt and looked out at the mess.

My daddy would skin the dead trunks with his axe and make shingles out them. I touched the pine tree, broke off a slab of gray bark and held it up to the light. I suppose it didn't much matter whether they'd had souls or not. Their souls were gone now, anyway. The storm had taken them away, and that was all there was to it.

Storms do whatever the hell they please.

~

Daddy was the tallest man in the bunch. He stood several inches above his friends; he was also the skinniest. His leather tool belt dangled loose on his waist. It wouldn't go any tighter; there weren't any more holes in his belt. Daddy's long legs walked on the high-pitched roof like a spider creeping up a wall. He held his hammer high, slack fisted, like a man who knew how to use it.

"I need shingles over here," Daddy yelled to the others. "Right there, and right there too."

"Coming right up, boss," one of the men answered.

"Tar over here."

"Yessir, boss."

Daddy swung his hammer and pounded a shingle.

My daddy was a skilled individual. He could do a little of everything. He wouldn't let you forget it, either. Anything from fixing loose hinges, to building a wood skiff. Because of this, the other men looked to Daddy to tell them what to do. They were in luck: Daddy loved telling folks what to do. Along with how to do it.

Daddy directed them here and there. He told them to fetch that box of nails there, to sweep this here. And they did as they were told. That morning, the group of men crawled every inch of our roof like a bunch of fire ants on a dirt mound.

"Hey, fellas," Mother called from below.

Mother came walking off the back porch steps carrying a pitcher of ice tea in both hands. The product of her only kitchen-talent. The thirsty men all stood up straight and looked down at her–they didn't give a damn about the tea.

"Come down here and get it," she said.

Mother made decent tea. And that counted for a lot in our part of the world. Here, sweet tea is as important as deviled eggs and Jesus. Without things like that, church potlucks would be impossible.

The men scurried off the roof, scraping the seats of their pants on the rough shingles. Daddy stood on the roof watching them, with a pipe sticking out of his mouth. His silhouette was slim and dark against the midday sun.

"Did the storm do much damage up there?" Mother asked Mullet.

"Naw, it don't look so bad," he said. "My roof looks a whole lot worse than yours do."

"Oh my. I'm sorry to hear that."

"Me too, blew my roof to itty bits."

"Can it be fixed?"

"Oh sure."

She poured a jar of tea. "Did it skin your roof clean?"

"Just about," he said, brushing wood chips from his gray beard. "Some rich fella up in Columbus will find flecks of my house stuck to his daily newspaper."

"How'd we get so lucky?"

"Well, I reckon you don't cuss as much as me, and y'all pray more than I do."

We didn't pray; in fact, we never prayed. We went to church occasionally, but that didn't mean a thing. Daddy wouldn't even say blessings for meals. He claimed he couldn't remember the words. Sometimes, when company came over, he'd say grace, but he sounded ridiculous doing it.

Another man came walking up to Mother with his hat in his hands.

"Would you like some iced tea, Roddy?" Mother said.

"Yes, ma'am, I would love some."

I liked Roddy. All he ever did was smoke cigars and talk about pretty women. He had the best dirty jokes this side of the Mason Dixon line. They'd make your hair curl.

Daddy came behind Roddy and patted his shoulder with a sticky black hand. "I sure do appreciate all the help," Daddy announced to the group.

Daddy's clothes were transparent with sweat, his soaked white shirt looked like a shroud. The moisture at the bottom of his shirt, made it stick to his stomach like old wallpaper. It gave away how skinny he was underneath.

"Damn, it's hot up there," Daddy said. "If we keep up this pace, we can start on Roddy's house before sundown. We certainly won't finish it, but we'll might could get a start on it at least."

"Much appreciate that," Roddy said. "I need shingles over my outhouse. Yesterday, the catbirds all watched me do my business through a hole in the roof."

The men laughed.

"Lord God Almighty." Mullet set his empty jar on the table and wiped his gray beard. "Catbirds must be hard up for entertainment these days. If they got nothing better to do than watch you take a whookie."

The men laughed again.

And that was the last time I ever saw Daddy.

6.

The mosquito crawled along Mister Roddy's face. Roddy didn't even know the mosquito was there, he didn't seem to feel it. Mosquitoes can be like that sometimes, difficult to feel on your skin. Except for bull mosquitoes, everyone can feel those.

The little fly searched for a place to insert his dagger on Mister Roddy's white cheek. It walked in a zig-zag pattern, wandering around. The creature finally chose the patch of skin beneath Roddy's left eye. Of all places. It must have been a good place to have supper. Mister Roddy's blood must've been richer beneath his eyes.

Mister Roddy kept talking there on our doorstep. He had no idea his eyelid was prey to a hungry fly. Or maybe Roddy did know the mosquito was there, maybe he just didn't want to swat at it. Maybe Mister Roddy had enough death for one day.

Roddy wasn't there to tell jokes, or to be funny. Mister Roddy came to bare news. Bad news.

The task was given to him because it was his house where the accident occurred.

My mother bawled, undignified.

Indecently.

Though, I couldn't hear her because she was standing near my bad ear. I turned to look at her. Her face looked like it had shattered into a thousand pieces.

"I'm sorry, Ma'am," Mister Roddy kept saying over and over.

I remember him using that particular phrase. It's an easy phrase to read on the lips, and I was watching his mouth.

"I truly am sorry," Roddy said again.

Mother collapsed in the doorway, her eyes shut, and her mouth gaped open like a well. Her head pressed against the door, and her silky yellow hair covered half of her face. A long string of spit fell from her open mouth, all the way down to her chest. Her dress had ridden high up onto her pale thighs, you could see her underwear. But she was unaware of these things, Mother was a few steps away from being comatose.

Mister Roddy did not look at her bare thighs. Instead he focused his gaze on me, wringing his hat in his hands. I'd never seen his happy face look so serious.

For the first time in his life, Roddy was without a punch line.

I wish I could remember all that Mister Roddy said on the porch that afternoon. But as you get older, bad memories become cloudier. I can't remember any details about how my father fell. Or how exactly the claw hammer punctured his chest.

All I can seem to remember is that God-awful mosquito.

~

"I don't want your damned money," Mother said.

"It's not much," Brother Willock said.

"I don't care, I don't want it."

Mother was stubborn as a blue-nosed mule.

Brother Willock closed his eyes, sighed, and straightened his suit. It was a nice suit, with not a wrinkle to speak of. I knew Brother Willock probably hated the tan suit. Willock was an outdoorsman in his heart, everyone knew that about him. He could out-hunt most any man in town, any season of the year, any day of the week. And he could do it with nothing but a slingshot and a piece of cotton.

Blindfolded.

Brother Willock once took down a deer that was the size of a pickup truck, way out in Cottonwood. The young boys in town idolized Brother Willock for his triumph. I was one such worshipper. I would've gladly paid a dime to see the gigantic buck on the wall of his Methodist church office.

"The church has money for you, just the same," Brother Willock said to Mother. "It's not much. But we always give money to new widows."

Widows. There was that new word.

"I don't want money." Mother wiped her face.

"I know you don't, but I'm leaving it with you anyhow; you can do what you like with it."

Mother curled up in the chair, her face worn and pale. She seemed unaware that Brother Willock was even there at all. She sat still as a stone, with tired eyelids, blinking. If it weren't for her soft responses, I would've thought she was a stone statue.

"I'm going to send a few ladies to help you with some of your day-to-day things. They've volunteered to help you for as long as you need them."

Mother stared at the arm of her chair.

"Did you hear what I said, Miss Lyla?"

Charity was a repulsive thing to my parents. They were bred to hate it. Most crackers did. It was a belief deep seeded in poor people's minds, like a kind of religion. More real than Jesus could ever be. There was no way Mother could have made the preacher understand such things, so she remained silent.

"Whatever help you need." Brother Willock adjusted his awkward necktie. "Just let the ladies do whatever needs doing. They're happy to help."

Mother was silent.

Emma Claire wobbled through the living room, her white tummy leading the way. She galloped up to Brother Willock, stared at him, and tugged on his knee.

She was a charmer.

"Hey, Miss Emma." He pinched her cheek.

"I don't need their help," Mother said. "We'll manage."

"Ma'am?" Brother Willock said.

"I said I don't need their help." Mother nodded toward me. "Quinn can take over Dale's boat. He knows what to do."

"Oh, of course y'all will manage, Lyla." Willock stood up and buttoned his coat. "But the church ladies are coming over just the same. You'd better get used to having them around. Because they sure as hell won't take no for an answer."

Mother looked at him with a vacant stare. Then she sighed at him; it was all she could muster.

Brother Willock rested his hand on hers. He said something to her in a voice that I couldn't hear.

She half smiled. Her manners were fake, and her smile was insincere.

So was mine.

When we accompanied Brother Willock to the front door, he stood surveying the open forest. He looked in every direction, probably hoping to catch a glimpse of a giant buck, or a huge boar.

"Say, Quinn," he said. "You ever catch any turkeys back in here?"

I shook my head. I'd never seen a turkey in our woods. In fact, the only time I'd ever seen a turkey was when Brother Willock killed one.

Brother Willock gestured toward the woods. "Old Jenkins and I used to hunt around here centuries ago, used to get wild turkeys from time to time. I remember I killed me one right over yonder."

I flashed another fake smile at him.

I was in no mood to talk about turkeys.

"Of course," he said patting my head. "That was many, many years ago. I's about your age back then."

Brother Willock thrust his hands into his pockets and looked at Mother.

"Y'all don't hesitate to call on me if you need anything, anything."

He stepped off the porch and tipped his hat to us.

"I mean it now, call on me, anytime."

Mother and I waved goodbye to him standing in the doorway.

When he was gone, Mother collapsed and sat cross-legged against the front door. She looked at all the damaged pine trees. They stood against the sky like busted twigs. It was a sky that seemed so hateful to her. She cried some, but not a lot, I don't think she had enough tears left in her to do that.

~

The eggs I prepared weren't good. But they were all I knew how to cook in the kitchen, except for toast. Daddy taught me to make eggs long ago, and I never forgot how.

When I finished cooking them, they were dried yellow. I heaped them on a plate and doused them in a thick dollop of ketchup. Just the way Daddy used to eat them.

Just the way I ate them.

I made toast too, but I burned it.

Emma Claire swung her feet underneath her chair like she was riding a bicycle. The table came up to her nose. She chewed her food loudly, holding a fork in one hand and a handful of yellow eggs in the other. She looked at me plain-faced and happy. Emma Claire was too young to know how to be sad. At least not for long.

Skills like that come with age.

The fork slipped out of Emma Claire's hand. The metal bounced on the ground with a clank. She crawled off the chair, bending over to retrieve it.

Emma had painted her face with red ketchup, like Indian warpaint. I should've known better than to slather it all over a toddler's eggs like that.

She was making a mess.

Emma Claire climbed back onto her chair. She plunged her hand into the pile of eggs as if she were searching for a prize in a box of Cracker Jacks. She fingered around, pinching her food, squashing it between her fingers.

I watched her.

Emma Claire.

Her face was fat and round, and she was as skinny as a chicken bone. Her big brown eyes and tuft of hair were dark as the ace of spades.

Emma Claire's eyes met mine, and it excited her. She flashed her teeth at me, bouncing on her rump, waving her hands in the air. I wanted to laugh at her, but I couldn't.

I wasn't able laugh.

I wasn't even sure I could digest my food.

Her red face was sticky with ketchup.

She had no idea she was fatherless.

Lucky her.

~

I stood by the casket, shaking hands with white-faced people walking through the line. Most of them muttering trite phrases and meaningless proverbs. All of us remembering Daddy.

I could still smell him, Daddy. Literally. I was wearing one of his shirts. It was about four sizes too big for me, but I wore it anyway. It was the only nice shirt he'd ever owned, a shirt that he wore on Sundays–if we went to church. The shirt smelled like he was right there in the room. I can't tell you why I wore the oversized thing to his funeral. I must've looked like a damn fool.

A tall, skinny man with tough skin and a slick of steel gray hair came through the funeral line. He was bound by a necktie. He shook my hand as if I were grown. But I wasn't grown. I was a thirteen year old boy who barely knew how to pee standing up.

I knew this type of man. He was the type of fella my father had worked alongside his whole life. There were hundreds of them in our town, maybe more.

My daddy was one of them.

They were gaunt men who ate lunch on a boat, or on the bed of a truck. Sinewy laborers who could tong for oysters in their sleep. Most of them drank homemade liquor because they felt it was their God-given right. They were men who taught their boys to kill a coon with a rifle and quarter it with a Buck knife. Men who shrimped in the dark and fished in the daylight. They trapped hogs in pinewood traps and caught catfish in woven ones. They killed squirrels with slingshots and did not own a single book. Except for the Good Book.

"Your daddy was a good man," the thin man said. His hand was thick and heavy, like an iron skillet. The knotty muscles in his forearm looked like twisted ropes around a stock of bone.

I pointed my good ear at him, he spoke to soft for me to hear him well.

"Yessir boy, your daddy always did right by everyone. No matter what it cost him, he always was fair. Ain't many men like him in the world."

I didn't say anything to the man. I couldn't dislodge the words from my throat. A lump of something blocked them.

The thin man was right, I suppose. My daddy had been proud of his morals; he'd worn them like a badge. That's how crackers were. And even though my mother hated to admit it, my daddy was a cracker. The crackerest cracker there ever was.

And he was proud of it.

Daddy's backwoods compass made him hate liars. With a purple passion. And braggarts, God, he hated them worst of all. He'd call out a storyteller, and whoop a cheat without even pausing to roll up his sleeves. I'd seen him do it on more than one occasion.

He believed in honest sweat, and frequent tastes of moonshine. He believed in hard work, and cheap tobacco. He liked blue crab, but he liked trapping them more than he did eating them. He would not tolerate common laziness in a man. And he wouldn't tolerate the uncommon kind either.

I suppose that these are the things that make a man good.

~

There was a knock at the door.

More people offering their respects. I went to the door and pushed it open for the thousandth time. This time Mister Fletcher Bookman and his wife Catherine stood on our porch.

Mister Fletcher wore a tie and held a paper bag of groceries. Catherine held a tin casserole pan draped in a dishtowel. Their little girls, Francine and Annie stood beside them, dressed in lacy, white dresses. They were the prettiest things this side of Florida.

"Good evening, Quinn." Miss Catherine extended her dish to me. "This is for you and your family, honey."

"Thank you." I reached out and took it from her. "We much appreciate it, ma'am. Much appreciate it, indeed."

I was acting as grown up as I could, using genteel phrases. Just in case Francine and Annie were paying attention to me.

"It's chicken and dumplings." Catherine glanced at the dish.

"Oh, thank you, ma'am."

Catherine bit her lip. "How's your momma doing honey?"

"Fine, I guess. She's already asleep now."

She looked up at her husband.

"Well, we understand that darling. Will you tell her we stopped by to check on her?"

"Oh, yes, ma'am. Thank you, ma'am."

She smiled. "We just came to offer our respects."

"Thank you, ma'am."

Miss Catherine bent down close to me. "You've got to be strong for your momma, Quinn. It's your job, now, to be the man of this house." She paused. "My daddy died when I was a girl, just like you, my brother had to take over for him."

I looked toward Francine and Annie and I felt my face get warm. Whether I was a man or not, I certainly hoped those pretty things thought I was.

"Give our best to Lyla." Mister Fletcher tipped his hat to me. "You tell her to call on me if she needs anything."

Miss Catherine shot her husband a look.

"Well," Miss Catherine interjected. "Better tell her to call the church first if she needs anything. Brother Willock is better at those kinds of things."

"Yes, ma'am. I will, ma'am."

When the Bookmans left our porch, I went inside, and shut the door behind me. I walked to the kitchen table and set the tin casserole dish down next to the others. Stacks of casserole tins covered the table like a puzzle, piled on top of each other.

People kept bringing us food by the truckload.

That's how it works. Down here where we live, death and food go together. If you're going to have the gall to let someone die, you'd better be prepared to accept a truckload of food in return. Here, food accompanies grief, hand in hand. It also accompanies occasions of joy, baptisms, and any trivial event between. But most especially grief.

The care packages that people sent us were not only a kindness. They were also a type of penance for the living. Most of the tin casserole dishes piled up on our porch people sent out of obligation.

Though, obligation is its own form of love, I suppose.

I wiped the sweat off my forehead and stared at all the bags of food and casseroles in the kitchen. I wasn't even hungry enough to eat them.

Not in the least.

I flipped off the kitchen light and walked to my bedroom through our dark hallway. My feet creaked on the floorboards. I looked at my bed; Emma Claire was already fast asleep on it, with her mouth wide open like an old man.

~

I didn't sleep well. Not at all. The nights were hot. I remember the sheets clung to my sticky body as I slept next to Emma Claire. It was a restless sleep. It wasn't losing Daddy that kept me up, it was the dank, humid air. That, and Emma Claire flailing about during her slumber. I lay sweating, splayed out on a damp bed beside her.

It was four o'clock when I awoke. I looked out my window. It was black as tar outside, with only the moon visible in the sky. I sat up straight in the bed, rubbing my eyes. I heard the muffled sound of sobbing coming from the other room. I walked out from my room, still buttoning up my jeans, into our dark creaky hallway.

It was Mother.

I saw her through her cracked bedroom door, seated on her bed. Her lamp was on. She sat limp, doubled over, heaving tears onto the wood floor. I wasn't sure if she was vomiting or crying. I suppose there's not much of a difference between the two sometimes.

Emma Claire came waddling out of the room behind me and stared at me like a piglet.

"Momma?" she whispered.

"Hush now," I said. "Get back to bed, Emma Claire, Momma's fine. You go on back to sleep now."

Emma Claire scurried back to my bedroom. She crawled back into my bed and went straight to sleep in a matter of seconds. I still don't know how she could manage to do such a thing. That little girl could sleep through an earthquake without having to get up once to go tinkle.

I walked out to our front porch and closed the screen door behind me, being as quiet as I could be. I looked up at the moon in the purple night sky. I loved the moon, I don't know why. It was so far away, but it somehow seemed like my friend. It wasn't altogether impartial to me. It even seemed to sympathize with me at times.

Not at all like the hot sun. It doesn't give a damn about anyone.

There were already newly-delivered casserole dishes on the porch that morning. Even at such an early hour of the day. There were bunches of them. More than the day before. They just kept coming, piling up like coffins, wrapped up in dishrags. Every day, people loaded our front steps with food. Cornbread, pound cakes, dumplings, biscuits, butter beans, collards, taters, and fried chicken.

They were our rewards for surviving.

And most of it would go to waste.

I looked back up at the moon and sighed.

Too bad that Momma didn't give a damn about food; we had more than plenty of it to go around. Most days she sat in her room. She hoped that Emma Claire and I would carry on, fend for ourselves, and make due without her.

And we did.

I picked up an armful of casserole tins and walked back inside. I pulled back the cover on one of the tins, smelling the aroma of fresh baked biscuits. They were still warm. I lifted one from the dish and took a bite.

Those first few weeks, Emma and I ate like royalty. Thanks to all the deliveries from the church ladies in town, our cooler was full. Our kitchen table heaped with pans of the finest food in the county. It was kind of them. It reminded me that people in town were thinking about us.

Even if it was only for just the week.

~

"Greetings, Quinlan," old McRyan said, crawling from his horse-drawn carriage. "I hope you are well on this Tuesday."

McRyan was a white-haired Indian with skin that looked like shoe leather. He traveled through our town from time to time. He sold vegetables and honey from the back of his rickety horse drawn carriage.

McRyan claimed he was Apalachee, but that was impossible. The Apalachee had disappeared hundreds of years ago. McRyan claimed that he was two hundred and forty-six years old, that he had been present when the Spanish had inhabited our area. No one knew much about him, except that he was old, and stone-cold crazy.

He shuffled his feet in front of me, hunched over at the waist, and I followed him to the back of his cart.

"Come look at what I have today, Quinlan." He lifted the canvas tarp from the back. He showed me the crates of leafy greens and ripe red tomatoes. He picked up a carrot and held it up to the light. Then he let me taste his collard greens and try a bite of his okra. In the back of the car were two skinny, dead coons. They were nice coons.

"Here is what I think you will like best." McRyan removed a big jar of amber-colored honey from one of the crates. The translucent honey was as brown as strong coffee.

"Here, taste it." He extended the jar to me. "Go ahead."

I dipped my index finger in the jar and then licked the honey from it.

"How much is it?" I asked.

"Oh no, Quinlan, I did not come to sell. I come to trade with you."

"Trade?"

"Yes." He bobbed his head up and down. His loose wrinkled cheeks wobbled. "As I have traded with your father in the past."

"But I don't have nothing good to trade sir."

"Before, in the past, your father traded with me the moonshine."

"Shine?" I laughed. "We got plenty of shine in the pantry." I lowered my head. "I reckon since Daddy ain't here to drink it no more, I can trade with you."

"Only if you want to, Quinlan."

I shrugged. "I suppose it don't matter."

McRyan put his crooked hand on my shoulder, and it felt heavy. His dark slitted eyes were black, worn soft by time. "You have lost your father."

And that was all he said.

He stared at me with eyes as black as calm river water, and he pointed upward.

I looked up at the blue sky above me.

"Quinlan, my people say, no man looks at the same sky twice." He waved his old hand. "It changes. Like all things. See, now it is different now that it was before."

I was silent, watching the clouds somersault over each other, my head tilted backward.

McRyan was as crazy as those coons in the back of his wagon. Maybe even crazier than that. But I appreciated his kindness just the same.

"You want me to go in and get the shine from the pantry?" I asked.

"Mmm hmm, yes I do. I will wait for you, Quinlan."

And he surely did.

7.

Somewhere along the way my pants, stopped fitting me. Before long, the bottoms of my pant legs landed just above my ankles, like flood pants. Meaning: in the event of a flood, my pants would fare just fine.

My arms were getting longer, too. Looking in the mirror was a horrible thing to do. The mirrors reflected a gangly goose with a long neck, big nose, and tight pants.

While it was true, over the last few years I'd gotten uglier, I'd also gotten stronger. I could tong for oysters all day, dock the skiff by myself, and I could lift almost anything. Good as any man could. A few girls paid notice to me, but I was pretty sure they were only gawking at how big my ears were.

The girls in our town transformed from awkward, lanky creatures into vestal vixens overnight. Their clothes were tighter too, but unlike me, it worked out well for them.

I worked like a dog each day, all day long. Emma Claire hated to see me leave for work in the mornings. She spent her days alone, entertaining herself with the feral cats in our backyard. They were her only friends. It broke my heart to leave her there by herself, but I had no other choice.

Money didn't earn itself,as my father used to say.

In the beginning, I brought her along with me on the oyster skiff. It turned out to be a horrible idea. She talked a blue streak the entire day, never pausing to even take a breath. Emma Claire would shout to the other oystermen in her giddy voice. "Hey!" she'd yell. "I'm Emma Claire, what's your name? How many years old are you?"

But the old oystermen didn't like talking about their ages.

In fact, oystermen didn't like talking at all.

"Don't leave me," Emma Claire said, holding me. "Don't go today."

"I have to, Emma." I peeled her arms from around my waist. "I need to earn money, I have to. I'm doing it for all of us."

Her wet face stared at me, the corners of her mouth turned in a frown. "Please, don't go."

"Emma, don't make this hard, it's not for long."

Every morning Emma Claire held me like this, squeezing me as tight as she could. Emma believed that when I left her presence I would die. I couldn't convince her otherwise.

While Emma squeezed me, I glanced back at Mother's closed bedroom door. Mother was a recluse.

"I miss you," Emma Claire said.

"I'll miss you too Emma Claire, but you have to let me go now."

"I can't."

"You have to, honey."

"No."

Mother hardly came out of her room; she lived in there. Sometimes she came out to join us for supper. She had to eat. But whenever Mother showed herself, she was usually too quiet to be noticed. It was like she'd become a stranger to us.

Whenever Mother would wander out of her room, which was rare, she looked uncomfortable. It was almost as if she was unsure about what it was that she ought to be doing. So she'd turn around, mosey back to her bedroom, then shut the door.

Sometimes, I'd hear Mother humming a song to herself through the walls. I could never tell what song she was humming. It was a strange melody. And even though she was in the other room, not more than a few paces away from us, I knew she was gone.

~

"We're in the money today," Mullet said.

The two of us worked side by side on the same skiff, adrift on the flat bay water. I beat the oysters with a culling iron. I knocked off the jagged barnacles from each craggy shell, one by one. After only a few moments, I'd filled a whole basket with them.

"Damn, Old Timer," he said. "You're a fast hand. Fastest I ever seen."

I couldn't hear him, but I could read his lips.

Often, Mullet would forget to stand on my right side when talking. I felt like a deaf boy whenever I worked alongside him. I'd never felt that way working with Daddy. Daddy knew where to stand, and how loud to talk so that I could hear every word.

The heap of oysters on the bow of the boat was enormous. The pile looked like a little obsidian mountain of jagged rocks. Mullet opened the tongs, spilling a load of rough oysters on the deck. I

Mullet set the huge tongs down and removed a little flask from his side pocket. He took a nip, wiped his mouth with his arm, and extended it to me.

I looked at him, unblinking.

"It's whiskey."

"Whiskey?"

"It ain't that shine your daddy drank. That stuff gives me bad headaches. I don't know how that old bird did it. Nasty stuff."

He handed me the flask, I sniffed it.

"Boy," he said. "If you don't deserve a swallow I don't know anyone who does. After these last two years, you're a grown man in anybody's opinion."

I put it to my lips and took a baby sip. It burned my throat and made me cough. The whiskey was pungent, but pleasant.

"Go ahead, Old Timer, take you a real snort. We both deserve it after having such a good day. It won't kill you."

I took a swig and handed it back to him.

My body got warmer from the drink. I smacked at the oysters and coughed a little. Mullet smiled at me. It was my initiation into a new club. He sat down next to me and took another pull from the flask before sliding it into his pocket.

He wiped his forehead with a handkerchief. My daddy had respected Mullet when he was alive, and that was a rare thing for Daddy to do. Sometimes Daddy didn't even respect himself.

When Daddy died, Mullet hired me to work with him. And so far, I'd worked two summers with him, and one winter. Sometimes we worked on his boat, sometimes on Daddy's old boat. Mullet paid me at the end of every week in big, heavy silver dollars. And every week I asked if he was overpaying me by an extra dollar. He swore up and down that the numbers were right.

I knew they weren't.

I saw Mullet move his mouth, and I wasn't able to read his lips this time.

"Sir?" I aimed my good ear at him.

"Oh, I'm sorry, I keep forgetting about your busted head holes, let's trade sides."

Mullet walked over to my other side.

He said in a loud voice, "Do you feel that breeze? Feels good don't it?"

It did feel good.

The bay breeze was gentle, but steady. The air smelled like dead shrimp, and mud, and I loved it. The wind is an oysterman's friend. It helped keep the wicked mosquitoes away from the boats on the water. Otherwise, the little bastards would eat a fisherman alive, one nibble at a time.

Mullet cleared his throat. "How's your momma doing?"

"Fine, I guess," The whiskey had loosened my tongue. "We hardly see her, though. She's always in her bedroom."

"Sounds about normal to me."

He tossed an oyster into the basket, picked up another and just stared at it. I watched him sitting there. Mullet was a short man with leathery skin. His brilliant blue eyes looked like crystal, and his legs were little stumps. He had a thick gray beard that made him look like one of Santa's elves.

If Santa's elves chewed plug tobacco.

"She don't want nothing to do with us anymore," I said.

"Yeah, I reckon that's about normal, too."

Mullet tossed a shell into the basket.

He changed the subject. "You know what happened to me the other day? I saw a goat in my front yard. A little doe."

"A goat?"

"Hand to God. I don't know where she come from. And when I goes to the back of the house, you know what?"

"What."

"There's another goat standing in the backyard too. A stout little billie, just staring at me. Goats got them weird eyes you know?"

Goats did have weird eyes.

"Hell," he said. "I don't know where they came from. Nobody seems to know where they come from. I don't know anyone stupid enough to have goats."

I laughed. It was the whiskey that was doing the laughing.

"So yesterday," he went on. "I spent all afternoon building a damn fence for them little things." He threw a tiny oyster overboard. "I don't know the first thing about goats. Not the first cotton-picking thing. I don't even know what they hell they eat."

He took another sip from his flask.

"But I got two of them now," he said. "Ain't that something?"

Mullet reached underneath his seat and brought out a bag of ripe full oranges. He reached in the bag, picked out a big one, and then tossed it to me. "I brought us some oranges today. God. Your daddy sure did love oranges."

~

The green, sticky sweetness of summer accompanies the most content time of year. It ought to be a season about peanuts, cotton, and fishing. Not about sadness. It's supposed to be a time when food is richer, brighter, when gardens show off. When speckled trout jump right into your boat and beg you to eat them.

My skin was dark that summer, not coffee-dark, mind you, but roasted-turkey-dark. Mullet and I had spent enough time out on the water that my skin was beginning to look as leathery as his. I liked to press my thumb on my skin and lift it to peek at the white underneath my thumbprint.

All the girls were dark, too, giving us boys a reason to notice them. As if we needed another reason. The good-looking girls were pretty, the plain-looking girls were even prettier.

All the boys in the baseball uniforms sat on the bench. Rory McAllister sat on the other end of the dugout, with his yellow hat on backward. He was a loud obnoxious boy, who had enough money to buy and sell whatever he wanted.

"It's true," Rory said, tossing his ball up into the air, and then catching it. "That's what I heard."

"Naw, Quinn's daddy wouldn't have jumped off a roof on purpose," another boy said. "No one in their right mind would do that."

"It's true. Downright sad, if you ask me."

The dugout was as hot and muggy as an attic. Double-hot if you were wearing a woven cotton uniform with a yellow number on it. The uniform never fit me right.

"I heard his daddy slipped. That's what my paw said," the other boy said.

"Your paw don't know squat. He didn't see it happen," Rory said.

"My paw knows stuff."

"Well, suit yourself, believe whatever you want."

"Wonder who'll marry Quinn's Momma, she's pretty. My daddy says she's arm candy."

"I heard his momma was a slut. Heard she used to screw Phillip

Sams from time to time while her old man was still alive."

"Well, I'd marry her anyhow."

"Shoot, she wouldn't want you. You're a little runt squirrel."

"I'd marry her a hundred times."

"You're a dummy."

"A hundred times a hundred."

The boys in the dugout didn't think I could hear them talking. They didn't even bother whispering around me; they thought I was practically deaf. The truth was, I was only partially deaf. There's a big difference between the two words–practically and partially.

I turned my head to look at Rory.

"I can hear you fools talking." I spat on the ground. "Plain as day, I could hear everything you just said."

The boys stopped their chatter and stared at me.

"I'm not deaf," I said. "Not all the way."

As if it made a difference to them.

They exchanged looks with one another, guilty looks.

"Aw, come off it, we didn't say nothing, Quinn," Rory said.

Then Rory bent his head down and whispered something to another boy.

"I could hear that," I lied.

"Oh yeah? What'd I just say, then?"

I was silent.

"Hey, Quinn," another boy said. "It's your turn at the plate."

He was right, it was up next for batting.

Rory wrinkled his face at me. "You going to get up to bat, or are you going to sit here and moan like a titty-baby?"

"I ain't no titty-baby."

"You are so."

"No I ain't."

"You are so. I'll bet you still got all your baby teeth."

The other boys bubbled with laughter at such a remark.

I stood up and chose a bat from the pile. I tapped it on the heels of my shoes. The chaw of tobacco in my cheek tasted like sweetened bits of leather. My head was swimming from the nicotine.

I exited the dugout and walked toward the plate. Frazzer, the pitcher watched me from his dirt mound with a smirk on his face. His scruffy, red hair poked from beneath his ball cap. Those big eyes he had followed me like darts as I walked to home plate.

I held the wood slugger high behind my head. My crouching batting stance was one I'd been working on all spring. I held my elbows up high, my legs spread wide apart, feet dug into the dirt. I wasn't a bad ballplayer. I was no Dodger, mind you, but I could hold my own.

Frazzer wound up and threw the ball.

His first pitch was bad.

"Ball," the umpire said behind me.

Second pitch: I swung as hard as I could and missed.

"Strike!" the umpire said with a wide open shout.

The third pitch flew by me like a rocket. Another ball.

Fourth pitch: I swung so hard I almost fell on my face, but missed.

The umpire threw his hand out to the side and yelled, "Strike two."

That old umpire was getting on my nerves.

The fifth pitch, I gave it everything I had. I swung so hard that I heard the tendons in my shoulder pop.

The bat and the ball connected with a loud, wooden *crack*. The baseball sailed through the air like an airplane. It arced over the dusty ball field and bounced over the back fence. I saw it roll through the weeds and into the forest.

"Run!" the catcher behind me waved his glove. "Home run, you dope. Run the bases, Quinn!"

My teammates in the dugout stood motionless in their dusty uniforms watching me. Their hands shoved in their pockets, and their white faces were blank. The brats didn't care to cheer. I was just a partially deaf cracker who'd hit a home run.

Home runs hit by crackers don't count.

I stood there, my legs locked like pine trees. I did not run. I touched my cheek and realized it was moist from my own tears.

The boys started to laugh like clowns.

Without warning, I flung the bat toward the dugout with all my strength. It helicoptered through the air and bounced off the chain link fence. The boys cackled like donkeys, but I couldn't hear them.

Sometimes it's good to be partially deaf.

I ran as fast as I could, lifting my knees high into the air, but I didn't jog around the bases. No. I sprinted off the field, down the street, and just kept going.

~

I kicked the dirt on the sandy road, swinging my arms as I walked. A puff of dust swirled around me. The wind caught the dust and then carried off to wherever it is that the wind goes to hide. Upward like a small tornado.

I looked into the sky and thought about the whirly-copters that Daddy used to make. He'd use his pocket knife to whittle them out of fresh pine sticks. Then he'd spin them faster than anyone alive could spin them. They'd fly as high as the clouds, and then fall back to the earth, like they'd been licked by the sky.

My heavy baseball uniform was suffocating me as I walked under the wide open sun. I was sure I was going to die a slow death by smothering in it. They'd find me dead, in my silly uniform. Then they'd say, "Quinn sure was a nice guy, damn shame about that hot uniform he had to wear. Killed him dead." And then some fool would answer, "I heard old Quinn was a titty-baby." I would haunt that fool for the rest of his natural life for saying such a thing.

Sweat dripped down my legs, under my arms. Only a few weeks earlier, I'd begun to notice that my clothes smelled horrible. Like old rotten onions. I'd never smelled quite that bad before. My body was changing for the worse, I smelled as pungent as a clam whenever I broke a sweat. I only prayed that some girl out there liked the smell of oyster stew enough to marry me.

I sniffed the arm of my shirt and it gagged me.

I kicked up another cloud of dust with my foot and watched it get tangled up in the wind again.

I thought about my home run. It felt good to smash the baseball with my bat, to feel the power of the wood in my hands. It would be the first home run of my entire baseball career. If you can even call it a career. I thought about retiring from the sport altogether. I didn't care if I ever saw Rory McAllister's sorry face again. Our coach, Tater, treated Rory like royalty because the McAllisters had money. It didn't seem fair. In fact, I was pretty sure it wasn't fair.

Still, our coach Tater was a nice man. He used to be friends with my Daddy when the two of them were boys. Tater owned the hardware store. His daddy, Mister Taylor, left the store to him when he died, and now Tater was modernizing things.

He had washing machines for sale in the front window. God help us. Washing machines. The things looked like something from another world. The young boys in town pressed their faces against the glass to look at them on display. However, the little boys were more interested in the advertisements than the washing machines themselves. The advertisements featured a busty blonde using the washing contraption. It was the closest thing to seeing a peep show you could get in our town. The Methodist women pitched a fit about those advertisements. They insisted that the ads were smut, and the coach finally took them down. All that, over a washing machine. I wonder what would've happened if he ever started selling women's bathing suits.

I looked forward to the day.

I felt embarrassed. I shouldn't have ruined the coach's game like that, throwing a tantrum. I was almost a grown man who ought to know better.

I don't know what part of my body that outburst had come from. I wasn't prone to pitching fits like that. Mother always said that I'd been the calmest baby she ever saw. She said I never made a noise at all when I entered this world. My sister, on the other hand, screamed like the devil had her by the ankle.

I saw a large shadow approach me from behind. I stepped to the side of the road to let the vehicle pass.

"Quinn," a voice said behind me.

I turned to see a dingy, red truck with a stuffed gator head mounted on the hood. It was driving next to me at a snail's pace. Mullet's head craned out of the truck window. The side of his cheek poked out with tobacco.

"Hop in slugger," he said throwing the passenger door open. "I'll give you a ride."

~

Mullet draped his arm out of the driver's window as he drove. He spoke in such a quiet voice that I couldn't hear him over the whir of the engine.

I didn't know Mullet, not well. Few people did. The only thing that people knew about him was that he was different. That was reason enough for folks to avoid him. And avoid him they did. Strangely, my daddy liked Mullet. It was something about the man's directness that Daddy appreciated. Daddy liked people who had the gumption to speak their own mind. Daddy also liked people who nipped at the bottle now and again.

Mullet did both.

I looked around the cab of Mullet's truck. Little swirl marks and floral designs decorated the truck from floorboards to ceiling. A mirage of paintings and drawings connected to each other, like an enormous tattoo. There were drawings of flowers, trees, fish, naked women, and numbers. My eye followed the trail of one picture into the next picture, and then the next. Before I knew it, the strange maze of art had me mesmerized.

"Hey." Mullet tapped me. "Don't you hear what I'm saying to you, Old Timer?"

"Sir?" I aimed my good ear at him.

"I said," he yelled. "Why didn't you whoop those boys' tails earlier?

They had it coming."

"Sir?"

He yelled louder.

"No," I said. "I can hear you fine, I just don't understand what you mean, exactly."

"The hell you don't. You threw that bat at Rory McAllister like you was trying to knock his block off." He spit into an old cup.

"You were at the ballgame?"

"Of course I was there. I go to every game."

That surprised me. No one came to our games except the wealthy parents who didn't have to work. And even they were slim pickings. Our little bleachers were lucky to have nineteen or twenty people.

On a good day, twenty-two.

"I ain't never seen you there," I said.

"Well, I don't exactly announce myself to the world." He chuckled. "I watch from over the back fence usually."

"But, why?"

"Well, that's a downright ignorant thing to ask." He turned to me. "Because I like baseball, that's why you dummy." Mullet wiped the brown spit off of his whiskers. "I used to play back in Columbus. Long time ago."

"You played ball?"

"Yes, sir."

"Were you any good?"

"Don't change the subject." Mullet shook his finger at me. "You should've made good on your threat and knocked old Rory McAllister sideways."

"Rory's a hateful wretch."

"All the more reason."

"He said cruel things."

"You should've made him take them back."

"Things about Mother."

Mullet was silent.

"Rory said that she was a slut. Said she was messing around with Phillip Sams while Daddy was still alive."

Mullet poked out his bottom lip and spit into his cup.

"Rory said things about Daddy too."

"Is that right? What'd that shit say 'bout your old man?"

"Said that Daddy jumped off the roof, fell on purpose."

Mullet slammed the brakes. The truck slid on the dirt road kicking up dust in front of the windshield. I flew off the truck seat, and into the naked lady painted on the glove box. The truck whined as he muscled against the steering wheel. He turned the truck in a wide circle.

"Well, now," he said. "Rory McAllister's going to have to pay for remarks like that."

~

The McAllister house was a gracious estate plopped right on the bay. It was steaming with wealth. A grove of blooming bushes and white magnolia trees surrounded it. The home's pristine lawn that looked as tight as a military haircut.

"Is this Rory McAllister's house?" I asked.

Mullet nodded.

"How do you know where he lives?"

"I did some work for the McAllisters, years back." Mullet threw the truck into park. "Never you mind about any of that. We got work to do."

Mullet opened the glove box and removed a little cloth bag. The bag jingled in his hands. He spilled it open and a slew of metal keys fell into his lap. He weeded through the mess and removed a handful of the brass keys.

"Listen up, we don't have much time." Mullet pulled a watch from his pocket. "The ballgame's almost over. It won't be long until the whole McAllister family's home. I don't want to be here when they're sipping on juleps, telling each other how smart they are. We have to haul ass if we're going to do this."

"Do what?"

"Just follow my lead, boy."

"Mullet, I don't want to do anything wrong."

"Don't you worry, Old Timer." He patted my shoulder. "I'll be the one engaging in all the evildoing."

We walked up to the tall wooden door. It loomed over our heads like a castle drawbridge. Mullet jammed a key into the slot of the door and fiddled with it. He rattled it back and forth. The latch clicked, and the door swung open.

"Eureka," he laughed.

We walked into the spotless home.

The floor-to-ceiling wood paneling made it seem as though we were walking into a mahogany-covered afterlife. A bulbous vase of fresh white flowers greeted us on a table in the entry way. It was taller than we were, and it smelled better than we did, too.

Mullet whistled. "This is fine-damn living right here."

I reached up and touched one of the flowers in the vase.

We walked into the kitchen. It was a large, white tiled room. High ceilings towered above us. The kitchen stove was big enough to cook an elephant on–or three. Mullet opened up the tall ice box. With squinted eyes, he scanned the contents of the cooler and removed a glass jug of milk.

"Hurry now, find me two glasses," Mullet said. "Not their good glasses, neither."

I went to the marble counter and pilfered through the cabinets. I'd never seen so many glasses in all my life. There were glasses of every shape and size. Round ones, tall ones, short ones, and long skinny ones. I picked out two of them and handed them to Mullet. He filled the glasses with milk and then took a sip from each. The white milk ran all over his thick beard, trailing down onto his shirt.

"Okay now," Mullet whispered. "Let's go find Rory's bedroom."

"Why are we whispering?"

"Because it's better than yelling."

The bedroom was upstairs. It was spacious. It looked like a wooden football field. The long and wide room sprawled outward in every direction. Baseball posters covered the walls, a radio sat on the nightstand, and there were mountains of magazines in every corner. I'd never seen so many pleasantries in one place before.

I inspected the small radio on his nightstand.

I figured Rory listened to baseball games on that fancy thing.

"Don't let jealousy curl your upper lip, Old Timer," Mullet looked toward the radio. "Won't do you no good."

"Me?" I set the radio down. "I ain't jealous."

"Mmm hmm, well you'll do good to stay that way, then."

Mullet searched the room, looking along the wood floor. He looked behind the furniture and felt underneath the bed. He opened up the door to the closet and looked around inside.

"This is what I'm looking for." Mullet grinned and knelt down. The metal floor vent was a grid-work of steel that looked like it belonged on the front of a Buick. The vent let out a rusty groan as he lifted it open.

"Give the milk here," he said.

He took one of the full glasses from me, and lowered it down into the vent hole, careful not to spill it. Then he drew back his hand from the crooked hole. Mullet shut the vent and looked at me with wide eyes.

"That oughta do it," he said.

"Do what?"

"Never mind. Find me another vent."

We searched the room for another heating vent, feeling along the floor. I found another big vent behind the dresser on the other side of

Rory's enormous bed.

"You do the honors this time," Mullet said, handing me the glass of milk.

I lifted the vent cover and set the glass of milk in the duct. Just like he'd done.

Mullet smacked me on the back and laughed. "Come on, let's giddy up out of here."

We scampered down the grandiose staircase to the front door like a couple of cats. We ran as fast as our legs could move, darting through the entryway in a flash. Mullet paused for a moment. He grabbed a white flower from the big vase and put the stem between his teeth.

He tossed another white flower to me.

"Here's one for the road," he said.

~

Mullet sped down the road as fast as the vehicle would run. The marshlands zoomed by the truck windows in a horizontal blur. I held out my shaking hand in front of my face. The adrenaline from our caper made me tremble like a blade of grass.

Mullet talked to himself in a quiet voice, or maybe he was talking to me, I wasn't paying much attention. I was too busy admiring the artwork inside the truck cab. The nude woman above the visor caught my eye. She reclined on a large daisy with an apple in her hands. The look on her face was whimsical.

"What's this?" I asked, pointing to the drawing.

He looked at the little painting. "Oh that? Why that's Lady Eve. Before she ate the fruit."

"You mean Adam and Eve?"

"The one and only."

"Aren't they from the Bible?"

"Yessir, she was the first woman alive."

"Ever?"

"She was perfect."

I imagined what a perfect woman would look like. That was easy to do, they all looked perfect to me. Even the bad-looking ones.

"Even though Eve was perfect, she made a bad mistake," said Mullet.

"A bad mistake like what?"

"The worst mistake anyone could ever make. She was misunderstood."

Mullet chewed on a mouthful of tobacco staring out the windshield. His jaws chomped, and he spit every so often. Mullet offered me the plug of tobacco without saying a word. I took the little brown brick and ripped a hunk off with my teeth.

"Mullet, what'd we do, exactly? To Rory, I mean."

"Well Old Timer, the beauty of our work is two-fold. First off, the milk will keep souring as the days go by. Each minute getting worse. After a few weeks, the smell will be so foul, Rory will wish he was sleeping in the outhouse."

I couldn't help but laugh.

Rory deserved every bit of it.

"What's the second thing?"

"Second thing is: the milk we hid in his closet won't just stink up his room. Since it's in his closet, it'll stink up his clothes, too. Rory will be waltzing around town smelling like a pile of oysters."

Mullet wiped spit from his mouth.

I could think of nothing better than Rory McAllister smelling like a pile of oysters. Just like me. I smelled like oysters every day of my life.

The laughter crawled all over me like a tickle. It started in my gut and rose upward into my chest like red in a thermometer. I threw my head forward and laughed until my stomach muscles were sore.

Mullet watched me laugh through the corner of his eye.

It was his gift to me.

~

Emma Claire stood at the window. Her face pressed against the glass in a kind of helpless boredom. The house was completely silent. It wasn't very tidy, either. Nobody ever cleaned it except me.

I walked through the front door and kicked my shoes off.

"Quinn," Emma Claire said, running over to me with her hands out.

I grabbed her by the arms and swung her in big circles. I wasn't able to scoop her up the same way Daddy did. He could lift her high up in the air as if she were a teddy bear. I wasn't as tall as he was, or as strong. I set her feet on the floor and noticed that she smelled like sweat and dirt.

"Have you been playing outside today?" I asked.

"All day." She smiled. "With Silver, Bits, Crystal, Tawdy, and Rocks."

"Rocks? You named one of your cats rocks?"

"He always hides from me behind the rocks when I chase him."

I'd probably do the same thing.

"What happens when you catch him?"

"I give him a bath. All of them had baths today. They don't like it."

"Well, that's because cats hate water."

"They drink water, though."

"That's different."

"Why?"

"It just is."

She didn't follow my logic.

I bent down and tickled her. "And now it's your turn to take a bath, you little sapsucker. And I know you hate bathing even more than the cats do."

"Hey!" Emma Claire let out a roaring laugh. "I'm not taking a bath!"

"Oh, yes you are, or I won't cook any dinner tonight, and you'll go to bed hungry."

That changed her mind.

"Bet you can't catch me!" she shouted, running from me, stomping through the house toward the bathroom. "Quinn can't catch me, Quinn can't catch me!"

I sighed, watching her run away

She was right.

~

The radio sat perched in the kitchen windowsill. It hummed sultry music through a tweed speaker, filling up the room. The sounds of southland jazz wafted through the atmosphere. The music made me feel warm. I liked the radio. I needed it on, even when I wasn't in the house. It made the dark, lonely place feel alive somehow. Alive in an artificial way, but alive just the same.

Emma Claire sat at the table and ate her cinnamon toast. She bounced her legs, humming to herself in a high-pitched voice. She like the radio as much as I did. If ever I turned it off, she'd fuss and point to it until I turned it back on.

Recently, Emma Claire had learned how to turn it on all by herself. Her little hand would clasp around the knob, and the radio would boom. The screaming clarinets and trumpets would scream until I came to adjust the volume.

While Emma ate, I sketched with a pencil on a scrap piece of paper. I attempted to draw a picture of Lady Eve, like the one in Mullet's truck. My drawing was terrible compared to Mullet's. My naked women looked like cheap smut.

"What's that you're drawing?" Emma Claire asked with a mouthful of food.

"Eve. From the Bible."

"Oh."

Each night before bed, Emma demanded cinnamon toast. I don't know how that habit started, but I'm pretty sure it was my fault.

"The Bible?" Emma Claire wrinkled her nose "What's that?"

"It's a big book."

She took another bite of her toast. "Have you read it before?"

"No. I can't read."

"At all?"

"Some words."

Emma thought about that. "Which ones?"

I shrugged. "Mostly just little words."

"Is my name a little word?"

"No. It's two words."

"Is your name a little word?"

"Yeah."

"I want my name to be a little word too."

If she could've been named Quinn Applewhite, she would've done that, too. She even slept in the same bed I did.

Emma never slept in her own room anymore. In fact, she refused to even go in there, not even during the daytime. Her room sat unused as lifeless as an old graveyard. The bedroom was a nothing but a storage room. It housed a few pieces of furniture, and a few bolts of Mother's old fabric. That was it.

"Where's Momma?" Emma Claire licked her fingers.

"Sleeping."

"Momma always sleeps."

I let out a big breath. It was true.

"Emma Claire, do you ever see Mother during the day? Does she ever come out of there?"

"Nope. Never."

We hadn't seen Mother in several days. I was sure she came out of her room when we weren't around. I knew she'd wandered into the kitchen at some point. The refrigerator was missing a block of cheese. The crackers in the cabinet were gone, too. She always took the best things from the kitchen. I'd taken to hiding certain things so Mother wouldn't steal them.

"Naked." Emma touched my drawing. "That girl's naked."

"It's all part of the Bible. That's why she's naked."

"The Bible must be a bad book."

"It probably is."

"What's the Bible?"

"It's a book for lawyers, I think."

"What's lawyers?"

"They make sure that people are miserable."

I'd heard Daddy say that once.

I crumpled my paper into a tight ball and started sketching on a fresh piece of paper. This time, I drew a daisy. Daisies are easy enough to draw, anyone can do a daisy. I traced the round petals onto the paper and then drew a circle in the middle of the flower.

My artwork wasn't as good as Mullet's.

Not by far.

"Oooh, that's pretty." Emma Claire pointed her buttery hand at the paper. "I like flowers."

8.

Two years went by as fast as a sunset in November. Two years didn't feel like a long time. And I suppose it wasn't, not really. It was just a little over seven hundred days. Seven hundred days doesn't even seem long enough to grow a tomato, if you think about it.

Emma Claire grew faster than anyone I'd ever seen in those seven hundred days. She sprouted like the woody weeds that grow in the ditches. Those weeds shoot up overnight. They look like small trees, like they'd make terrific bows and arrows. But they don't work for that sort of thing. They're far too papery and soft.

I know this from experience.

Emma Claire spent her days playing in the backyard behind our home. The feral cats chased her, parading themselves behind Emma Claire like committed disciples. She built forts out of palmetto leaves and decorated them. She told stories to the cats and sometimes dressed them in doll's clothes.

I'm sure they loved the doll clothes.

Once, Emma Claire threw Silver into the bay. His little paws swatted at the water, a feline attempt at the dog paddle. The cat's head bobbed up and down like a popping cork. I saw the whole thing happen through the kitchen window. I ran outside, jumped into the water and plucked the drowning cat from his peril. He thanked me by scratching the Holy Jesus Jeremiah out of my forearms.

Silver never went near the bay again after that.

Neither did any of his feline friends.

Emma Claire loved the bay. Often she stood looking at it, her eyes wide open, to see how far she could see.

On a good day, you could see six miles. That's what the old fishermen often said. Six miles in each direction. The large cool water makes you glad somehow. It stretches out into the greater world, reaching the crevices of the unknown. It fills the largest troughs, connecting itself to everything. I wished I was a poet sometimes, so that I could write about it.

But crackers make terrible poets.

Especially crackers who can't read.

"I got a fish!" Emma Claire yanked backward on the cane pole.

The speckled trout tried to shoot underneath the boat. Emma Claire muscled against the fish with her young arms, cranking her reel.

"She's a better fisherman than you are, Old Timer," Mullet said.

When her fish got closer, I reached over the side of the boat. I lifted the fish out of the water and flung it into the basket. The trout flopped, twisting and beating its body against the braided wicker.

"I'm a fisherman," Emma Claire said.

"That's right, baby." Mullet rubbed Emma Claire's head. "You're the best one on the damn boat."

"A lot better than me," I said. "In fact, you're embarrassing me."

"Am I really better than Quinn?"

"Hell baby, you're better than both me and Quinn put together."

That made her head swell up like a watermelon.

She dropped her line into the water again, looking to outdo herself with a bigger fish than the last.

The truth was, Emma Claire was the world's biggest copycat. Whatever I did, she did. Whatever I liked, she liked. She fished whenever I fished. She followed me like a shadow and even ate the same blue crab I did. I took care of her the best I could. I taught her to tie her brambly shoes and washed her clothes every four days.

That girl could stink worse than an old Billy Goat.

Emma Claire held on to her cane pole with both hands. She watched the tip of the pole, just like we'd taught her to do. She watched for the slightest movement in the water.

Mullet was right, Emma Claire was a good fisherman. Or rather, a good fisherwoman. She had the fiery spirit of a hunter, and the arrogance that it took, too. She would lock her eyes on the tip of that pole and hypnotize a fish into swallowing her hook.

All of a sudden, my own rod bent downward in a grand arc, like it was going to snap in two.

"Fish!" Emma Claire shouted. "Look Mullet, he's got a fish!"

I gripped my pole tight, without even pausing to consider what had happened, and I fought against my reel as it zipped. The little wooden boat rocked back and forth with my movements.

"Give him some more line, Old Timer." Mullet was calm, he tucked a bit of tobacco in his cheek. "You're going to have to wear this big one out."

"Quinn's got a fish!" Emma chirped. "A big one!"

"Alright, baby," said Mullet. "Lower your voice or you'll scare the rest of the fish away."

So she whispered, "Quinn's got a fish."

I braced my feet against the side of the boat and let the line shoot underneath my fingers. The metal reel buzzed like a machine in my palm, warm from the friction. I pulled against the fish and cranked him backward toward the boat. He shot forward again, in an S formation. I reigned him back. He shot sideways, and downward again.

"What's happening now?" Emma Claire whispered.

Mullet spit overboard. "Quinn's trying to concentrate, let's give him a minute, baby."

The fish came near the surface. Its glowing body zipped beneath the thin green layers of water. I yanked the line and lifted it out of the water and into the air. The fish was as big as a Buick.

"Holy Pharaoh and Moses." Mullet pushed the brim of his cap up. "Look at the size of that thing."

It was the biggest redfish I'd ever caught. As long as my ever-loving leg. Its head was as big around as a football. It jerked from side to side, dripping in the sunlight like a giant column of muscle.

"Am I still a better fisherman than Quinn?" Emma Claire asked.

"Always, baby," said Mullet.

She took comfort in knowing that.

~

We rowed toward the shore. My happy disposition could've set the woods on fire. I looked at the humongous fish by my feet; it was too big to fit in any basket. It shimmered pink in the sunlight like a monster, with a round, fat body that filled up the entire hull of the boat. Emma Claire could not keep her fingers off of the great fish. She stroked it like one of her cats.

"We got company." Mullet glanced toward the shore.

He was right. Parked on the shore was a shiny black car, with sparkly hubs, and a chrome front. The car looked like it belonged in a magazine ad. Its doors splayed open, and its radio blared music into the atmosphere. Young girls and boys romped around in the shallow water. They splashed each other, laughing in loud voices.

"Look," Emma Claire said. "Look at the kids playing."

"They ain't kids, baby," Mullet said. "They're teenagers."

"Teenagers."

Mullet patted her head. "That's older than a kid, younger than a grown-up."

"I'm a teenager, Mullet?"

"No baby, you're a cricket."

The young men in the group tossed a ball back and forth on the shore. The boys displayed their bare torsos in the sun, strutting like seventeen-year old roosters. Their female companions were in multicolored bathing suits, laid on the shore, watching the boys. There wasn't a cracker in the whole bunch.

When we neared the shore, I leapt out of the skiff. Mullet and I slid the dinghy onto the sandy grit, using our shoulders. The boat hissed as it ground against the shore.

"Any of those jokers friends of yours?" Mullet asked.

"Lord, no."

"Well, they sure are loud. They're scaring all the fish away from my new favorite fishing hole."

I looked at the teenagers, I knew one of them. My cousin, Phyllis. She lay on a beach blanket, letting the sun burn her white skin like girls often do.

"Is that Phyllis Ronsman?" Mullet asked.

"Yeah. She's wealthy as the day is long."

"Good God, I beat her daddy, Slip Ronsman, out of two-grand, ten years ago. One of the biggest wins of my entire life. I thought I was a hundred-feet tall."

I believed it, too. The only thing Mullet liked more than gambling, was gambling.

I lifted Emma Claire out of the boat and set her feet on the sand. She was much heavier than she used to be. Emma Claire was a bonafide girl now. She had her own opinions, her own way of fishing, and her own set of little, muddy cracker-boots.

The moment her boots touched the ground, Emma Claire darted over to the teenagers. She kicked up wet clumps of sand behind her. I reached after her, but it was no use. Emma was like a bloodhound who'd spotted a crippled squirrel.

She watched the colorful group of teenagers with wide eyes,

shaking her hips to the music and moving her feet. Then, she bent forward and yelled at the top of her lungs, "My brother catched a big fish y'all! It's so, so big!"

Emma Claire held out her hands, showing the teenagers the relative size of the fish. "Even bigger than this!"

The group of teenagers stopped what they were doing. They watched the three-foot-tall girl holler like an Apalachee. My face either turned white or red, there's no way I'll ever know for certain which color.

"It's a huge fish!" she yelled again. "Come look!"

I ducked my head down and considered leaving for the mountains to start a new life for myself.

Emma Claire turned around and then ran back to me. I bent down and picked her up, looking into her big cow brown eyes.

She was lit up like a bolt of electricity.

"Hey, Quinn, I told those kids about your big fish."

"Those aren't kids, Emma Claire," I said. "They're teenagers."

~

The freckled girl was about my age. She had freckles, all over, too. Not just on her face, but on her shoulders, arms, and chest. I don't think I'd ever seen that many on a person before. There must've been billions of them—no, trillions. Maybe gazillions. I can't be sure. They all ran together, like copper-colored buckshot.

The girl's white bathing suit covered her, but it felt indecent to stare at her for long. Quite indecent. Furthermore, I was nervous to be standing so close to a young lady wearing so little.

Nervous in a good way.

"Did you just catch that?" Freckles asked.

I couldn't hear the girl's voice in my bunk left ear. I didn't want to tell her that I couldn't hear her. She might start to think I was missing other important pieces of my body, too.

"Ma'am?" I said to her.

"Darling," Mullet interjected. "You're going to have to stand on Quinn's good side, he can't hear a thing out of that left ear."

My odds at impressing her were slowly dwindling. I fought against the impulse to duck my head down and melt into a puddle of fish pee.

"Oh, I had no idea." The girl walked to my other side. "Is this better?"

"Much better, yes." I gave her a smile.

The girl before was a friend of Phyllis'. Phyllis happened to be a distant cousin of mine, but the truth is, I didn't know Phyllis that well. I saw her at Uncle Sky's house for reunions once each year, but we never said much to each other. She was from a richer part of the family than we were. They were not crackers. In fact, they weren't even made of flour.

"That fish is enormous," Phyllis yelled to me, cupping her hands over her mouth. "Huge."

"I can hear you fine, Phyllis," I said. "You ain't got to yell."

"Sorry, Quinn," Phyllis said.

"It's okay, just talk slow and loud."

I looked down into the boat at the fish. She was right. The big thing sprawled out like Goliath himself, only with fins. Now and then, it would let out a big flop that made the girls jump back and shriek.

Their screams made Emma Claire giggle.

"I've never seen a redfish that big," the freckled girl said. "He's a real lunker."

Mullet and I looked at each other.

Most girls didn't know the difference between a redfish and a coffee mug, let alone use the word lunker–it was a technical term.

"A lunker?" Mullet said.

"What?"

"Nothing," I said. "It's just, not everyone uses that word."

"A lunker," Emma Claire repeated. "What's that?"

"Freckles is right," Mullet said. "It's a lunker alright, the biggest red I've ever seen. Thing weighs more than you two young ladies put together."

"What about me?" Emma Claire said.

"You?" He looked at Emma. "Shoot, you're a sack of feathers, baby doll. You don't weigh nothing."

"Yes I do, too," Emma said. "I'm so heavy."

The freckled girl reached out her hand to touch the slimy fish. She touched her index finger on the slick wet skin. The gills of the creature opened and closed, gasping.

"What're you going to do with it?" Phyllis asked.

I shrugged. "Eat it, what else?"

"All of it?" the freckled girl asked. "How will you eat it? It's so big. There's enough here to feed a whole army."

Mullet looked at me and winked his eye.

"She makes a good point Quinn, reckon we'll need some volunteers to help us out. It's too much fish for the few of us."

I decided to move to the mountains and change my name.

"Oh, let me help," the freckled girl said. "I can help eat it."

"Me too," Phyllis said. "I can help, too."

"Well now." Mullet put his hands on his belt. "You ladies sure about that? You'll have to do your fair share of eating. Won't be easy. It'll be hard work."

"I love fish," the freckled girl said. "I can eat as much as any boy."

I doubted that very seriously.

"You hear what she just said, Quinn?" he said. "That sounds like a challenge to me. Old Quinn here can eat more than any boy in town."

She turned to me and held out her hand. "My name's Sonneta Ann, but everyone calls me Sonnet."

And that's exactly what she was.

~

The fish laid flat on the big wooden table. It was a table that Daddy had built out of scrub pine for cleaning fish, squirrel, and coon. It was stained crimson and brown from years of use. Gutting a fish had been our victory ritual when he was alive. It was the most fun part of the whole ordeal.

It made me sad to clean the fish without Daddy standing nearby. Like something was missing. I liked to imagine him standing there while I worked, watching me. His thumbs hitched in his belt, puffing on his pipe. Sipping on a jar of shine.

The sad fact was, Daddy had been dead for several years, and I was starting to forget his face in my mind. I forgot his nose first, then his ears and eyes, and then I forgot what shade of brown his hair was. That's how it happens. One piece at a time. Then, one day the person has disappeared from your memory altogether. Like they never even graced the earth.

The fish was hard to clean. It's difficult to cut up a fish that's the size of a tree trunk. This is especially true when using the wrong kind of knife. My little blade wasn't up to the task. It was dull and rusted over.

I was a lazy sharpener.

The fish guts spilled out of the great beast like soft purple jelly. Carefully, I slid the knife along the fish's white belly. The rubber skin parted behind my dull blade.

"That's a big one," Mother said leaning against the post.

I turned to see her watching me. Mother's hair looked like she'd just woken up. Her eyes drooping. She'd lost the thin layer of baby fat that had once covered her face.

"Yeah," I said. "He's a lunker."

I loved that word more than ever before.

She walked closer to the fish, admiring my carving-work. She'd never cut an ounce of meat in her life, such things impressed her.

They reminded her of Daddy.

"I'll bet he tastes good," she said. "I can't wait to eat him tonight."

She touched a pool of dark fish blood.

"Well, actually," I said. "I was planning on taking the fish to Mullet's tonight since he helped me catch it. He's having some friends over for a fry."

Mother looked at me with a flat face.

"That's odd," she said. "Mullet doesn't have any friends."

I was quiet. "Well, it's just a little dinner," I finally said. "Nothing much."

She looked me up and down, studying the tender stubble on my jaw. I think it reminded her of Daddy too.

"I see," she said. "And what about my supper tonight? Am I to go without while you party with your friends?"

"No, I'm about to start some for you, soon as I'm done here."

"You are?" Mother leaned against the post and folded her arms across her chest. "What are you going to cook for me?"

I nodded toward the fish. "A little of this."

She eyed the big thing.

"Well, I don't want to eat here tonight, all by myself, I want to go to your party."

I stopped cutting. "You wouldn't know anybody there."

"So what?"

"I just don't think you'd have any fun."

"Fun?"

"You won't know a soul."

"Well, I know Mullet. And I've known him longer than you have."

I let out a breath, and picked up the severed head, it dripped dark purple blood onto my shirt. Mother watched me fling the head into the garbage can.

"So, I'm not invited, is that it?" Mother asked.

"No, it's not that, I just don't think that you'd enjoy yourself."

She tightened her eyes. "I suppose I'm the one who feeds Emma Claire tonight then? I'm supposed to put her down to bed since you're leaving us?"

God forbid.

"No, ma'am," I said. "I was going to bring Emma Claire along with me."

Mother's nostrils opened up, and her face tensed.

She walked closer to me, eyeing the big slabs of pink meat on the table. "Okay then. So this is all about a girl? That's what this is all about?"

Mother was an expert in this field; I didn't stand a chance against her.

"No it's not about a girl."

"It's not?"

"No, it's not."

"Is she pretty?"

"There's no girl, I told you, it's a fish fry, with some of Mullet's friends."

"Who is she?"

"There's no girl."

Mother scoffed. "What's her name?"

"I said there's nobody."

Mother butted her hands against my shoulders and pushed me.

I stumbled backward and dropped my knife on the ground. She picked up the giant tail of the fish and threw it at my chest. It thumped against my sternum. Then, she hurled the whole fish carcass into the dirt.

My trophy plopped in the dust like a stone.

"You goddamn liar!" she yelled and her voice broke. "I know you're lying to me. I'm not stupid."

I stood there, without a word.

She stomped toward me and jammed her finger into my throat. "You're not going to any goddamn party. You're staying home tonight."

~

Emma Claire sat cross-legged on the floor. She played with the wooden blocks I'd made her last Christmas. They were wood scraps from the mill I'd dyed with food coloring. To her, they were the finest play things money could buy.

I got the idea for the blocks from a friend of mine. My friend had built an entire maze out of old wood from the mill. He'd put lizards in the maze, and we'd place bets on which one would make it to the end fastest.

I made a lot of money off those lizards.

I sat on my bed, lost in a swirl of anger. I wasn't sure if my thoughts were good or bad, righteous or unjust. The only thing that I was absolutely sure of was that I ached inside. I didn't want to miss a chance to see the freckled girl again. She was the loveliest thing I'd ever seen, and she had such a stunning vocabulary.

Lunker.

My self-pity mingled with hazy images of the girl's buckshot shoulders. I closed my eyes and thought about her auburn hair, it was the color of a rusted piece of metal. If God would've wanted to make anything more perfect, he couldn't have.

I leaned back onto my pillow looking at the ceiling, my deaf ear ringing like a bell. It always rang. Always. My bum ear hummed like a million crickets in unison. I was used to the sound, I never even payed attention to it to tell you the truth. The only time I noticed the ringing was when I was in my own whirlpool of thoughts.

When I was a child, with ear infections, Mother said I'd stay up half the night moaning in my room from the ringing. I'd bled all over my pillow like a stuck pig. But I didn't even remember that.

I closed my eyes again and thought of the freckled girl's peppered shoulders. I remembered her swimsuit. The straps were almost as white as her pale skin.

What a suit it was.

The ringing in my in my temples spread through my skull. It crawled through my face, down my jawbone and into my neck. Then, it spread to the rest of my body, until it enveloped me in its deafening sound.

"Hey, Quinn!" Emma shouted.

Her voice startled me out of my daze.

"What is it Emma Claire?"

"Are we eating fish with those kids tonight?"

"I don't know."

"I thought we were going to a fry?"

I shook my head. "Probably not."

"Well I want to go."

"I don't think it's going to work out tonight."

"Why not?"

"Because, Emma, Mother doesn't want us to go."

"I don't care what she wants," she laughed. "I want to go."

Emma Claire was defiant as a slug.

"Come on," she said. "What are you waiting for, dummy? Let's go."

I looked out the window beside the bed. The sky was turning pink outside as the sun started to lower. I could feel my resentment toward Mother rising as the sky became redder.

"You're right, Emma Claire." I stood up from my bed and took her by the hand. "Let's go."

~

Emma Claire sat next to me in the passenger seat. She touched the big hunks of fish wrapped in black and white newspaper. The fish steaks sat between us on the seat. Emma moved her finger along the printed words on the newspaper wrapping. She pretended that she could read, mumbling.

"What's this word say?" asked Emma Claire.

I looked at her finger. "I have no idea."

It was too small, and too long for me to read.

"Quinn, how do you spell my name?"

"Your name?"

"Yes."

I thought for a moment. "Well, I don't know exactly, but I know that your name starts with an E."

"What else?"

"I can't remember for certain. I know that Claire starts with a C."

"E. C.," she said in a staccato voice was.

"That's right. Those are your initials."

"What are those?"

"Initials are how you sign your name, if you sign a contract. Well, it's how you sign your name if you're a cracker."

"What's a cracker?"

"Never mind."

She turned around and looked out the back of the truck window at the sun going down. The brilliant orange sunset was Emma Claire's favorite thing in the world. It was one of the few pleasantries that we could afford to have almost every night. She propped herself on her elbows and gazed out the rear window. She watched it like it was the first time that she'd ever seen it.

"E," Emma said again. "How do you spell E?"

"You can't spell E, it's just a letter. Letters are what you use to spell the words with."

"What about your name? How do you spell your name?"

I knew that one. I could even spell it backward.

"Q-U-I-N-N," I said.

"Wow. You're good. What about Mother's name?"

I shook my head. I knew how, but I wasn't about to spell that one. Not for a long time anyway.

Emma Claire and I had left the house without a single word from Mother. Mother hadn't even tried to stop us from leaving. In fact, she didn't even know that we were gone yet. Mother was too busy locked away in her bedroom to know what went on in the rest of the house.

"You're smart," Emma said. "How do you know all this stuff?"

"I went to school when I was little. For a few years."

"But now you're old?"

"No, I'm not old. I'm only seventeen. That's not old."

Emma Claire sighed. "I want to go to school like you did. For a few years, like you."

Emma would've renamed herself Quinn Applewhite if she could've.

Like a lot of oystermen, Daddy had pulled me out of school after the fifth grade. I'd helped him on the boat since then. Money was money, and we never had enough of it. My extra set of hands on the little boat meant more earnings. More earnings meant that life could be just a touch easier for the family.

Like most men who worked the beds, I'd grown up thinking I had a crippled brain. I thought I was as dumb as a pine knot. But sometimes, I wondered if I had a sharper mind than they allowed me to believe. I wondered what might've happened if they had left me in school. Maybe I'd be a great writer, a famous baseball player, or even a politician.

No. Definitely not a politician.

Maybe a writer.

I looked over at Emma Claire, she watched the sun.

The poor girl had never darkened the doorway of a school. And if it was up to Mother, she wouldn't go at all. It seemed like a shame. Emma's mind was as sharp as a circle hook.

"Is that true, Emma Claire?" I asked. "You want to go to school?"

Emma Claire shrugged her shoulders.

She'd forgotten all about school already.

"Well," I said. "I think it's a great idea. You could learn numbers, learn to read, make some friends your own age."

The only friends Emma Claire had were feral cats.

"Friends?"

"Yeah, kids the same as you."

No one would ever be quite the same as her.

She moved closer to me, crawling on top of the pile of news-wrapped fish steaks between us. She kicked her shoes off, flinging them down onto the truck floorboard. Emma leaned her head onto my shoulder, closing her eyes.

"I already got a friend," she said.

~

Mullet tended the big iron pan, watching the onions crackle in the grease. The trees towered over his house. They broke up the peach-colored sky with their straight dark shapes. I stood beside him, watching him fry, my hands shoved deep in my pockets.

"Get over there and talk to her, you stupid ass," he said flipping the onions. "What're you doing here with me? I'm ugly as sin."

"I'm nervous," I said. "I don't know what to say to her."

"You can talk about how ugly I am, if it makes you feel better about yourself."

"But she's so, so. Well...."

"I know, I know, Romeo. So go over there and talk to her then."

"I can't."

Mullet stabbed me with the spatula. "I said go."

The two young women sat on a big swing suspended from a gnarled limb, rocking back and forth. They smiled at Emma Claire, who was making broad sweeping gestures with her hands. She was telling one of her stories. Probably about her cats. Emma Claire used her hands whenever she spoke, it was how she talked. Everything she said was intense and required movement.

The girls were good listeners. They watched Emma carry on and gave her their complete attention.

Sonnet's white legs were like long, freckled stilts. Her knees were knobby, bigger than normal knees. She had two awkward ankles that were thicker than common ankles.

"Get your ass over there." Mullet elbowed me again. "Or I'm gonna tell the girls that you ain't got no ding dong."

"Huh?"

"You heard me."

I had no idea if Mullet was serious or not, I decided to do as he suggested. I couldn't have the whole town thinking I had nothing under the hood.

I walked over to the girls with my hands in my pockets. The throbbing sound of my heart pulsed in my right ear. I'd developed the terrible habit of quietness whenever I became uncomfortable. I hated that about myself. I wished I could talk up a blue streak like Emma Claire, but I usually found myself tongue tied when asked to discuss anything more than fishing.

"Hey, Quinn," Emma Claire greeted me. She was ablaze with energy. When she saw me, she ran and hurled herself through the air. I caught her flying body and held her like a dangling monkey.

"Emma Claire is quite the informant," Sonnet said.

"Yes, I'm sure she is," I answered. "What's that?"

"She's been telling us your entire life story." Sonnet tossed her hair over her shoulder and bore her brilliant green eyes into me.

"Well, I apologize for that, it's a boring story."

"No, we're having a lovely time hearing all about you."

"She might be feeding you lies. Emma Claire likes to embellish things."

"I do not!" Emma Claire shouted. "I only like relish at Christmas."

"That's not what I said, Emma."

"Quinn," Emma Claire said. "Do you think Sonnet's pretty?"

I winced, and I'm certain I turned as red as a crawfish.

Abso-damn-lutely I did.

She was prettier than butter a stack of cakes.

But all I said was, "Sure."

Sonnet laughed and pinched Emma. "Well, I think you're beautiful, too, Emma Claire. I wish I had your long, dark hair. I've always wished I had dark hair."

I was glad God never granted her wish.

Beautiful girls like Sonnet were several cuts above me. They never paid me any mind. The only attention I ever got was from cracker girls. Cracker girls were lanky things, with screwy teeth, and big ears.

This girl was no cracker.

I wasn't even sure why a girl like Sonnet had agreed to come to the silly fish-fry supper. She could've had any boy in town that she wanted.

I knew that.

The sad fact was, oystermen like me ended up with the daughters of oystermen. That's the way things were. Loggers ended up with the daughters of loggers. Mill-workers ended up with the daughters of mill-workers. Boys like me found companionship with women who worked hard like I did. Women who worked too hard to have time to be pretty, with hands that were pruny and rough. Oystermen, loggers, and mill-workers married their own kind, those were the rules. There was no point in fighting it.

"Can I get y'all anything to drink?" I asked.

Emma Claire fell into me, burying her face in my stomach.

"Me," Emma Claire said. "I want sweet tea, please."

"Okay," I said to Emma. "Thank you for saying please."

The girls giggled at that.

"Sweet tea for Emma," I said. "What else can I get?"

"We'll both have tea also," Sonnet said rising from the swing. "I'll help you get them."

Emma Claire turned to follow us, but Phyllis pinched Emma

Claire's rear end.

Emma Claire squealed at her.

"Emma, have a seat next to me," Phyllis said. "I want to hear more about the cats that live behind your house."

"You do?" Emma shouted.

Emma Claire had a lot to say on the matter.

Sonnet and I walked up to the porch, our shoulders almost touching. It seemed illicit standing so near to her. I kept my head down, trying not to stare, watching the hem of her white dress move back and forth against her freckled shins as we walked.

They were smooth as enamel.

"Emma Claire is hysterical," Sonnet laughed. "You're everything to her aren't you?"

"I suppose so."

"I'm not that close with my brothers. I feel more like their babysitter than I do their sister."

"I can understand that."

"I'm sure you can, but it's different with you and Emma Claire. You seem like her guardian, like her father."

"I guess in a way, I am."

Sonnet smiled at me, and my heart nearly split wide open.

"I think that's awfully brave of you," she said.

I was anything but brave. This girl ought to've seen me during a hurricane. I had a hard time just holding my bladder during such events.

I lifted the big glass jar of sweet tea from the table. The jug was big enough to hold a baby pig inside. Must've weighed fifty pounds. As carful as I could, I poured the tea into old jelly jars, spilling some on the table. Sonnet wiped up my mess with a towel.

"So, where do you live?" Sonnet asked.

"Over there, just up the road two miles."

"It's beautiful here."

"Yeah, it is."

"I love it here."

I poured tea into her jar. "What about you? Where do you live?"

"Oh, we've just moved to Port Saint Joe. My daddy just got a job there, he's a mill-worker."

I dropped the jug of tea, and it shattered on the porch.

9.

It was late, dark, and it was humid. Our porch light was the only light for miles–except for the moon. Emma Claire and I had the house to ourselves. It would've been completely quiet, if it weren't for the chorus of bullfrogs.

The frogs sang together in awful harmony. Their hoarse voices did not blend well together. Daddy used to call our place the frog mating grounds, and he would say it without a hint of irony. During the spring and summer, the frogs would overrun the area like a plague. There was a benefit to their invasion. Frogs ate the mosquitoes, and we ate frog legs.

Everybody had something to eat in the end.

I loved frog legs, lean and chewy, I could cook them in my sleep.

"I'm done." Emma Claire pushed her plate away. "I'm unquestionably full, I couldn't eat another bite."

I picked her plate up and lifted the half-eaten frog leg off it. Emma Claire had gotten into the habit of using curious words. Her newest word was *unquestionably*. She used it in almost every sentence she said. It was something she picked up in one of the books from school. I still didn't have a handle on what the word yet.

"Did you finish your homework, Emma Claire?" I stacked the silverware on top of the empty plate.

"Unquestionably."

"Does that mean yes?"

"I said, 'Un question-a-blee.'"

"I don't speak Spanish."

"It means yes."

I lit the stove and tossed the dishrags into the big pot.

When Emma and I were alone in the house, it was peaceful. It was our nightly routine since Mother had begun working at the grocery store. Emma Claire and I had grown to enjoy the peace. And it was peaceful when Mother was away. When Mother was home, her restless energy made everyone in the house fidgety. We liked it better when she left the house to us.

For the past few years, Mother had started exploring the world. She'd leave home at sunset, and return late at night. We didn't know what she did when she was out and about, but we knew it had something to do with men. Most of the things Mother did usually involved men.

The oyster-grunts at Norma's would talk about Mother when they were good and tight. They spoke about her like Mother was a piece of white meat. They'd hush their voices whenever I walked by, but it was usually too late. I'd already heard them.

After a long string of men, Mother finally attached herself to Carl Plight. Carl owned the grocery store. He gave Mother a job there, and it pacified her. Carl seemed nice enough, from the few times that we'd met him, but he was no Daddy.

Sometimes he'd come over to the house in the evenings and stay for hours. Mother and Carl would lie next to one another on the sofa in the evenings. They'd prop their feet on the table, and nurse glasses of expensive liquor. Carl told ridiculous jokes that weren't even funny. The more he drank, the less funny his jokes became. Afterward, they'd lock themselves in Mother's room. Emma and I could hear their grunts and moans through the walls. It was enough to turn my stomach sideways.

"I like frog legs," said Emma. "But not as much as blue crab legs, blue crab is my unquestionable favorite. Unquestionably."

"You'll have to explain what that word means to me again. I thought you just said that it meant yes."

"It means, no questions."

"About what?"

"It means *undeniably*."

"Huh?"

She opened her mouth wide. "Emphatically."

"What'd you just call me?"

"Oh, never mind, Quinn."

Emma took after Mother with her sharp mind. Mother could've gone on to be a school teacher if she'd've wanted to. God knows, she was smart enough to do it.

She just enjoyed laziness better.

Mother was generally quiet around me and Emma Claire whenever we saw her. We didn't know the woman who stocked groceries at the grocery store. The only time we saw her was at morning meals, right before I carried Emma Claire off to school. Mother was usually too exhausted to say much in those early hours. Before she left for work, Mother would massage her temples, lost in her mug of coffee. Mother complained that I made her coffee too weak. But then, she liked to complain about most things. It was one of her talents.

Once, just to give Mother a jolt, I made her coffee as thick as pine tar to tease her. I used triple the normal amount. That coffee was strong enough to power a boat. But my mother didn't know it was a joke, she thought the sludge was delicious. The joke was on me.

"Okay, Emma Claire," I said. "Go wash your unquestionable hands and get ready for bed."

"That's not how you use the word. You sound unquestionably ridiculous saying it like that."

"I thought you said it meant no questions."

"It does."

"Then do as I say and go wash your damn hands."

I got her with that.

Emma fell asleep fast in my bed. It was one of her many skills. It was like God put a switch in her brain, one that she could flip on and off at will, like a lightbulb. She lay in bed every night and commanded herself to sleep in only a few minutes. I envied her for that. I wasn't like her at all. God didn't make me that way; sleep was hard to come by.

After Emma Claire went to bed, I walked out onto the front porch to have a gander at the moon. I tapped a pack of cigarettes against the butt of my hand. The squawking frogs screamed loud enough to make anyone feel deaf. Like a bunch singers in church who'd forgotten the words.

I lit my cigarette and pulled the smoke inward.

Sometimes, I wished our house had a phone. We were too poor for that. I wished that I could call Sonnet. I wanted to see how her day went, to see if she needed anything. To hear her voice. She was my steady girl, and I needed her.

Sonnet's parents had a phone, but Sonnet was the only one who ever used it. All she did was talk on the damn thing. She burned up the party line every day, keeping up with fresh gossip. As a result, she knew everything there was to know about our area. Even things about folks I'd never heard of.

I watched the blue smoke exit my mouth, drifting upward

A frog hopped onto the porch and looked at me. He was a big one. He was lucky I wasn't in the hunting mood; his legs were as thick as a rooster's.

I looked into the night sky and I wondered about Daddy. I wondered where his soul might've gone off to if his spirit was intact or not. Perhaps he was out there, somewhere, in the great beyond. Maybe out there with the frogs, croaking. I doubted the pie-in-the-sky stories from church were true. I had a hard time envisioning Daddy with wings.

Still, I didn't give a damn either way, I just liked to wonder.

I wondered if people came back to earth after they died. Maybe as trees, or as animals. Maybe all the animals in the world were once people like Daddy had thought. Maybe his wish had been granted, perhaps he'd come back as a heron. I would've come as no surprise to me; he was half heron when he was alive.

Me, I still wanted to come back as a squirrel. And the more I thought about it, the more the idea suited me. Squirrels seemed like the most liberated creatures in the woods. They'd fly from limb to limb without the faintest of fears to inhibit them. Dauntless, furry things, free from worry. Fast, agile, and invisible–if they want to be. I could enjoy living that way. That is, as long as I was able to avoid brats with slingshots, or some joker toting a rifle.

I exhaled another tuft of smoke. Two bright headlights bobbed toward me, zipping down our driveway. Chunks of gravel made popping noises underneath the car's tires.

The car came to a halt and the passenger door swung open. Mother's blue shoes stepped out of the car before the rest of her did. She was nothing if not sultry. She emerged looking like a lady of the night. She walked to the other side of the car and leaned into the driver's window.

Mother lingered there for a few minutes whispering God-knows-what to Carl. Her smooth legs looked violet in the moonlight; she never showed her legs like that when Daddy was alive.

Carl Plight saw me through the windshield. He raised his arm out of his window. I waved in return. It was a kind of obligated greeting that neither of us meant.

Especially me.

Mother slapped the hood of the dark car and then frolicked up the porch steps. Her shoes clapped on the wood porch. She waved goodbye to Carl. He backed out of the drive, and his red taillights got smaller, fading into the black.

"Hey, you," she said. "How's it going?"

I shrugged.

She held her hand out. "Mind if I bum a smoke?"

I could count on one hand the number of times my mother ever bought her own cigarettes. It was too much trouble.

"Did you have fun with Carl tonight?" I gave her a cigarette.

"Oh yeah, unquestionably."

~

The morning brought a dewy heaviness that saturated our house and clothes. It was a clammy sticky moisture, but the truth was, we didn't notice it. We lived with it. It was always there. The only time we noticed the dampness was during winter season. Then the humidity was more like frost. It made your skin as cold as the backside of a corpse.

Mother stood in the kitchen with her hands on her hips, screaming at the top of her lungs. The whole house expanded beneath her bellows.

"You can't wear that to school, young lady!" Mother shouted.

"I will wear it!"

"You'll do as I say!"

"No I won't!"

"Oh yes you will, I'm your mother, dammit!"

Mother and Emma Claire fought with tenacious skill. They were good at it, and could carry on for hours sometimes.

I walked into the kitchen to see Mother and Emma Claire in a standoff. Mother stood blocking the screen door, her legs spread wide. We weren't going anywhere until the two of them finished their private war.

"Don't tell me how to dress!" Emma Claire hollered.

"You look like white trash. I won't allow my own daughter to go to school looking like a rag doll."

"I am not white-trash!"

"Well you certainly look like it, wearing that."

"Hey, what's going on?" I interrupted, walking into the kitchen.

They both stared at me.

It wasn't anything new to see them fussing like that. Mother and Emma Claire fought like the Devil and his mule. It was their favorite thing to do to pass time.

"Quinn," Mother said. "Tell Emma Claire that she is not going to school in that god-awful dress. It has a hole in it."

As if I had any influence over that fiery little girl.

"Unquestionable," Emma Claire said. "This is simply absurd and unquestionable."

"Wait," I said to Emma. "I thought that word meant something else."

She ignored me. "Tell Mother that she's not the boss of me!"

"I am the boss," Mother snapped. "Quinn, people will think that she's trash. Is that what you want, Emma Claire? To be a good-for-nothing cracker?"

I failed to see how that mattered at this stage in our lives. Everyone knew we were poor as clams on Friday.

"Come, now," I said. "Let's all calm down, there's no need to shout. Even if we are crackers."

"I ain't no cracker!" Emma hollered. "Maybe you both are, but I'm not!"

"Emma, hush," I whispered, bending down to inspect Emma Claire's dress. It was one of her only dresses, she wore it all the time, even outside to play. "I don't see a rip anywhere."

"It's right there," Mother said. "By the neckline."

My eyes traveled to the neckline, and I saw it, near the white collar, a little tear the size of a penny.

"Oh fiddle, Emma Claire, Mother's right, let's get you changed. Hurry up now, or you'll be late."

"She's a hateful woman." Emma Claire shook a fist at Mother. "Emphatically hateful!"

"Now, now," I said. "There's no need to swear, Emma Claire."

Emma Claire stomped down the hallway as hard as she could. It sounded like a rhinoceros in wooden clogs was doing the two-step in our house. Mother followed behind, stomping just as hard as Emma Claire stomped.

"What did you call me you, little brat?" Mother said. "You horrid little bi–"

"You're not my mother," Emma Claire cut her off. "You don't want me, you don't even care about me."

Mother said nothing.

"It's unquestionably true." Emma Claire's face was becoming swollen with tears. "You don't love me. Never have. Probably never will!"

Mother was quiet. She did not bother to correct Emma Claire.

"You can have my stupid dress!" Emma stripped her dress off in one sweeping motion. She tugged the garment over her head, wadded it into a ball and flung it at Mother. "There, light it on fire, if you want!"

Emma Claire stood there in the hallway in her panties. Her chest heaved with anger, and her ribs showed through her thin pale skin. She looked like a white water bug.

"I hate you!" shouted Emma. Then Emma Claire thought of the worst insult she could utter. It was something she didn't even understand yet. Not all the way. "I hate you, you whore!"

Mother looked at Emma Claire with enough venom to take down a horse. Her voice became quiet and low:

"Well, I hate you too, and I wish I never had either of you. You're both just two big mistakes."

Emma Claire sneered. She ran into my bedroom and slammed the door.

Mother did the same thing, darting into her room. She slammed the door behind her in an identical theatrical manner. The walls of our clapboard house rattled like sheets of paper.

I stood alone in the hallway.

Mother's angry voice came muffled through her bedroom walls. "You've both ruined my goddamn life, I hate you both!"

"That goes unquestionably double for me!" Emma screamed.

~

Emma Claire's bright red dress was a nice one. It was one reserved for special occasions. A little too fancy for school, but it was all she had. She'd almost grown out of it. It was small on her, but no one noticed.

Everything was getting small for her.

Her whole world, in fact.

Emma Claire was getting taller each day. Her legs were stretching into lanky cane poles. Her hair was changing too. It was long dark hair, grown halfway down her back. Overdue for a cutting.

I was the one who cut Emma Claire's hair. The last time I cut it, I'd made it uneven. Cutting hair was a lot harder than it sounded. It's hard to cut thick hair in a straight line. When I was finished with her, Emma Claire looked like she'd fallen headfirst into a mill saw.

But Emma wasn't bothered by my butcher-cuts. At such a young age, she cared little about fashion. She cared more for her books than she did her appearance. Whenever I mangled her hair, I'd hide my disaster by braiding her locks the same way I spliced ropes on my boat.

No one was the wiser.

"Have a good day." I waved to Emma Claire. "Learn something important and then tell it to me."

"Bye, Quinn."

"Unquestionably."

"That's not how it's used."

"I'm working on it."

"Well keep trying."

Bite me, you little brat.

Emma Claire flitted away and pounced up the school steps in her red dress. She toted her books behind her with a leather strap that held them together. I recognized the leather strap as my old belt. That made me smile. Emma Claire must've raided my closet to find that thing.

Resourceful little thief.

I went to light a cigarette when I noticed a figure standing outside the window of my truck. Startled, I turned my head to see Miss Rachel knocking on my window. If she'd've been a man, I would've rolled down the window to speak. But Miss Rachel was a lady.

I kicked open the door and leapt out of the truck.

Miss Rachel smiled at me. "Hello, Quinn."

"Hi, Miss Rachel, how are you today?"

I focused on Miss Rachel's mouth, pointing my good ear in her direction. She spoke so soft and quiet, it was hard for me to hear a single word she said.

"How's business?" she asked.

"Oh fine," I said. "It's been a good season so far."

"That's marvelous. And your mother, how's she?"

"Oh she's okay; you know she works at Carl's now."

"Yes, I'd heard that."

I'm sure everyone had.

I smiled at her. I didn't know what other conversational pleasantries to offer Miss Rachel. I was a cracker, not a socialite. But Miss Rachel was a sharp stick; she knew who she was dealing with.

"You look good, Quinn," she said.

And I thanked her for the sweet lie.

In a way, Miss Rachel was my boss' wife. I sold my oysters to Miss Rachel's husband Harold, and only him. Just like a lot of oystermen did. Harold had been an oystermen in his early days, working the beds like the rest of us. Then, he'd started his own packing and shipping company. His company was a blistering white-hot success, and we all respected him for it. Harold's success trickled down to us.

And he treated us well.

Harold was a city councilman too. And even though oystermen don't know a lick about politics, it made us feel good knowing he was on the council, using his voice.

"I'm worried about Emma Claire," Miss Rachel said.

"You're worried?"

"Yes, I'm worried that Emma Claire is bored."

I ran my hands through my hair. "Yes ma'am."

"The truth is, she's bored senseless in my class."

"I think I understand."

"No, I don't think you do. You see, Emma Claire is bored because she's smart, and her studies are too easy for her."

"Easy?"

Miss Rachel nodded her head. "Far too easy. Emma Claire breezes through everything, faster than the other students do."

"I'll tell her to slow down."

"No. Don't do that, Emma Claire isn't doing anything wrong."

I was quiet for a moment. "Then why's she in trouble?"

Miss Rachel laughed. "She's not in trouble, not at all. She's smart."

It came as no surprise to me.

I knew Emma Claire was smart. Since Emma Claire had been a five-year-old, I'd taken her into town with me to do business. That girl knew how to count exact change better than I did. Emma Claire also knew the names of every player on the Yankees. She listened to the radio games with me all the time. Miss Rachel wasn't telling me anything I didn't already know.

"You're saying that she's...."

"Utterly brilliant," Miss Rachel said. "The most brilliant child that I've ever seen, to be quite honest."

The pride welled up in my belly, rising through my chest.

"With permission, next year, I'd like to advance her."

I cocked my ear closer to her. "Advance her?"

"Quinn, what I mean to say is, I want to move Emma Claire to the seventh grade. She's already learned everything that elementary school has to offer. She needs to stimulation."

Stimulation.

A big word like that sounded unquestionably serious.

In that moment, I began to think about Emma Claire's little face, her fat pink cheeks and dark eyes. I thought about how she liked piggyback rides and the hand-slap game. About how she despised mint, but loved candy canes. That never made any sense to me whatsoever.

"It won't cost a thing, if that's what you're wondering," Miss Rachel said. "Everything will stay the same for Emma Claire's day-to-day studies. She'll just graduate sooner than the others."

Miss Rachel stopped talking and stared at me.

"Quinn, do you understand what I'm saying?"

I couldn't answer her.

Miss Rachel embraced me in the parking lot, like one of her students. She stroked the back of my head with her hand.

"Oh, Quinn. I know you must be so proud."

I was.

Prouder than I'd ever been.

I'd never meant to start crying in front of a lady like that.

It was an indecent thing to do.

~

Emma Claire and I drove down our little dirt road toward home. The path cut through the woods like a dusty creek, right to our front door. I looked through the windows at the green trees. The pines diffused their green scent into the air. Bright green lizards made themselves at home on the long branches. Green palmetto fronds waved to us. Green katydids chirped at us. Green, green, green. Green everywhere.

While it was true that our family was poor, we were lucky. We had a house on green land; that was more than a lot of crackers had. Especially oyster-grunts like me. The land jutted out into the bay like a continent. It was the most valuable thing my family would ever own. We were lucky to have it.

My Granddaddy had come by the huge plot of land long ago when he was a young man. He was smart as a whip. A money-savvy young thing who gambled better than the Devil himself—or so people have told me.

Folks said my Granddaddy was hell at a card table. They said he had more luck than a team of rabbits missing their feet. Granddaddy would show up to card games dressed in raggedy clothes. Inside his ragged jackets, he had hundred dollar bills sewn into the lining. I never knew why he'd done such a thing, but it sounded mighty clever.

I would've loved to inherit one of his old suits.

My truck brakes squealed as I pulled into our driveway. Emma Claire and I both stared at Carl Plight's car parked in front of our house.

We frowned together in unison.

I don't know what it was about Carl Plight that neither of us cared for, it was hard to pinpoint. It wasn't that he was a bad man, he wasn't. In fact, Carl seemed as decent as anyone could be. He'd given Mother a job at his grocery store, and now she was finally earning a little of money.

God knows, I was grateful to Carl for that.

The thing was, Carl Plight was a graceless man. His awkwardness could make even a politician uncomfortable. And Carl never knew exactly which words to say to me. He stumbled over his sentences like he had a full bladder and a mouthful of peanut butter. So, instead, he'd just look at me with his big bug-eyes. Then, he'd say something like, "You been doing much fishing?" to which I would always answer, "You bet your ass."

"Aw, Carl Plight?" Emma moaned. "Again?"

"It appears so."

"How wonderful."

I nodded. "Unquestionably."

~

Mother met Emma Claire and me on the porch. She was covered in white flour and dressed in a frilly apron. One that I'd never seen before. She looked ridiculous wearing such a thing.

"Quinn," Mother said. "Help me. I've made a horrible mess in the kitchen."

I refrained from saying anything sarcastic. What I wanted to say was something about how she ought not mess with skillets. Or flour. Nothing good could come of Mother being anywhere near a bag of flour.

But I held my tongue.

Mother squatted down to Emma Claire's eye level. She put her powdered white hand on Emma's shoulder.

"Emma Claire, I owe you a big apology. I was angry this morning, and I said things I didn't mean. I don't hate you." Mother paused. "I want to say I'm sorry."

Emma Claire glanced at me, but said nothing.

"You too, Quinn." Mother looked at me. "I owe you an apology, too. I shouldn't've said what I said. I love you both. I am grateful to God for you both. I'm so grateful."

Mother was a little drunk, too.

Mother pulled Emma Claire into herself and embraced her. She drew her eyebrows together, wrinkling the skin on her forehead. Emma Claire wrapped her arms around Mother, but didn't squeeze.

Then, Mother stood up and brushed a strand of hair from her face. There were spots of flour on her cheeks.

"Now I want y'all to be sweet to Carl," Mother said. "He's my boss and my good friend. Try to make him feel like he's right at home, you know how uncomfortable he can be."

God yes we knew.

But this would never be his home.

~

The kitchen was a wreck. Flour covered the counter in what looked like a biscuit suicide. The grits on the stove had burned, stuck to the bottom of the pot, charred black.

There's nothing in the world worse than a pot ruined by a grit burning. Except maybe, death by a million splinters. Or being half-eaten by a gator. A grit-burning is the ultimate disaster. The grits weld themselves to the bottom of the pot like tiny chunks of iron. There's nothing you can do to save the pot, you might as well throw it away and forget about it.

"See, I've made a mess," Mother explained. "I was trying to make biscuits and grits so that we could all have a nice dinner for once."

I lifted the spoon out of the skillet. "And I take it this was supposed to be some kind of gravy?"

"I know, it's horrible," Mother laughed, removing her apron. "Can you take over from here?"

"I suppose."

"Oh good, I'm so relieved."

"Well, that makes one of us."

Mother sighed. "You're not mad at me are you, Quinn?"

"No, but you'd better get out of here before you hurt yourself with a rolling pin."

Mother and Emma Claire left the kitchen. They waltzed into the den to join the notoriously amiable Carl Plight. There, Emma would be engaged in an enlightening conversation about the rising price of turnips.

She never liked turnips.

I dusted the counter. I pinched the mixture of butter and flour together between my fingers and wondered how to tell Mother about the good news. About Emma Claire's advancement into the seventh grade. I wondered if I ought to attempt to tell Mother at all. The truth was, I didn't know if Mother would be happy for Emma, or not. Mother could sometimes be indifferent to good news that didn't involve her.

Her self-centeredness was an unpredictable animal that did whatever it wanted. Sometimes, the best way to rain on a parade was to invite Mother to join the procession. And she would suck the fun right out of it. There was no way to know if Mother would be happy, or be jealous-green as a gecko.

I rolled the buttery dough out like a slab. Then I used an upside down jar to cut the biscuits, like a cookie cutter. These would be big biscuits. I might've been a Florida cracker, but I could sure as hell make a good biscuit. Biscuits were my claim to fame. I didn't have many.

Sonnet had even taken my biscuits to the Baptist church picnic once. They hailed my biscuits as the best thing to hit the town since the invention of the shrimp.

"Is there anything I can do in here?" Mother walked into the kitchen to refresh her drink.

"Do?" I asked.

"Yeah, before I go back out there and join the battle in the living room."

"No, I think you've done more than enough in here already."

"I know, it's bad, I'm sorry."

"You ought to have bought a layer cake and left it at that. Carl would've been happy with a layer cake."

"He hates cakes." She rubbed my back. "Thanks for saving the day."

I could smell whiskey on her breath.

"You're welcome," I said, rolling the slab of dough on the counter.

Mother walked over to the table. She sat down and pressed the cold glass against her sweaty forehead to cool herself off.

"How are things with you and Carl?" I asked.

"He's okay, I guess," she whispered. "Some days I like him, some days I don't. You know how it goes."

I knew her.

"Well, what about today?" I asked. "You like him today?"

"It's early yet. I think I like him today."

"Well, look on the bright side, there's always tomorrow."

She laughed and then let out a hiccup.

I knew the truth, and I suspected that Mother knew it too. Though, she'd've never admitted it to herself. Carl Plight was a way for Mother to pass the time, and that was all. He was free entertainment.

For that reason, I almost felt sorry for Carl, having to deal with Mother as his lover. Mother was the most unsatisfied person in the world, forever ill at ease. Emma Claire and I were stuck in her world with her.

"He's been good to me though," Mother added. "I'll give him that. He's a good man."

"Good?"

"Oh, you know, he treats me good at work."

And it probably bored the hell out of her.

"He's a good boss," she said. "Treats everyone fair."

"Oh, well that's decent of him."

"Yes, I suppose it is."

Decent people bored her.

I watched her as she looked out the kitchen window into the darkness. She wasn't always that self-centered. But when Daddy died, he dragged the selfless half of her into the ground with him. The other half of her, the half that still lived, that was the selfish half.

That half was alive and kicking.

Mother rubbed my back while I added fresh cream to the pot of grits on the stove. The cream transformed the grits from light yellow to snow white. The only acceptable color for white grits.

"Grits must have cream in them," I told Mother. "Or else they're bland as bark. If you ever try to make grits again, remember that much. I beg of you."

Mother smiled. She wasn't thinking about the grits.

"Quinn, Honey," she said. "Honey, I know I'm a...."

The liquor was loosening that tongue of hers.

Mother paused and looked into her glass.

I looked back at her and realized that it was all Mother could say, and it was good enough for me.

At least she knew.

~

I could see Sonnet standing on the shore, dressed in pale green. It was the same green color as the fancy key lime pies they served at the inn. She wore her long cedar-colored hair pulled back, hanging behind her head. She did not wave at me, nor did she smile, she just watched us as we neared the soggy beach. Her pale shins and thick ankles poked out from beneath her dress. Those awkward-shaped legs were the best two things God ever made.

Except for those two green eyes.

"There's your honey." Mullet pointed.

"I see her."

"Sure is a pretty thing."

"Unquestionably."

"Huh?"

I wrapped the dock line around my arm, making a spool of rope on my elbow. Mullet stood on the back of the boat, pushing the skiff with a long pine branch. He stabbed the limb into the water and pushed our skiff forward, like a gondola.

"Sonnet's a good girl." Mullet wiped the orange spit from his unkempt beard.

I grinned. It was an understatement, but I let it slide.

"You're lucky to have her," he said. "My paw always told me there're two types of women in this world. There's the kind of woman you take for a wife, and there's the kind of woman who ruin your life." Mullet laughed. "Reckon you already know that though. Better than anyone."

Another understatement.

"What about you, Mullet? Why aren't you married?"

Mullet spit off the side of the boat and said nothing.

He was my best friend, and I realized that I knew nothing about his past. Nothing whatsoever. He never talked about women, children, or grandchildren. In fact, he was mute on all matters of his own history.

Once, when he was good and high on shine, he mentioned a woman named Vivian. But it ended there. And I never asked another question about it.

Vivian.

I'll bet that woman had stories.

Wherever she was.

Mullet jumped off the boat with the dock-rope in his hand. I jumped off the rear of the skiff, my boots splashed in the shallow water. We muscled the heavy boat up onto the gritty shore with our shoulders.

Sonnet waved at us.

"Pardon me, Quinn," Mullet said. "But I need to steal a hug from Freckles over here."

Mullet stomped out of the water. He opened his arms and squeezed Sonnet as tight as he could.

"Good God Almighty," Sonnet said. "Your beard stinks. Someone needs to give you a bath." Sonnet pushed him away, and he cackled like a mischievous piglet.

"Mullet doesn't bathe," I said. "It's against his religion."

"I do, too." He took off his hat. "Once a month, come rain or shine. It's a ceremony, really."

"You know what." Sonnet said. "I actually believe you. It's no wonder you have such a long beard. I suspect you roll in fertilizer to make it grow."

"Shoot," Mullet said. "Ain't no use bathing, it only attracts mosquitoes. They won't touch you if you smell like shit."

"You've got it all figured out, don't you, Mullet?" said Sonnet.

"Not everything, but damn near all of it."

Sonnet changed the subject. "Look, I came down here to tell you two the news, I couldn't wait any longer."

"News?"

"Not good news." She made her face serious.

"What do you mean?" I said.

She tilted her head. "God, I don't know how you could've missed it. It's all everyone is talking about, it's been on the radio all day today."

"And on the party line?" I suggested.

Sonnet shrugged.

"Well dammit, spit it out Freckle-Face," Mullet said.

She bunched her eyebrows up. "America's just joined the war."

10.

The old men who sat on Laddie MacLean's front porch, listened to a small radio on a table. From time to time, his porch would be full of old codgers who gathered to hear the news from it. All the men listened with ears wide open, cigarettes between their fingers. They took turns shaking their heads, mumbling things like, "Have mercy," or "What's this world coming to?"

Laddie sat on his porch swing, presiding over the whole business. He'd rock back and forth, talking back to the transistor radio. It was as if he was having a conversation with it. It was distracting. But no one dared to hush Laddie—it was his porch.

"I just don't understand," Mister Laddie said, his pipe jammed in his teeth. "Why ain't we killed that Hitler yet? Seems like the only solution."

"Mmm hmm." One of the black men nodded.

"Hell, we got airplanes, there's got to be a way to snipe that old Kraut and end it all."

"Mmm hmm. That's right."

Laddie sipped his glass. "This war's been on for two damned years. They've had plenty of time to figure out how to kill that bastard."

I leaned against the porch railing, listening to him shout over the radio. Mister Laddie was deafer than I was, everything he said was like a siren.

"Reckon so," a black man said.

"Don't you know it," another man chimed in.

The sun poked through Mister Laddie's magnolia trees. The translucent leaves looked like clusters of fat emeralds.

I enjoyed being around the old men in our town. They didn't seem to mind that I was a partially deaf cracker with a stir-crazy Mother. But more than that, I liked to watch fiery Mister Laddie get riled up about little things.

Old Laddie could get to hollering in the blink of an eye, about any subject. I once saw him get hopping mad over a plate of under cooked butter-beans. He was so worked up that he had to pour himself a stiff drink to wash them down.

Laddie sneered. "Our president is an idiot," said Mister Laddie, and the men on the porch all bobbed their heads in agreement. No one ever disagreed with Laddie, even if they secretly disagreed with him.

"Well," a black man said. "The way I sees it, old Hitler's kept under lock and key. Ain't no way to sneak a bomber in to nab him. Not when he's under lock and key."

"We're America, boy." Laddie waved his hand. "We got the best army in the whole damn world. We can do anything we please."

The black man stopped talking, recalling the Laddie's butter-bean incident from the previous year.

"Lord God, these is scary times," said another man.

"Sure enough right," Mister Laddie said. "Scary as hell."

The old men had a point. The war scared us. We didn't even know what we were scared of exactly, but we were scared just the same. And every morning brought new fears, like the world might go up in a puff of smoke.

Mister Laddie cleared his throat in the loud way old men often do. He said, "I suppose you all heard we lost Chadley Billman few days ago." Laddie spoke as if Chadley Billman had belonged to us all.

"God Almighty," one man answered.

"Heard they buried him over in Europe."

"Jeezus Lord."

"Yep." Laddie pressed his thumb into his pipe. "I heard Chadley still had his rifle in his hands, never even fired a bullet."

"Mercy."

Mister Laddie looked over to me. "He was about your age, Quinn."

The thought made my blood run as cold as ice tea.

"Mmm hmm," the black man said. "That sure is damn sad."

It was sad.

Damn sad.

Gossip, like the kind done on Laddie's porch, brought the worst headlines. News worse than the radio and the newspaper combined. News of fresh death. Young deaths. Every day.

When the first war-death occurred, I kept track of all the fatalities that followed. They were my peers. I'd grown up with them; it seemed like the right thing to do, to keep score.

For my friends.

Lucas Hill was our first, followed by all three of the Ferry brothers. Then, my own cousin, Tig, was shot over in Italy. Tig was four months older than I was. We used to hunt Mister Fallers' chickens with homemade slingshots together.

He was hell with a slingshot.

Buster Hamms was next. God, I still remember when he taught me how backflip off the swing by the river. His sister was the first girl I ever kissed. Rora. Rora was a wreck when I saw her at Buster's funeral.

After Buster came the two Peck boys. Then came the death of their Uncle Brill, a sergeant in another outfit. Frazzer was next. Our old baseball pitcher. Only one day after him our third-basemen died. Their deaths hit particularly close to home for me.

I didn't eat right for a week after that.

It was then I quit counting deaths. I didn't want to hear about anymore them. Not ever again. Each boy killed was someone who talked like I did. We all had the same brown hands and sun-bleached hair, and we were dropping like flies.

I bent down and stabbed my cigarette on the porch step.

"You taking off, Quinlan?" Laddie asked.

"Yessir. I reckon I'd better quit loafing and get to work before the day's up and disappeared."

"It's Saturday, boy, hope you ain't working yourself too hard."

"No, sir, just came into town to get lightbulbs is all."

Laddie tapped his pipe on the edge of a flowerpot.

"You stay on US soil as long as you can Quinlan, you hear?"

"Yessir."

I intended to do my best to make that old joker proud.

On my way into town, I walked past the Henry Grady building. A tall brick building in the middle of town. Sonnet worked there as a seamstress. The building was filled with young ladies who did their part in the war effort. They labored on the sewing assembly lines like a team of oxen.

By day, they sewed tents, awnings, and canvas bags for the troops. By night, the girls would entertain the visiting soldiers. They'd sit on the soldiers' laps, laughing at their jokes, drinking free beer.

I walked along the sidewalk, watching my shadow on the pavement before me. A group of boys in metal helmets shot past me. They chased one another, darting along the sidewalk. They aimed their wooden rifles at each other, making explosive sounds with their mouths. One of the boys dropped his gun. He clutched his chest and wrinkled his face. The boy pretended to shrivel up and die right there on the grass. He made all the appropriate sounds that go with such an event.

I remembered playing like that once, with my cousin Tig.

Only, we used slingshots.

The war was everywhere. It was all people talked about, preached about, or thought about. It seemed everything in our town revolved around the distant battle. I wanted to forget about it, but it was nigh impossible to do. The war was in every sentence, and on every face. American flags flapped in yards, and war posters peppered the shop windows like wallpaper.

I pushed the door to the hardware store open, the bell on the knob jingled. I noticed the colorful sign in the front window advertising war bonds. An illustration of a grinning Boy Scout on the poster, with a sword in his hand. He looked so happy. I wondered what in God's name he was smiling about.

Maybe he liked swords.

"Howdy, Quinn," Miss Taylor greeted me. She sat behind the counter with her white hair bunched up on top of her tiny head.

"Hi, Miss Taylor," I said.

Miss Taylor stood up from her stool and turned her radio off. "How's your Momma and sister doing?"

"Oh, they're good, Emma keeps taller."

"I've noticed that. Lord, she looks just like your daddy did."

Emma Claire was my daddy's twin.

"You know, Quinn, I remember your daddy when he was a little thing. He used to help Tater raise worms out in the woods behind our house."

My daddy could raise more worms than Christ, himself.

"Mercy," said Miss Taylor. "Your daddy was so skinny. I used to tell him if he didn't eat more, a stiff wind was going to knock him over one day. I reckon you take after him, skinny as you are."

I reckon I did.

"And how is Miss Sonneta Anne?" Miss Taylor asked.

Only old folks called Sonnet by her full name.

Before I could even answer Miss Taylor, the bell on the door rattled behind me. Into the store walked a man in a tan-colored uniform. He removed his cap revealing short cropped blonde hair. He walked right up to the counter, stepping in front of me.

"I'm looking for cigarettes?" he said in a yankee accent.

I stepped aside. "Go ahead sir, I'm in no hurry."

He flashed me a false grin. "Right," he said, and then looked back to Miss Taylor. "You got any Luckys in this place?"

"Yessir." Miss Taylor smiled. "We have all kinds of cigarettes."

"Good, I'll take some Luckys, three packs."

I guess words like please and ma'am, weren't yankee words.

All the yankee soldiers attending the training school at Carrabelle visited our town. The soldiers were young men from all parts of the nation. Some were Southerners, but not many.

The military boys flooded the streets, looking for a quick romp in the hay. They hoped to find temporary solace within our borders. Sometimes they'd go to the docks and look out across the water. Often with a bottle in their hand. I wondered what they were thinking about.

But then, I didn't want to know.

For days at a time, the sidewalks would be overrun with loud, confident men. Men with funny accents, dressed in drab uniforms. They'd sit on overturned buckets and tell their war epics to the young boys in town. Each enlisted man wore that wide eyed look on his face. Like he'd already seen the whole world.

Or like he was about to.

The soldiers all wanted the same basic things during their free time. Things like cheap hooch, cheery music, and to hook arms with a girl for the night.

If not a girl, maybe her mother.

I left the hardware store with lightbulbs. I also bought a carton of One-Eleven cigarettes, and some licorice for Emma Claire. That girl loved licorice more than mud soup. Cigarettes and licorice were inexpensive pleasantries. God knows, we were glad for such things. When I arrived home, I wheeled my truck in to our driveway and threw the truck into park. I leapt out of the vehicle and hiked to our mailbox. I flicked my cigarette butt into a puddle of water and watched the water bugs zip away from it. I opened the mailbox and removed a stack of three envelopes, then rifled through them, one after another. It didn't matter what they said, I couldn't read them very well. I could only read small words. Then, one envelope in particular caught my eye, an official looking one.

From the US Government.

~

Sonnet and I parked beneath our favorite live oak near the water. The tree spiraled toward the sky. Its craggy finger clawed like a knobby witch's hand. My truck was close to the bay's edge. It had once been my daddy's truck, and I loved it. It was a clumsy heap of metal, covered in pretty red dust.

It reminded me of him.

We stared through the windshield at the colors of the sky. There was nothing we liked more than to watch evening take hold of the bay.

I was not my usual self. It was hard to ignore the ache in my stomach; it gnawed inward on me like a hungry boar. I hadn't broken the news about my letter from the US government to Sonnet yet.

She was in too good of spirits.

Sonnet had spent the entire ride to Port Saint Joe talking up a cloud. She told me all about her mother and her brothers. She talked about the Baptist church social. She was particularly proud of her squash casserole that she'd prepared for the event.

She had every right to be.

It was a legendary casserole.

Sonnet liked to talk about whatever that came to her mind. She spoke in one long stream of sentences. About the woman in Sunday school class, who always argued with the teacher. About Felina Williams, who Sonnet hated like the plague. Felina was Sonnet's mortal enemy ever since the missionary bake sale. Felina stole credit for organizing the event and Sonnet never forgave her.

The bake sale had been Sonnet's idea.

The hussy.

Sonnet reclined in the truck, her white feet propped up on the dash, slouched in the passenger seat. She was the happiest thing I'd ever seen. Not a trace of sadness in her eyes.

"What time does the picture start?" I asked, peeling an orange with my pocket knife.

"Six thirty, but you know how I like to get there early to get a good seat."

"Yes, I know."

"It's just so hard to find a good seat with all the people."

I thumbed my knife along the orange. "Well, on a nice Saturday like tonight, everyone will be there."

"That's why we get there early."

"You're an unsung genius." I tossed the peel out the window. "I reckon with all those people in one room, we'll sweat like dogs."

"Probably."

She didn't mind sweating one bit.

"That doesn't bother you, to sweat like that?"

"Nope, I love the movies, hot or not."

And she did.

The theater was still a novelty to her. When they built it in Saint Joe a few years back, it became the hottest thing in five counties.

Everyone paid twenty cents to sit in the dark room, sweating buckets, dazzled by the faces flickering on the silver screen.

As stunning as the movies were, I had little interest in the films, especially all the war footage they rolled before each movie. The black and white reels showed dirty faced men, smoking free Lucky Strike cigarettes, romping through foreign French pastures, rifles slung over their shoulders. The soldiers were probably already dead by the time we saw their grinning faces. They looked almost happy.

Almost.

I ate my orange, looking out the windshield, and then sighed.

"Sonnet, I suppose I ought to tell you the news. I guess now's as good a time as any."

She turned her head and looked at me.

Her bone-serious green eyes.

I did not look at her. "I got a letter in the mail today."

"Letter?"

"In the mail."

She shot up from her seat while I dug the folded envelope from my pocket. It made my palms cold and clammy just to hold.

"You haven't even opened it yet," she remarked.

"No."

"Why not?"

"Scared, I guess." I wiped juice from my chin with my sleeve. "I thought it would be best to let you do it."

"Me?"

"I wouldn't be able to read it nohow."

Without wasting a moment, she ripped it open with her thumb, and slid the letter out. The folded thing was covered in text that I couldn't decipher. It brandished an official-looking stamp. She read the letter quietly to herself and then gathered her eyebrows together.

She read it again.

"Oh my God," she said under here breath.

I nodded.

I knew.

I'd known a slew of boys who'd gotten the same letter. The government made all the boys register at the Post Office. We'd stood in a long line and put our names in the hopper like we were playing a game. Since that day, we all expected our time was coming.

Sooner or later.

Sonnet set the letter in her lap and looked out the passenger window. "Do you want me to read it aloud to you?"

"No."

"But it's important."

"Yeah, I know."

She covered her mouth. "I think I'm going to be sick."

I spit an orange seed out the window, then reached out and took her pale hand. It was soft, covered in freckles, not at all like my brown ugly hands. My fingernails knuckles were as thick as pine knots.

"You don't want me to read it to you, you're sure?" she asked, turning to me.

I shook my head.

She studied my face with her tense eyes.

"Oh, I hate this goddamn war." She tucked the letter back into the envelope and flung it onto the dashboard. "What are we going to do? What are you going to do, Quinn?"

I had no idea.

I looked at the oak through the windshield. The huge tree glowed red in the sunset. A scene grander than any black and white picture show could ever be. I thought about all the colors my human eyes were able to see. Ancient colors the Apalachee had named in their own language long ago.

I turned toward Sonnet. "I'll tell you what we're going to do. You're going to teach me how to read and write, dammit."

~

My bedroom shimmered blue from the moonlight pouring through the window. It was a full moon, and the bright light in the bedroom made it hard to sleep. Though, I had other things on my mind too.

I glanced upward from my pallet on the hard floor. Emma Claire was fast asleep in my bed above me. Her mouth was wide open, making dry raspy sleeping sounds.

That was my place. There on the floor. I didn't mind it. I lay on the ground every night, staring at the ceiling. I counted the smudges and water spots accumulated up there. I traced along their shapes with my finger.

I imagined myself huddled in a European ditch. I could see myself with a cold rifle, with muddy hands, a photo of Sonnet tucked in my shirt pocket. I imagined bullets, voices screaming, and the sounds of explosions in the distance.

I thought about Ricky Flount, a boy my age. He'd been all too excited to get shipped off when they called his number. Ricky was ready to leave our oystering world behind him. He wanted to see something bigger, to be free.

To hold a government rifle.

Ricky had a bunk ear like mine; in fact, he was even more deaf than I was. In elementary school, the teacher made the two of us sit together at the same desk. She thought our two good ears would equal one able-bodied student. They didn't. We heard a quarter of everything the old hag said. Didn't matter anyway, we knew our daddies would pull us out of school as soon as we were old enough to scratch our privates.

But our deafness was where our similarities ended, we were nothing alike. Ricky was a fierce, short young man. He was always fussing with someone to prove his toughness. Trying to make up for his disability.

Once, Ricky got into a fistfight with Cornelius Hill because he thought Cornelius called him Tricky Ricky. Ricky hated that nickname. Ricky fought hard, but lost. Cornelius crawled Ricky up one side and down the other. Beat him like a stepson.

When the walloping was over, Cornelius and Ricky were still as tight as ever. It didn't affect their friendship in the least. I couldn't understand how such a thing was possible after a fistfight. Boys like Ricky were different than me. They were fighters.

I wondered if Ricky was alive.

Emma Claire's lanky arm dangled over the edge of the bed. She snored like an old man. Her grunts came and went in the same rhythm as the tide. I thought about what would happen to her when I left. Emma Claire was almost the same age I'd been when Daddy died.

She was a teenager now. She was awkward and tall. She could gut a fish without my help, but was still afraid to sleep alone. It was one of those things that didn't make good sense.

I looked at the ceiling again. I thought about all the happiness our family had lost over the years. All the happiness I'd lost. I reckon it didn't matter in the end, I wasn't using it anyway.

Emma tossed on the bed above me, sleeping in her convulsive way. She was one of those sleepers who kicked and waved her arms in the night. It was dangerous to fall asleep near her. That girl had smacked me with her flopping arms many times.

When she was younger and we shared the same mattress, Emma Claire gave me a bloody lip. It happened in the middle of the night, her hand fell onto my face. It scared the living Jesus out of me. I thought I'd been shot with a twenty-two.

I looked up at her slack hand, hanging limp over the edge of the covers. I held my own hand up to hers. Her hand was almost as big as mine own.

God.

She was almost a woman.

~

"Sound it out," Sonnet said.

My pronunciation was that of a two-year-old reading the dictionary. I tried to force the words out, but they weren't coming.

"That's it. You have to break the word up into big chunks," she said.

It didn't help.

I sounded out the syllables. I pushed them out of my mouth like cement blocks. The words tumbled from my fat lips. It was as though I was attempting to speak foreign language.

Backward.

"That's good," she encouraged me. "It's coming back to you, I can tell."

I wondered how on earth she thought such a thing.

I looked up at the sky. I found it a strange feeling not to be out in the oyster beds, not working during such weather. I hadn't put in a full day of work since Roosevelt had the gall to draw my number.

Since my draft call, I spent every moment of the day with Sonnet. I breathed her in. I wanted to memorize her face so I could see it whenever I closed my eyes.

"Quinn." Sonnet tapped her pencil on the page. "Dammit, focus now or I'll stab you in the eye with this pencil."

I liked it when she cussed.

It suited her.

We read out of a children's book that belonged to her. She used it in the first grade. Inside the book were illustrations of a boy climbing a tree. He played with his dog, running, and skipping rope. His name was Dick, and he was a happy little towhead who had the world by the scruff of the neck.

Lucky Dick.

"That's good," Sonnet said. "No shame in reading it slow."

Speak for yourself.

"See Dick run," I read the words with a heavy tongue.

"Very good."

"See Dick jump."

"Good, nice and slow."

"Dick. Can. Climb–climb a tree."

"Good."

"See Dick fall out of the tree and break his ever-loving neck."

"Hey, it doesn't say that."

"Dick is dead."

"Quinn, stop it."

"Poor Dick."

Sonnet was a talented teacher, patient, better than any I'd had in elementary school. Our childhood teachers were horrid. They knew we were cracker-boys. They, like us, knew we were going to be fishermen, loggers, and mill-workers. They didn't force-feed us anything. To be fair, there would've been no point in it.

My father thought the same way they did. Like many poor people, he didn't place much importance on education. To the impoverished, reading and writing were like fancy cars. Sure, they were amusing, but far too expensive for a cracker to own.

"This word right here." Sonnet touched the text on the page. "It sounds different than it's spelled. It's a hard one."

"Lag," I said.

"No, I'll give you a hint." She tapped her lower leg. "It sounds like the word calf."

I looked at her thick shin and forgot all about reading.

"Pay attention, Quinn, sound it out."

I squinted at the page. "L-L-Laugh?"

"Good. See what you can do when you focus?"

"But, I don't get it, what does Dick have to laugh about?"

She rolled her eyes at me.

It was hard to focus on the colorful illustrations and black text in the book. All I could think about was my own grim future, one where I'd be holding a rifle not meant for hunting. I imagined myself dressed in drab green, my head clad in iron, stiff boots not yet broken in. I had tender feet, I wondered if they'd let me bring my own boots.

Likely not.

"How about this word?" she said.

I concentrated. "Hmmm."

"Come on, you can do it."

 No I couldn't.

"I know you can do it."

I wasn't so sure.

"Read the word for me."

Coming right up, Sarge.

I focused on the lines of text, squinting my eyes at them. All the letters looked the same, more or less. Like gibberish.

Sonnet put the pencil down and slumped into her chair. She stretched her neck forward, smoothing her coarse hair. Then she took a breath. "Quinn, you're never going to learn how to read in two weeks. Not if you don't push yourself."

I stared down at the word. I focused all my energy on it, willing it to bounce off the page.

Nothing happened.

Sonnet pulled her mess of hair over a shoulder, inspecting the ends. She was giving up on me.

It happens to the best of us.

"Shout?" I said.

"Hey, that's it." She sat up straight. "You're getting it."

I collapsed in my chair and let out a groan.

"You should be proud of yourself, Quinn. You're improving."

"But I don't know any big words yet," I said. "Real words. You know, so that I can write letters when I'm gone."

"Oh, you don't need to know big words to do that. You can still say a lot with little words."

She touched my cheek with her warm hand. "Little words like love. Words like you. Me. Us."

Those weren't little words.

~

Four empty bowls littered the table. Everyone had eaten their fill of oyster stew. It wasn't bad eating. Everyone liked it. Oyster stew was the easiest thing I knew how to prepare; we ate a lot of it in those days. Sometimes, I didn't have the wherewithal to prepare an elaborate meal. So we ate basic stew instead. It's nothing but cream, butter, and oysters.

Simple. Elegant. Lazy.

Sonnet helped me cook. She was lightning fast in the kitchen, and could handle a knife better than I could. She sliced onions and garlic faster than a scalded dog.

I still hadn't told Mother or Emma Claire about the draft letter. I didn't have the courage. I suppose I didn't want to say it out loud. It pained me to mouth the weighty words. I didn't want to release them into the air for the rest of the world to hear. Still, I owed it to them, it was too important to ignore.

I cleared my throat and set one hand on the table.

"I have something to tell you both," I announced.

Emma Claire looked me dead in the eye.

"Well," Mother said. "What a coincidence, I have something I want to tell as well."

Sonnet and I exchanged looks.

"Okay, you go first Mother," I said.

Sonnet squeezed my hand and nearly cut off my circulation.

Mother sighed and gathered her emotions. "Carl fired me from the grocery store. He and I are finished."

"Oh my God." Emma Claire threw her arms up.

Mother narrowed her eyes at Emma Claire.

"It happened yesterday," Mother continued. "He didn't even have the nerve to tell it to me in person. He had Gregory do his dirty work."

"Is it for real this time?" Emma Claire said.

"Oh, it's for real."

Emma laughed. "Mother, do you even know what reality is?"

"What's that supposed to mean?"

"Figure it out."

"That's quite enough, young lady."

Emma scoffed at her.

Mother looked down at the table, I saw a tear fall into her empty bowl. The poor woman had been toying with Carl, off and on, for the last few years. She'd had lots of these conversations with us.

"I'm tired of being taken advantage," Mother said. "I deserve someone better than him."

"Gimme a break." Emma Claire smacked her forehead. "You know, I don't blame him for breaking it off."

"Hey. Why do you say that?"

"Because you've slept with every greasy jerk at that store. Everybody in town knows that. Why would Carl want you?"

Mother's face tensed. "How dare you."

"Me? How dare me?"

Emma was getting wound up tighter than a pocket watch.

"How dare you," Emma shot back. "Nothing ever changes with you. You want one thing, then you change your mind. And you make us all miserable for it."

Mother's volume of voice was getting louder too. "Why do you torture me like this?"

"Torture you? You've got it backward. You're the tormentor."

Mother wore a confused look. "I don't do ever anything to anybody."

Emma conceded. "For once you're right. You don't. You don't do anything."

"Huh?"

"You don't do a damned thing!"

"Emma Claire."

"Nothing! You're hopeless!"

I'd finally had enough.

I pounded my fist on the table and shot up from my seat. My chair rocketed behind me, falling backward on the ground. The air in the kitchen grew still. Both Mother and Emma looked up at me.

My face was hard. I wanted to say something, to shout at them, to scold them for being selfish. I tried to speak, but my words got stuck in my throat. I stood with an open mouth, unable to coax out a sentence.

So I closed my eyes.

"I'm taking Sonnet home," I said. "It's getting late."

I took aim with the rifle and pulled the trigger.

The entire forest canopy erupted. Birds flittered from their nests, scrambling for safety in the top branches. The squirrel darted along the trunk of the pine, peering down at me with black doll eyes. Its little rib cage expanded with each rapid breath.

I missed.

I lowered the rifle and decided to let it go.

"You're letting it run free?" Sonnet whispered. "I didn't think hunting worked that way."

"Naw, I'm not going waste ammunition on that little thing. I'll let him live to fight another day. He might be someone's granddaddy anyway."

"Huh?"

"You know, if humans come back as animals."

"Are you feeling okay?"

Our boots made deep impressions in the soft mud as we hiked through the woods. A blanket of furry pine straw covered the forest, sweet scented and thick. The saw greenbrier crept up the trees like thin snakes. The vines pointed leafy spindles at us as we passed by.

The days seemed shorter, like blips of sunlight. Morning was followed by twilight, then dusk, then morning again. Each day shorter than the last. Only a few hours long. Before I had a chance to wake up, the day was halfway over. The soldiers in town told me it was all very normal. They said that the days would slow down to a snail's pace once I was in a uniform.

I believed that.

We marched along until we found a clearing. Sonnet sat down on a tree stump and crossed her legs, watching me. She never accompanied me hunting, but she'd insisted on it that day.

War makes people do strange things.

Sonnet didn't say but a few words while we meandered through the forest. The sanctuary of longleaf pines lends itself to quietness. I imagined that the Indians long ago would've been as quiet as the trees when they hunted. That would've been back when the woods belonged to them, and only them. Long before civilized man trespassed with his noisy thunder-sticks.

I shouldered the rifle, aimed high, and felt the weapon's weight in my arms. Another squirrel zipped through the treetops, prancing from limb to limb. The rifle popped, and the forest awakened with the shot. Birds and animals evacuated the area, all at once, leaving the state of Florida forever.

The furry squirrel fell limp to the ground.

I hoped it wasn't someone's granddaddy.

Sonnet walked over, lifted the squirrel by its tail, and placed it into the bag. I wrapped my arm over her shoulder and pulled her near to me. I kissed her cheek and inhaled her smell. Her skin smelled like stale sweat and strawberries.

She gave me a soft grin.

Soon, I would report to the induction office in Tallahassee. There I would surrender myself to my government, to Selective Services. I would become a publicly-owned man. I would eat what they told me to eat and go to the bathroom when they permitted.

And die if they commanded.

But that wasn't for a few days yet.

We walked home through the woods. We knew that on that particular night we would not talk of war, or dying. That night we would eat. I would cook squirrel, with gravy. Gravy so thick you could mortar bricks with it. I would dice the meat up into small pieces and serve it up steaming hot over a bed of rice. And biscuits, I would make my famous biscuits for her.

Biscuits were Sonnet's favorite.

~

Emma Claire sat on the porch. Her knees were drawn into her chest, and she was crying. Emma was not a pouter, in fact, she rarely cried. If ever she did break down and sob, the world shook on its foundations.

She made certain of it.

Emma tucked her face in her knees when she saw us. Sonnet

tromped up the porch with the bag of squirrels in her hand.

"Emma Claire," Sonnet said. "What's wrong?"

She didn't answer.

I knew how to fix that.

"Okay," I said. "We'll leave you alone, Emma Claire."

Emma wasn't about to let me off that easy.

"When were you going to tell me?" Emma Claire lifted her head and drilled her dark eyes in me.

She ignored Sonnet altogether.

"I'm going inside to start supper." Sonnet zipped inside, the screen door slapped behind her.

Emma Claire paid no mind to Sonnet. "When did you get this?" Emma held the letter in her hand. "You're leaving in less than a week."

"How did you find that?"

"Oh, please, I know where you keep your hoarded money. It's under the floorboard behind your dresser."

I needed to find a new hiding place.

I sat down next to Emma Claire, dug a pack of smokes from my pocket.

"Quinn, how could you be so selfish, not to tell me?"

Selfish.

We had different definitions of that word.

"Well," I clicked my lighter shut. "The fact is, I did try to tell you and Mother, a few times."

"You didn't try hard."

"I guess not."

"So, you were you just going to disappear one day? Was that your plan?"

I shrugged, I never had a plan.

"God," she moaned. "What's happening?"

I reached my arm around her and drew her near to me. Emma Claire sobbed into my bad ear, I couldn't hear her, but I could feel her heaving on my neck.

"Don't leave me, Quinn. Don't."

I patted her dark hair, noting how long it was. It was overdue for a good butchering.

"I have to." I looked at her in the eye. "They don't give us a choice, Emma Claire."

"But you can run away. They'd never find you."

"Now, that's ridiculous."

She sat up straight. "No it's not, it's perfect."

And to her young brain, it was.

"That wouldn't be right, Emma." I exhaled. "That's not the way I am."

"You could do it for me."

"Unquestionable."

"That's not how the word's used," she said, sniffing.

What was it about that word?

"Quinn, if you go, if you leave, to fight, you could be—" She paused. "I can't bring myself to say it."

I exhaled a stream of smoke through my nostrils. "Killed?"

She cried.

"There are plenty of things worse than death," I lied.

She turned to look at me. Her tears gave way to anger. She shoved the letter against my chest with a thud, knocking me backward.

"Just forget about it." She wiped the tears from her face. "You don't care about me anyhow. You've got Sonnet now, and she's all you care about nowadays."

"Oh, Emma, don't do that."

"You know, I wish you'd leave right now, get out of here, just go and die already, get it over with."

I reached out to her, but she swatted my hand away.

"Don't touch me," she said. "Don't you ever touch me again. You're not my father, you're not my anything. You hear me?"

She stormed off from me with her hands on her hips, stomping her feet on the wooden porch. The whole clapboard house shook beneath the power of her steps.

Sonnet emerged onto the porch, with a damp dishrag in her hands.

"What on earth happened?" she said.

I stabbed my cigarette butt onto the deck and flicked it into the woods.

"Oh, don't worry about her," I said. "She's just upset."

"So I take it she knows?"

"God yes, she knows."

"Well, I'm sorry it went so bad."

I stood up and embraced Sonnet. I closed my eyes. Sonnet was nothing like the dramatic women in my household. I was grateful for that.

"Will she be okay?" Sonnet asked.

"Emma Claire will be just fine. Now let's go inside and eat someone's furry, little granddaddy."

"Huh?"

~

120

The night was thick and wet. Sonnet and I slept in the woods, right near the water. It was the only place where we could be together the whole night through. We didn't want to rouse her family's Baptist suspicions. Her family was more devout than mine.

My family wasn't religious. Far from it. In fact, I'm certain the Baptist pastor warned his male parishioners about my mother.

Sonnet and I held each other and petted one another's teary faces. It was a bitter night, a wonderful night, all wrapped up in sadness. We'd made love, but there'd been no comfort in it. We were both too enveloped in anguish, our bodies didn't care one way or the other. We ached. It was a pain that neither of us could identify as either good or bad.

"I'll miss you, Quinlan." Sonnet pulled the covers sung beneath her neck.

"Oh Sonnet, I'll miss you more."

"No you won't."

"Yes I will."

"No, you will not."

I let her win.

One of us was right, that was all that mattered.

I kissed her, and I felt her mouth on mine. She was smaller than I was, but more powerful. She grabbed my shoulders so hard that she hurt me, clutching at me, pulling me. I looked at her in the dark, but could only make out her shape, her lean silhouette. She blended in with the darkness.

"You're going to think of me every night," she said, lifting her head from the pillow. "Right?"

"How could I not?"

"Well, I know that men get lonely."

"What?"

"Well, when men get lonely, you know, they go out looking."

"I'm not that kind of man."

No one existed in my world but Sonnet.

Furthermore, if ever another girl had pursued me, Sonnet would've ripped her head off and chucked it into the bay, without pausing to kick off her shoes.

The girls in town all stayed the hell away from me.

And that suited me just fine.

I couldn't see Sonnet's face, it was too dark. She laid her head back down onto my chest. I knew I was fading from her a little more with each second. I was halfway to Europe. And even though Sonnet was right there in my arms, she was fading too. Already one of my distant memories. More memory than she was flesh.

"I'll think of you every second of every day," she said. "For as long as I live. Forever."

"That goes double for me."

"Triple for me."

"Whatever comes after triple, that goes for me."

"Quadruple."

"There's no need to swear, young lady."

She laughed and pressed her cold nose against my stubbly cheek. I closed my eyes and thought of how she would live in the letters she wrote to me. She'd stay tucked in a foot locker at the end of my government bunk. Her photograph, would remain stuffed in my shirt pocket. They'd find her picture when they found me, lying dead in the Italian mud. They'd comment on what a nice-looking girl she was and wonder what on earth she was doing with a boy so ugly that he had to sneak up on a mirror.

I could hear her breath in my good ear.

It made me sad to think that I was ruining her life, and she was ruining me. It would've been easier if we'd never have met at all. At least then, maybe, I'd've gone off to Europe without a care in the world.

Sonnet held me tight and wrapped her arms around me. She pushed herself close. I could not tell where her cotton dress ended and my faded denim began. Then she pressed her face into mine. I tried to speak, but my voice didn't work.

It didn't matter what I said in that moment anyhow. I was holding her, and that was well enough.

She cried, her briny tears dripped from her cheeks, and rolled onto my shoulder.

Then she yawned.

Sleep nipped at us both, but we kept shaking it off. We lay still, forcing ourselves to stay awake. Neither of us wanted to disappear into our hazy dreams. We wanted to be present, right there.

With one another.

Something wonderful happened that night, in our souls. Something matrimonial. I don't know much about how the law works, Lord knows I don't. But that night we pronounced ourselves properly married. It was a cracker-wedding, mind you. And there weren't any witnesses except the bullfrogs.

But it was a wedding by God.

Same as any other.

In the morning, we found ourselves covered in cold dew as the sun peeked over the tree line at us. I stared at the orange ball in the sky with weary eyes. I wished that a sudden hurricane in the Gulf would extinguish the sun like a little candle.

Sonnet rested her elbows on my chest and looked down at me. Her bloodshot eyes were pink and green.

"Today," she bit her lip. "Today's the day I lose my husband."

~

Mother and I stood on the porch. I held my tote sack over my bony shoulder. I wasn't sure the Army would let me keep my bagful of belongings, but the draft letter said to bring a bag anyway. It was a bag Mother made out of an old flour sack years ago. Back when she still gave Christmas presents. She'd even put my initials on it. Q.A.A. Quinlan Adam Applewhite.

The initials were fading.

"Oh, Quinn." Mother took a draw from her cigarette and pulled it from her mouth. "I just can't believe you're leaving. It ain't fair, it just ain't fair."

I wish I could've disagreed.

"I guess it's about time," Mother said. "About time I learned how to cook, finally, learn how to make my own dinner."

We both laughed.

We both knew how absurd such a statement was.

I heard gravel breaking underneath the truck tires. The red truck with the gator head inched down our driveway.

Then I heard something behind me, in my good ear. I turned to see Emma Claire's face behind the screen door. Emma watched Mother and me with sad eyes. She pushed the door open and walked with her head drooped. It was her version of an apology, and her timing was perfect.

I encircled Emma Claire and wrapped my arms around her.

She did not speak a word, and neither did I.

Her silence said a lot more than her words could've.

My mother stomped out her cigarette, wearing a feeble smile. She pulled me to her one final time and squeezed me. I heard my back pop as our hearts pressed against one another. We stood there, separated by nothing more than bone, muscle, and fabric.

"Goodbye, Mother," I said.

It was then that my mother's face split wide open, and she cried like a baby.

I rarely called her Mother.

~

Three of us crammed in Mullet's truck like sardines. Sonnet rested her head on my shoulder.

We drove past the corn fields and cotton. With each mile, the trees became thicker. Pine trees gave way to fat oaks, tufted with green bushels of leaves. Healthy and tall. The dirt highway cut through the northern fields like abandoned paths in the woods. Mullet's old truck rattled like it might shake apart into a million pieces.

The interconnected paintings inside Mullet's truck were like old friends of mine. Throughout the years I'd seen them thousands of times. Nude Lady Eve stared down at Sonnet and me. She looked like she was apologizing for what she'd done to humanity.

It was only an accident.

She didn't mean anything by it.

When we arrived to Tallahassee, we drove through the city like a mule at a dinner party. Slow. We looked for the War Induction office, but all the stone buildings looked the same.

New.

The Selective Services building was a big, brick one. There were cars and buses scattered around it. The pavement was swarming with young men, some of them my age, some older. They walked around in nervous circles, puffing on cigarettes. Their nerves, like mine, had ruptured, spilling fresh adrenaline into the air.

I looked around at the large city. It was the second time in my life I'd ever been to Tallahassee. The place was bigger than anything I'd ever seen. On every corner were complicated structures, works of stone sculpture, with statues and flourishes. The buildings in Tallahassee were much bigger than the faded clapboard buildings in my hometown. Our humble town stood cracked and chipped with salt air, like it wouldn't last one more stretch of bad weather.

Sonnet pulled me near to her and pushed her forehead against mine. The bones of our skulls knocked together, and I felt the warmth of her breath. She held me there, staring at my mouth, breathing in and out. She said nothing, but I knew what she meant.

I was thinking the same thing.

Mullet stood beside the truck with his hat off, and he shook my hand. His little hands were like tough oven mitts. He watched me with serious eyes and a cheek full of chaw.

"Give them hell, boy," he said. "Give them hell."

I knew not to answer him; it would've undermined his words.

The Selective Services room was air-conditioned, and it felt like a refrigerator. I'd only seen air conditioning once before in my life, at Michael Banks' home on the other side of our town.

The Banks family lived in a huge Antebellum estate on the water. It had shooting columns, a high roofline, and tall stained glass windows. Their kitchen had an air conditioner. Once, I held my face up to the thing. Jesus, it liked to freeze my nose clean off.

The young man sitting next to me stuck his hand out.

"Name's Dirk," he said.

I turned my good ear toward him. "Pardon?"

"Said my name's Dirk, what's yours?"

"Quinn." I shook his hand.

"Nice to meet you, Quinn, where're you from?"

Dirk was nervous as a flea.

"Eastpoint," I answered.

"Oh yeah? Don't know where that is."

There's no reason he should've.

"Eastpoint is small."

"I'm from Columbus, myself. Ain't exactly small, but we get bored just like small town folks do."

I had no idea what he was talking about. I'd never been bored a day in my life.

"Quinn, I'm nervous, how about you?"

That was putting it mildly.

"I'm doing okay," I said. "As long as they don't stick any probes in me, or shove a needle in my neck."

"First time at a doctor?"

"Yep."

"Me too."

The war induction office was dreary, with hanging tin lights and brick walls. The room was overrun with a mess of silent boys. No one but gregarious Dirk said much. And Dirk made up for the collective silence with his river-mouth.

A curly-haired nurse emerged from the door.

Every man looked at her with a half-smile and stood to his feet. The girl had more curves than a billiard ball. It didn't matter though, we were almost too nervous to notice such things.

Almost.

She glanced at her clipboard and called my name. I rose from my seat drawing the eyes of the entire room. I couldn't shake the feeling that

I was a head of livestock. A longhorn, getting ready to have a visit with the butcher.

"Hey, good luck, Quinn," Dirk said.

"Thanks, you too."

Dirk smiled, and I noticed his eyes were bloodshot.

Even more than mine.

I followed the nurse back through the corridor. She took me past the hallway of exam rooms. I trailed three feet behind her like a lost puppy. The curly-haired girl turned and smiled at me before opening a door that led me into a small room. In the room was the physician, seated on a chair, reading through his notes.

The physician introduced himself to me and I pumped his slender hand. He was a pale man with a shiny head trimmed in a wreath of white hair. He didn't have the hand strength to open a jar of jam.

"Okay, let's get to it," the physician said. "Remove your clothing, please, and put these on."

The nurse handed me a pair of white shorts that looked a few sizes too small for a four-year-old.

"Right here?" I asked. "Right now?"

He nodded and looked down at his notes.

The nurse turned her back while I gave the doc a free show.

When I finished changing into my lingerie, the doc inspected me like a mechanic. It was as if he were searching for leaks on an old Ford. He weighed me, measured me, looked at my tongue, and patted my elbows. He even investigated my head of hair. Then, he sat me on the tall, cold, metal table. He shined lights in my eyes and made me read large letters on the white sign.

"Can you read those letters?" he asked.

After all my studying with Sonnet, I could've read the *Declaration of Independence*.

He struck my knees with a little hammer and watched my legs bounce with delight. The whole thing reminded me of how Daddy used to inspect a hound puppy. He'd inspect their hips and then check the roofs of their mouths to see if they were black or not. Black-mouthed dogs were guaranteed good animals. Pink mouthed animals were only good for companionship, nothing more.

I had a pink mouth.

"Do you have depression?" the doc asked.

"No sir, I don't think so."

"Good, good."

He wrote on his board and then looked up at me. "Okay, remove those shorts."

"My shorts?" I glanced at the curly-haired nurse. "But you just had me put them on, Doc."

He smiled. "Yes. Now please take them off."

I dropped my shorts and showed the old man everything I had to offer this world. Then, he surprised me. He inspected my vulnerable regions with his cold rubber gloves. The curly-haired nurse did not turn her head this time. She intended to get her money's worth.

The old man groped my genitals in his palms, and was not gentle about it, not in the least. I looked over at the nurse in the corner of the room again.

She was smiling at me.

"Mister Applewhite, I'm looking for the Great Impostor," he said fondling me. "Have you heard of that before?"

"Sir?"

"The Great Impostor." The doc stood up and removed his rubber gloves with a snap. "It's another name for syphilis. You can pull your drawers up now."

"Sir?" I said again, pointing my good ear toward him.

"Syphilis." He cocked his head. "Do you know what that is?"

"No, sir."

He looked at me, taking his glasses off.

"Son, why do you keep turning your ear to me like that?"

"This is my good ear." I slid up my shorts.

"Your good ear?" The doc pulled a little tool out of his pocket and inserted it into my ear. "Which ear is your good ear?"

I tapped my right ear. "This one."

"Carol," he said. "Bring me the fork."

The nurse rose from her chair and burrowed through the drawer. She handed him a silver wishbone-shaped object.

The physician tapped the metal fork and then pressed the stem of it into my forehead. It tickled, vibrating above my eyebrows.

"What do you hear when I do this?" he asked me.

"Ringing."

"In which ear?"

I touched my right ear.

"What about now?" He tapped the fork again and pressed the stem near my left ear. "Do you hear anything in the left ear?"

"Sir?"

He furrowed his brow. "Hmm, I see."

The doctor looked down at his clipboard and scribbled out a paragraph. Finally, he sighed, then handed me the clipboard.

"Okay, Quinlan, sign this please," he said.

I wrote my name down on the line in my neatest handwriting.

"I'm sorry, son, but I'm classifying you as Four F. Do you know what that means?"

"No sir, I don't."

He put his hand on my shoulder. "Look, I know you want to serve your country, Mister Applewhite. But I can't let you into the US Army. Not with that." He pointed to my ear. "That thing would get you killed in a jiffy."

The world started spinning around me all of a sudden. I felt like I was on one of those merry-go-rounds. The kind the traveling carnival folks brought to Saint Joe several years ago. They called it the Magic Wheel of Fun. I paid a nickel to get sick as a dog on that thing.

"Sir? I don't understand."

"Now, don't lose heart son," he said. "You can still help your country in other ways." He patted my leg. "But Four F means that you're going back home. I'm sorry, but you'll have to sit this war out."

He tore a sheet from his clipboard and handed it to me.

"Finish getting dressed, and Carol will see you out."

I stood up, staring at the paper in my hands.

"Mister Applewhite," said the doctor, looking over his glasses at me. "Try not to look so relieved, please. It's bad for business."

11.

Over the next few summers, I watched my favorite pine tree die. It didn't happen right away. Trees don't die right away. Only if lightning strikes them. Even then, they can go right on living, scarred in unusual ways.

No, my favorite tree died a little each day. It was pine beetles that killed it. They did it in a torturous manner, gobbling up the tree up one mouthful at a time.

I hated those little bugs worse than taxes.

The tree wasn't an exceptional climbing tree. None of its limbs were near enough to the ground for that. It wasn't a shade tree, either; it didn't have enough greenery to be one of those. But that's not why I liked the tree.

I liked the big tree because it was a gracious, ancient pine, with a trunk as thick as a wagon wheel. It had held its place in our front yard for a few hundred years. It was a piece of our world, and it was part of my permanent memory. It was an object we looked at every day. It had been here when the Apalachee had. The tree had endured storms, floods, fires, and the hateful Spanish. Such things had made its skin rough and thick.

All of that would've made my skin thick, too.

Long ago, when my granddaddy won the land, the pine would have been a few inches skinnier. Maybe only as big around as a soup kettle back then. The older it got, the fatter its base became.

Daddy told me most of the pines on our property were a few hundred years old. The thicker ones, like my favorite, were likely three hundred years old. Three hundred. I couldn't comprehend numbers that big. Sonnet explained the arithmetic to me once. She said that a tree three hundred years old would've dated all the way back to the days of

Columbus.

I had no idea Columbus, Georgia was so old.

At first, I noticed the black pock marks multiplying all over the body of the pine. Then, the tree's bark began to shed in huge chunks, shattering on the ground below.

God, it made me sad. It was like watching an animal die.

After a few summers, most of the bark had fallen off the tree. The pine became faded, gray, and naked. Its soul left it. It escaped like a ghost through the bullet holes the beetles bored into it.

Soon, the lifeless top limbs looked like stone snakes. They became dry, and there was no foliage left on them. They released their needles into the breeze and gave up the last ounce of their life.

And so it went one summer, that my tree finally died.

I had to cut it down with an axe.

~

Emma Claire's new male friend and I stood on the porch together. We waited for her like obedient labradors. He was a stocky boy with a tuft of coal black hair and pale skin. I eyed him up and down, examining his build.

His shoes were new and un-scuffed.

So were his face and hands.

"That looks like it must've been a big tree." He directed his gaze to the big stump in the front yard.

I shrugged. "It was."

"Must've been, what, a hundred years old?"

"Try three."

He whistled.

The boy on the porch rocked on his heels, with his arms folded. He carried himself with a stiff neck and an easy walk. His face had a permanent smirk on it. His clothes looked like they were fresh off the department store shelf.

"Mind if I bum a smoke?" he asked.

I removed a cigarette from my shirt pocket and handed it to him.

He jammed the cigarette between his lips and looked at the tree stump again.

"I'm Quinn," I said, extending my hand.

"My name's Shelby, but everyone calls me Scrubs." He shut his lighter and did not offer his hand.

"What do you do, Scrubs?"

"Nothing right now, I just graduated last year."

Just as I thought.

Young and lazy.

He sucked a chestful of smoke from the cigarette. "My father wants me to go to work for him, but I want to join up. I'd love to go kill Germans."

Young, lazy, and rich.

In the driveway was Scrubs' fanciful green car, sparkling like a glossy advertisement. The chrome on it looked like a mirror reflecting the full power of the sun. He was too young for such a car.

"So, how do you know Emma Claire?" I asked.

"Oh, she's a friend of Jesse's."

"So you're Jesse's brother?"

"Yep, Jesse's my baby sister. Only she's not a baby anymore."

"Nope, she's not."

He laughed. "Jesse's a full blown woman now."

She was a rich brat is what she was.

Jesse was my least favorite of Emma Claire's friends. Snotty and patronizing. But Scrubs was right about one thing, Jesse was a young woman. So was Emma Claire. She'd become a woman overnight. She was long and lean like a lamp pole.

"All the boys in town want Jesse." He smiled. It was a knowing smile, too old for him to be wearing. A flat-faced, privileged grin. One that crawled up his cheeks and settled into his affluent blue eyes.

"So, what about you, Quinn?" he asked. "What do you do?"

"How's that?"

I turned my ear toward him.

"I mean, for a living, what do you do?"

"Oh, I'm a hambone."

"A what?"

"An oysterman."

He nodded like he understood.

I sighed. "I'm afraid that I'm a cracker, just like my sister is."

He tilted his head back a little.

There was that look of his again.

I stared again at his shining vehicle in the driveway. Its fat white tires were covered in the red dust from our little dirt road.

I realized I was behaving rude toward him. He couldn't help being so rich. I resolved to try to give this boy a chance, to try to accept him with open arms. Maybe he really was a nice boy.

"That's a fine looking horse." I glanced at his car.

"Yeah, my father just bought it for me, I don't like the ugly color. I really wanted red, but it would've taken two months to order that color. I'm still mad about that."

I flicked my cigarette into the woods.

To hell with it.

No more chances for this boy.

"Hey, you want me to show you the air conditioner?" He tapped the ash from his cigarette. "I've only used it twice."

Scrubs hopped off the steps, walked up to the vehicle. He opened the door with a broad sweep of his arm.

But I was already gone.

~

"This ain't going to be a bad house when it's done," Brother said.

I would've answered Brother, but I was holding too many nails between my lips. I pounded one into the wood with a hammer.

"Nicest house in the whole damn county, if I do say so myself." Brother patted the side of the structure.

Brother was Sonnet's daddy.

He was all freckles and sass.

I don't know why people called him Brother. No one could seem to agree on how the nickname came about. Someone told me it was because he followed his older brother around like a shadow when he was younger. Someone else said it was from growing up in the Baptist church. Everyone in the Baptist church called each other Brother-So-And-So, or Sister-such-and-such.

Brother's real name was Reginald, but he hated the name Reginald. No one ever called him by it unless they were fixing to lay a walloping on him. To me, he was either Brother or sir. And he hated the name sir more than he hated the name Reginald.

So he went by Brother.

"Nicest house in the county, my ass." Mullet swatted his hammer at the clapboard. "Quinn's terrible at framing a house, and you can quote me on that."

"Is he that bad?" Emma Claire asked.

"Lord Almighty," Mullet said. "Before we came along, this house was as catty wampus as a bag of snakes."

"It wasn't that bad," I defended myself.

"The hell it wasn't, this thing was as crooked as a politician."

"Well it wasn't all my fault, it's horrible bowed wood."

Mullet laughed.

He wasn't about to ease up on me.

Brother and I held the strip of wood siding against the framed house. I beat the nails into it one at a time. The wood was uneven, and scrubby, you could get a splinter just by staring at it. It was going to be a small home. A little wobbly, but by God it would be ours.

Almost all the wood we used for the house was scrap lumber. Things Sonnet's Daddy brought home from the mill where he worked. Most of the rough timber had to be squared with a hand plane before it was ready for use. Some boards were too short, some were too bowed, but most were just knotty as hell.

"Crooked or not," Brother stepped in. "Quinn's going to be living right here on the water. That's fine living in anyone's book."

"Reckon you're right," Mullet said.

Brother wiped his wet face. "Shoot, I ain't never lived on land this nice before. Hell, I've been paying landlords since I was fourteen years old. Renting any house I could find. Just to live in squaller."

Mullet shook his head.

They belonged to the same fraternity in that regard.

Brother laughed, then said, "I've paid landlords since I was a boy. Hell, I pays'em now. I reckon I'll pays'em when I can't stand up straight all the way. When I'm so old, I'm messing all over myself."

"Don't matter one way or the other." Mullet spit onto the ground. "Long as your bills get paid, that's all that counts."

Brother tucked the hammer in his belt. "I throws all my bills in one big drawer. Then, once a month I reach down in the drawer with my eyes closed and pick one out. When the collectors calls me, I tell them they'll have to wait for their month. Same as everyone else in the drawer."

We all laughed at that.

Partially because it wasn't a bad idea.

Hearing Brother talk about rent made me glad to know that our house was ours. No bank or landlord would ever have a damn thing to do with it, not if I had my say in the matter.

I was a cracker.

Crackers don't trust banks, teacher, or doctors. Some trust preachers, but not me. I trusted them least of all. You could call us hillbillies, and we were, but we were self-sufficient ones. I'd rather live under a thatch roof than let a bank into my life.

And you can quote me on that.

The new home was right on the crest of the bay. If you stood in just the right spot, you could see Mother's clapboard house to the east. Her house was about a quarter mile away through the woods. Both houses were on the same plot of acreage my granddaddy gave my daddy long ago.

Granddaddy was a hopeless gambler. The old man won everything from pocket-watches to people's daughters during in his time. I had a pocket-watch he'd won, but it didn't work. I kept it hidden, with my stash of money and other valuables. I also kept Daddy's old pipe in the box. The watch and the pipe both reminded me of the men who'd come before me. To me, the men were characters from fairytales. The pipe and watch made them seem real.

Even though they weren't.

Not anymore.

Daddy said that Granddaddy won our land from a Spanish gentleman in Quincy. He'd won it in a game of cards, the whole thing. My Daddy loved the land. This acreage was his crowning glory. It was one of the few things he was proud of–except for his coon stew.

"It's going to be a fine house." Brother stood back and looked at the structure. "It took some doing, but we got it all square."

"I couldn't have done it without your help," I said.

"Naw." Brother sniffed. "You could've. It'd just be ugly as hell."

"Well, I much appreciate it, just the same."

"Don't mention it, I'd do anything for my daughter. And since I can't kill you for stealing her, I might as well help you build a house."

I patted him on the back. "It's as much your house as it is mine Brother. I mean it."

Brother cackled in that way that older men do. "Don't tell me that, boy. I'm liable to show up on your front porch with my wife and all my younguns in tow, ready to move in."

I chuckled and prayed he was joking about that.

Brother nodded toward Mother's house in the distance. "I know your momma and sister will be glad to have y'all so close. Y'all are tight neighbors now."

I wasn't exactly excited about that.

Mother and Emma Claire's house was closer than we preferred. But It was better than being trapped in the Brother's house like we were. We'd been living with Sonnet's parents for the past two years. And Sonnet was about to lose her good mind.

Sonnet's two younger brothers gave us no privacy. They pressed their greasy ears on our bedroom door at night, hoping to hear us making love. Sometimes, when I knew they were listening, I'd start moaning, pretend we were.

Sonnet hated it when I did that.

Sonnet's brothers weren't a problem though, they didn't bother us, not bad. Not compared to Sonnet's mother Rena. Rena was about to cause Sonnet to start drinking as a hobby. Rena fussed and henpecked about everything Sonnet did.

And everything she didn't.

It was downright entertaining to watch the two of them fuss. Though I'd've never admitted such. I would've gotten my teeth knocked out if I'd said that.

Poor Sonnet never won. She always lost arguments with her mother. It was just the way it worked. An unwritten rule. Each night before bed, Sonnet fantasized about cramming various objects down her mother's gullet. It sent her straight to sleep.

Emma Claire stood up and stretched her arms into the air.

"Why didn't you build more bedrooms?" she asked me.

I beat a nail with the hammer. "What do you mean?"

"Only two bedrooms?"

"Sure, what's wrong with two?"

"It's too few, if you have children, I mean."

"More bedrooms takes money honey," Mullet interjected. "Old Quinn ain't as rich as you think."

"Yes he is." Emma Claire leaned back against the truck, extending her egret-like legs. "Quinn's rich, he saves his money like a packrat. He's got plenty of it tucked away."

Brother scoffed. "Quinn's married Honey, don't matter how much he got. He spends his money like it's on fire. You'll learn that soon enough, darling."

I hoped later rather than sooner.

"Oh, I'll be married one day," said Emma, "and my husband will be even richer than Quinn."

There was no doubt about that.

Emma Claire attracted the attention of the boys in her small high school class. That girl could've had her pick of the litter. The boys bumbled and stuttered like fools whenever they were around her.

But the joke was on them.

Emma Claire was no walk in the park.

I stood back several feet and surveyed my little house. It sat beneath the large umbrella of longleaf pines. The trees splayed their large arms out, shading the house from the white-hot sun. It was nothing more than a glorified shack sitting in the blotchy shade.

But dammit, it was mine.

"When do you think it you'll finish it?" Emma Claire asked.

"As soon as you finish painting the outside of it," Mullet answered.

"That's the last step of the whole project darling."

Emma made a face. "Me? I'm not painting that thing."

"Why not?" Mullet spit. "Hell, we've all been pitching in. What makes you different than us? You're Quinn's own sister."

"It's not my house, that's why."

"Good God," Mullet said. "You kiss your momma with that mouth?"

What a strange thought. Emma kissing Mother.

"Quinn can paint his own house." Emma declared.

Mullet pushed the brim of his hat up. "Suit yourself, baby-doll. I suppose Quinn and Sonnet ain't never going to invite you over for supper. Not if you don't help do any work."

"Wait a minute," Emma said. "I've changed my mind."

"Nope, it's too late now. No supper for you."

"But, I want to help." Emma looked at me. "Quinn, I've decided I want to pitch in."

"Sorry, darling." Mullet tucked tobacco in his cheek. "I sure hope you like your mother's cooking. Because that's what you'll be eating from now on, baby."

Emma Claire looked at me.

She knew I wouldn't rob a fly from a spider.

~

One of the feral cats watched me from behind Mother's kitchen screen door. It whipped its tail from side to side. The gray cat sat bone-still, staring at me with curious eyes.

I sat at the kitchen table and looked down at my textbook. I tried to focus, but it was hard to concentrate over the noise of the bullfrogs. They were out with a vengeance that night. They croaked like an army of miniature men.

The frogs didn't come out at Sonnet's parents' house, not ever. The nights were dead-quiet there. I wasn't used to total stillness like that. It was strange. The only noises at Sonnet's were from her brothers Crick and Blair, wrestling.

Giving each other bloody noses.

My mother's place was tranquil and familiar to me. The back porch was where Daddy taught me to clean dove, fish, and coon. The den was where I first learned to walk with my lanky pair of legs.

I wiped the humidity from my forehead. It was sticky and hot that night. Sonnet had opened all the kitchen windows, to let in the wet evening air.

"Two halves equal what?" Sonnet looked at me with wide eyes. "Come on, you know the answer to this."

"A whole?" I tapped my cigarette on the rim of the ashtray.

"Okay then, so now what about these?"

I paused, looking at the page.

"Three and one eighth?" I sighed a breath of smoke. "Hell, I don't know, fractions are hard."

"No, try again." Sonnet touched her pencil on the page.

I stared at the numbers, then shrugged.

"Come on," she said. "Don't give up that easily. There're no distractions here. You have no excuses."

It was true, Mother's house was quieter than Sonnet's. When we studied at her mother's kitchen table, her mother buzzed around, interjecting comments during our lessons. Rena liked the sound of her own voice. The woman did not know how to stay quiet. I was certain Sonnet was going to kill her own mother with an eraser one day.

"Try again." Sonnet handed me the pencil.

I wrote the fractions onto the paper.

"Good," she said. "That's right. Maybe we need to study here at your mother's more often, where you can focus. You're already doing better, without distractions."

"But wouldn't that make your mother awfully lonely?"

Sonnet curled her lip. "That woman don't know how to be lonely. She's always nosing up in someone's business."

Namely Sonnet's.

It was true. At Sonnet's house, the only place I felt comfortable was inside our bedroom. It was the only spot in the small home that we could claim as our own. It was about the size of a broom closet.

I set my pencil down.

"Three and two-sixteenths?" I said.

"Nope." Sonnet grabbed the pencil and corrected the arithmetic on the paper. "You need more practice. But you're doing better."

"I'll never pass the damn test."

"Don't say that, give yourself credit. Stay positive. You've come a long way, you'll pass. We just need to study fractions some more, is all."

"What's the use?" I stabbed my cigarette out. "I'm dumb as a box of wet sticks."

"You're going to do fine. Don't talk like that or I'm going to show you where you can store your textbooks."

She was convincing when she wanted to be.

She closed the book. "I think we're finished for tonight."

I moaned. "Thank God."

My brain had turned into a puddle of pine tar.

"Is there anything else you want to go over before we call it quits?" she asked. "Anything at all."

"Yes, I'd like to learn how to become as smart as teacher."

She raised one eyebrow. "That's impossible."

"I thought you told me to stay positive."

"Positive, not unrealistic."

The floorboards creaked behind us. Mother walked into the kitchen. She folded her arms, and leaned against the doorway, watching the two of us.

"How's it going in here?" Mother asked.

"Good," Sonnet said. "You'd be proud of Quinn, he's doing great."

Mother flashed a half smile.

Pride was something Mother rarely felt for other people.

She reserved such emotion for herself.

"So, you're ready for your big test?" Mother asked.

"I don't know, I sure hope so."

"Oh he's ready." Sonnet patted my shoulder. "We've been studying this stuff since last December. He'll pass with flying colors, I know it."

"Is it a hard test?" Mother asked.

"Is there any other kind?" I stretched my arms above my head and let out a yawn. Then I looked at the clock above the sink. "I didn't realize it was so late. Where's Emma Claire at this hour?"

Mother shrugged. "I guess she's still out with that pretty-looking boy."

I lit another cigarette. "You mean the horse's ass."

~

The empty high school was like a graveyard that weekend. Lifeless, except for a few of us dumb crackers roaming around inside. We were a handsome lot of fellas. We'd shown up with our number-two pencils in our front shirt pockets to take a test.

And tin mugs for our tobacco spit.

David McGee walked beside me down the sterile hallway. Our boots squeaked on the polished floor. David had grown up working the oyster beds with his daddy, like me. He had the same dried sandy hair and tough brown skin that I had. The same slow drawl too. Though, I think he talked even slower than I did. Sometimes I had to wait a whole ten minutes for him to finish a sentence.

We passed by the deserted classrooms and peeked in the windows like nosy children. The hallway was lined with dozens of metal lockers against the walls. I looked at the rows of them, stacked up on themselves. I knocked on one. It rumbled like a huge bass drum.

"What in the hell you think they keep in there?" said McGee, walking beside me. "You reckon they have changes of clothes for every subject?"

"What do you mean?"

"In the lockers. You know, one shirt for math, one for geography, and such."

"Maybe they keep their hunting rifles in there?"

McGee smacked his forehead. "That's it, why didn't I think of that? Of course they do. Where else would they keep them?"

We were two excited young men who had the world by the tail for once in our lives. We would make fun of dumb high-schoolers as much as we pleased. We had new diplomas, we could do whatever the hell we wanted.

The world was our oyster.

"McGee," I said. "Was that test hard for you?"

"A little." McGee thumbed a pinch of chaw into his cheek. "The section where we had to write out two hundred and fifty words 'bout liked to kill me."

"Yeah. It was tough as nails."

He leaned over and spit into a garbage can. "Shit, I don't never say more than two hundred words in a whole goddamn day."

I believed him.

"Well," I said. "For me, the writing part was fun. Hard as hell, but fun."

It was true. I'd always fancied myself a writer. I'd just never had a reason to write. That–and I didn't know the alphabet all the way through.

"Not me," McGee said. "Writing's 'bout as much fun as wading through a pot of boiling pine sap."

I rubbed my sore eyes. "God, I thought the arithmetic was the hardest."

"Naw, arithmetic's easy."

He said his words as slow as pond water.

I shook my head. "Maybe for you McGee, but not for me. After a while, all the numbers on the page started mushing together. I couldn't make heads or tails of any of it."

"Arithmetic don't never give me no trouble, all that done made perfect sense."

I could not fathom how such a statement could be true for old David McGee–who still cooked meals on a campfire. And I imagine that he thought the same thing about old Quinn Applewhite.

Who often did the same thing.

McGee spit again. "It's all the damn reading and writing that I can't never wrap my mind around. I can't spell worth a cuss. I'm surprised I even passed."

But we did pass.

And we were kings for it.

The double doors made a loud crashing sound as we swung them open. We walked outside into the bright daylight like new men. I waved goodbye to McGee, and then scanned the parking lot, shielding my face from the sun.

I saw Sonnet, sitting on the roof of my truck in the far distance. She looked like a statue from far away. She sat with her knees touching her chest, her arms wrapped round her legs. Her bare feet were the color of new magnolia blossoms.

Her feet were always bare.

Sonnet didn't care for shoes. She looked strange if ever she actually wore them, bound up and cramped.

Sonnet sat there like one of those circle-framed silhouette portraits. The kind rich people hang in their dens. She didn't see me approaching, she was too lost in her own thoughts. Too preoccupied to notice a lanky, big eared, high school graduate walking toward her.

I decided to surprise her.

I crouched down and slid off my boots, then hurled them over the side of the truck as hard as I could. They sailed through the air and plopped into the flatbed with a loud bang. The sound liked to startle the Holy Ghost out of her.

She looked down at me from her catbird-seat and sliced her green eyes through my chest.

"You silly-ass! You scared me half to death."

"You know, I've always wondered what happens if you get scared half to death twice in a row."

"Try it again, and I'll show you."

She didn't appear to be joking.

"Well come on with it," she said. "How'd the test go, did you pass?"

I shrugged my shoulders.

"Do not tease me, Quinlan, or I will make you bleed."

I did not altogether doubt that.

I climbed onto the truck tailgate, my bare feet moist on the rusted metal. I crawled up and sat beside her. My dungarees scratched on the metal roof of my truck. I scooted next to her until our thighs were touching.

Sonnet leaned on my shoulder. "Tell me how the test went or I'll hurt you, and then bury you alive out behind our new house."

I was silent.

"Quinn, I'm serious." She sat up straight and looked at me. "You tell me, right this instant."

I frowned at her, then closed my eyes.

"Oh my God, no." She brought her hand up over her mouth. "You failed?"

I remained silent, removing the folded envelope from my pocket.

"You fool." She drew back and punched her little fist into my shoulder. "How could you tease me like that?"

"Hey." I held my shoulder. "That hurt."

But she was not concerned with my well-being.

Only my diploma.

Sonnet snatched the envelope and removed the paper certificate. It was a surprisingly light sheet of paper, trimmed in gold.

With my name on it.

"Oh my God." She sighed, running her finger along the gold leafing on the paper. "It's beautiful."

And she was right.

It was a downright handsome piece of paper.

12.

The water was as smooth as a bookkeeper's rump; there was not a breeze to speak of. I looked over the side of my boat at my own reflection in the water staring back at me. I looked like an ugly blue heron with fat ears.

"Hey, Quinn, is there any more of that coffee left?" Scrubs asked.

"Right there." I pointed beneath his seat to the tin thermos.

Scrubs retrieved the container.

It was Emma Claire's birthday, and the sun was as strong enough to fry an egg. We spent the day of her birthday on the water, in an eight foot long skiff, with cane poles in our hands.

Just the way she wanted it.

She was a lot like me.

Emma Claire loved to fish. It was one of the few places where her mouth ran quiet and her mind slowed, right there on the water.

Much to my disappointment, she brought Scrubs along with us for the outing. She begged me to be gracious toward him even though he had the personality of two-week-old chicken salad.

Scrubs was from the other side of the water, and he acted like it, too. He had grown up learning to appreciate expensive things, and expensive people. People like Scrubs did not go fishing. When people like him wanted a fish, they asked for one. And they usually got it on a sliver plate, with a little glass of Scotch whiskey on the side.

I looked at him sitting there on the other side of the boat. The smirk he wore aggravated me. He poured the coffee into his tin mug and screwed the cap shut. Then, he reached into his back pocket and removed a shiny metal flask. He garnished his coffee with a few pours and flashed a smile at Emma Claire.

She smiled back at him.

"A little early to take a swallow, isn't it?" I asked.

"Naw." He took a sip, then passed the mug to Emma. "It's Emma Claire's birthday. Anything goes today."

So that's how it worked.

I was from a different school of thought. I was an oysterman. To earn a sip during the daylight hours, you had to first work like a dog. And sweat like one too.

Scrubs hadn't done either.

Not one day in his life.

While Scrubs nipped from his bottle, he fiddled with his pole like an epileptic. The boy couldn't have sat still if his life depended on it. Emma Claire and I both sat calm, paying close attention to the tips of our rods. Our lines dangled in the water. With quiet minds, we thumbed through the pages of our thoughts.

Scrubs stood up. He wobbled the boat and cast his line as far as he could throw it. Then he sat down on the seat with a plop and stared out at his lure.

"You didn't bring a hat, Scrubs?" I commented.

"Naw, I don't need one."

He'd be sorry about that.

"I don't see what the big deal is," he said. "About fishing."

Emma Claire smacked him on the chest with a dull thud.

"Hush, now," she said. "It's my birthday. I can do whatever I want today. Don't complain."

Scrubs laughed at her with a cackle, not altogether unlike a bird.

"I just don't see what's so great about it," he said. "I think it should be called waiting instead of fishing. That's what it is. A bunch of waiting around."

This kid was priceless.

"Just shut up and fish," Emma said.

Scrubs took another sip.

"You know," I said. "There is one way to cure boredom with fishing."

"There is?"

I nodded once. "Time-tested, through millions of years."

"How?"

"By catching a goddamn fish."

Emma Claire looked at me and I stopped talking.

Scrubs' frustration was understandable. The boy hadn't caught a fish all morning, and it had dried up his enthusiasm. Too bad for him. Emma Claire and I were having a spectacular day on the water. We reeled in hogs from every direction. After an hour, Emma had caught two speckled trout, and one ladyfish.

She was on a roll.

Suddenly, Emma Claire's rod bowed downward again, her reel whined out a high-pitched scream. She didn't make a face. She worked the beast back and forth like a woman who knew her way around a rod and reel. She tugged at it and then cranked up the slack, back and forth. Her lithe wrists were nothing if not coordinated.

She pulled the fish closer to our boat and finally lifted the wild thing out of the water. It gleamed like a piece of silver, twisting back and forth in the air. Then she flopped the bright trout into the wicker basket and closed the lid.

"Nice one," I said.

"But he's not a lunker."

God, I loved that word.

I suspected I always would.

"That fish'll eat just fine," I said. "Especially with hushpuppies."

She laughed. "That's because anything eats good with hushpuppies. Even boot leather."

I'd never tasted boot leather, but my sister had a point.

"Well, I think it's a fine birthday fish," I said.

"Thank you, Sir Quinlan of the River, esteemed fisherman."

She tipped her hat to me.

I pretended to understand what she said.

Scrubs did not see Emma Claire's fish. He was too busy fidgeting with the fishing rod in his hands. He cranked his reel, letting the clicking sound pollute our silence. It sounded like a ratchet wrench. I exhaled in aggravation and wedged a cigarette between my lips. That boy was beginning to annoy me worse than room temperature beer.

Scrubs stood up again, jolting our boat side to side. He threw his line out into the water with a splash.

"Scrubs," I said. "You know, you don't have to keep casting your line out like that. You'll get a better response from the fish if you relax."

He looked at me with vacant blue eyes.

"How about you fish your way, and I'll fish mine?"

I bit my cigarette in my teeth and imagined what he'd look like wearing the jaws of a gator as a helmet.

I took solace in that image.

~

I drove us home through the hot sunshine. I sat alone in the truck cab, with my arm draped across both seats. I watched the blurry marshlands zip past my windshield in a streak. They were striped colors of gold and green.

Emma Claire and Scrubs sat in the bed of the truck close together like turtle doves. I could see him sipping from his flask in the rear view mirror while she leaned against him.

He was burnt to a crisp.

It was God's little gift to me.

I looked at the basket of fish on the passenger seat. They kicked and twisted like angry devils, unhappy about their fate. They fought against their ultimate end with all their might. They were fighters.

We all lose in the end.

The fight in between is all that counts.

We caught five fish in total that day, nice looking animals, too. They would make a fine birthday dinner for Emma Claire later that night. Nothing on earth was finer than fish. Not even making love, or early morning cigarettes.

Or both at the same time.

Our broken family didn't have many traditions, but we did have a birthday tradition. We bookended each birthday with a heap of fried fish and boiled crab. Every year I attempted to surprise Emma Claire with a mess of blue crab, but she was never surprised. She always knew it was coming. Every year.

I was predictable.

That particular year, I'd caught eight blue crab altogether. I had them hidden beneath Mother's porch in a big bucket of water. I caught one large male that looked as big as a horse cart—with pinchers.

I hoped Scrubs would choke on the thing.

I watched Scrubs in the rear view mirror, burnt red as an apple. Emma Claire saw me watching them; she poked her tongue out at me and wrinkled up her forehead.

Still a child.

She crawled forward and rapped on the back window with her knuckles. I reached behind me and slid it open.

She popped her head through. "How're things going up here?"

"Fine as wine."

She pressed her finger on my neck to test my ugly tan.

"You never get sunburned. You're brown all year round."

"It's not as glamourous as it sounds." I stabbed my cigarette in the ashtray. "How's Red Man doing back there?"

"Oh, he's fine. Just sunburnt."

Damn.

I was hoping it was worse than that.

"I wish I were brown all year round, like you," she said.

"No you don't."

She rested her chin on her hands and looked straight out the windshield of the truck. She let out a sigh, a satisfied one.

"Mother told me about your diploma," she said. "Said you went and took a high-school equivalency test."

I nodded.

"Was it hard?" she asked.

"Hard as a row to hoe."

"But you passed?"

"By the hair of my chin."

"Well, I'll bet Sonnet is proud of you," she added.

I turned to face Emma Claire. "Yes, I think she is."

"Well then, that means that you've graduated before me. I hope you're happy, you little ass."

I was.

She thought for a moment, then said, "Hey, but I caught two more fish than you did today. At least I'm still a better fisherman than you are."

Emma Claire was nothing if not competitive.

And I loved her for it.

~

Scrubs leaned against the post. He watched me insert my knife into the soft white belly of the dead fish. The wine-colored blood leaked out of the fish, sticky on my fingers. I plopped the guts out onto the wooden table. Scrubs scrunched his nose and said something I couldn't hear.

"Say again?" I tilted my right ear toward him.

He cupped his hands over his mouth. "I said that's gross."

"You don't have to shout."

He shrugged. "I said that's gross."

"I know, you've said it three times now."

I looked down at the fish on the table. I tried to forget about the sunburnt donkey standing there beside me. I concentrated on happier things. I imagined my family seated around a small supper table for Emma's birthday. Each of us stuffed tighter than ticks.

Me especially.

I slid open the drawer and removed a meat cleaver. It was a huge rusty blade, big enough to hack up an oak tree. I lifted it high up in the air and hammered it down onto the wood table, lopping off the fish's head. The head bounced off the table, landing in the dirt.

Scrubs leapt back a few steps.

I bent down, picked up the head, then tossed it into the bucket. The metal rang like a bell with the direct hit.

"So, where'd Emma Claire run off to?" I asked. "She likes to help do this part."

"She does?" his face bunched up.

"Sure, she loves to gut a fish."

"Why?"

"Oh, I don't know, maybe because she likes blood."

"Huh?"

"We crackers like blood."

It wasn't an exaggeration.

Not in the slightest.

I slid the knife along the skin of the fish. "She's good at it, too, she can clean a fish without tearing it up, that's an art, you know."

He didn't know.

Nor did he care.

I took the pink hunks of meat, set them aside, then flung the skin into the bucket.

"Hello, boys," I heard Emma Claire say behind me.

I turned to see Emma Claire walking toward us. She wore a crisp white evening gown that came all the way down to her ankles. Her dark hair was drawn up into a loose bundle behind her head, and she wore a string of pearls. I recognized the white-heeled shoes she wore; they were Mother's. Emma Claire came closer to us. She hiked the sides of her dress up, tip toeing over the red dirt.

"Well, my stars." I set the knife down.

Scrubs turned to see her walking toward us and let out an indecent whistle.

I could've gutting him for it.

"You like my new dress?" she asked.

I wasn't sure if she was asking Scrubs or me, so I didn't answer.

"Yes, ma'am." Scrubs slid his hands around her waist and held her close to him. "You look good enough to eat."

She pecked him on the lips.

"What do you think, Quinn? About the dress?"

I nodded my head and smiled.

She was as pretty as a placemat.

"Mother helped me make it," she said.

"It's mighty fine," I said.

"We worked on it for two whole days." She looked at Scrubs with a silly grin on her face. "Two long, full days."

Mother was faster than that.

Emma Claire must've slowed her down.

Scrubs stroked her bare white shoulder with his finger. "I think my parents will be impressed."

"Parents?" I asked.

"Oh yeah, I forgot to tell you, Quinn. Scrubs' parents invited me over their house for a birthday dinner tonight. I won't be here for dinner."

~

The sky was like a painting. Brilliant golds and purples streaked sideways above us. One thing I like about the Floridian sky: it changes with every passing moment. Always has.

Always will.

Before he traded me for moonshine, Old Mister McRyan would sometimes tell me no man could look at the same sky twice. He said everything was changing and replacing itself, bit by bit. He was right. I'd never seen a sky look as beautiful as the one above me did.

And I'd never see one like it again.

I hugged Emma Claire and wished her a happy birthday. She draped her arms around me and squeezed me tight. She crawled into Scrubs' car and tucked her white dress around her in the bucket seat. I closed the door for her.

"Hey," I said to her from outside the car window. "It's still your trout. We won't touch it until we're all sitting down together. Maybe we'll even have some blue crab too, you never know."

Emma Claire smiled at me from behind the glazed car window and gave me a thumbs up. Her face was mature, but it was the same smile that she'd had since birth.

Mischievous.

Scrubs fired up his car, and it hummed like a baby lion. And just like that, they were gone. I watched his red taillights disappear down the driveway in the dusky evening. The screen door squealed behind me as it swung open, and Mother walked out.

Without saying a word, I handed her a cigarette.

She only came out to the porch to smoke.

"Thanks," she said.

"She's gone." I motioned toward the driveway. "On her own birthday."

"She never told you?"

"Nope, I guess she doesn't tell me much anymore."

The squatty, big-eared baby who named the feral cats, who climbed the oaks behind our house, who dangled upside down like a monkey, who wasn't bothered by fish blood, who was too afraid to sleep alone, had changed.

She was a girl in pearls now.

"I know." Mother inhaled her cigarette. "She don't tell me much, either. But I knew she was going tonight."

"You knew she was going over there?"

"Mmm hmm." She sat down on the front steps and tapped her ash onto the ground. "That's why we made the dress. I forgot to tell you."

How considerate.

I hitched my thumbs in my pockets and let out a breath.

"Oh, cheer up, Quinn, she can't be your little girl forever."

I glanced over at Mother. She was lean, her features were sharper than they used to be. She let out a breath of blue smoke that rose upward and evaporated into the air.

"Don't worry." She looked up at the sky. "Scrubs is a good kid. And he's so damned handsome."

I did not respond, neither did I concur.

Not in the least.

~

Sonnet and I walked up the wooden steps into our half-finished stilted house. It was beginning to look like a legitimate home. Less like a shack. If you used your imagination, you could almost see it painted white. Complete with green shutters and a wraparound porch.

"Oh, it's going to be lovely." Sonnet touched the rough yellow post and ran her hand along it. "So very lovely."

"Careful," I said. "Don't catch a splinter."

She walked over to a wall and stared out of the window.

"The kitchen will be over here?" she asked.

"Why, Miss Applewhite, the kitchen can be wherever you want it to be."

She walked to the other side and spread her hands out. "What about here?"

"Sure. If that's where you want it."

"Well, I suppose it's your decision, you're the one who cooks. You're the chef."

"Not anymore. I've been promoted to dishwasher."

"I thought you were the dishwasher and the chef."

"No, it doesn't work that way, I can't be both."

"You can, if the house president say you can."

She walked over to me and slung her arms around my shoulders, leaning her head into my chest. The crude charm of our new home liberated us, made us lighter. We held each other underneath the open roof, waltzing from side to side. Neither of us could dance a lick, but we were good pretenders.

I looked down at the wood floor and watched the raindrops start to fall. They made little polka dots on the floor. The pitter patter sound became louder with each droplet.

"We'd better take cover," I said.

The words had not left my lips before the sky opened up and poured onto us. Sonnet yelped and covered her head. She darted down the platform to the truck. Her dried, coarse auburn hair turned dark, soaking up the rain.

"Come on!" Sonnet yelled. "Hurry up!"

I crawled into the truck, slammed the door, and shook my wet hair like a dog. The drops of water flung all over the truck cab in every direction.

"Hey." Sonnet slapped my shoulder. "You're getting me all wet, you big fool."

"How's that?"

"Don't play deaf with me, your good ear's facing me."

"Ma'am?"

Sonnet looked out the window.

"Hey, look." Sonnet gazed out the window. "Who's that over at your mom's house?"

~

"Isn't it a little early for Scrubs to be dropping Emma Claire off?" Sonnet said. "School's not out yet, it's still the middle of the day."

I squinted through the truck window. I could see the fat white tires of Scrubs' fancy green car in Mother's driveway.

"You're right," I said. "It is odd."

I pulled my truck beside his car.

The rain battered my metal hood. Crashing sounds of water engulfed all other noise. Sonnet leaned over and said something to me, but the rain was too loud to hear. I hopped out of the truck and shut the door behind me, clomping up the house steps. I eased Mother's front door open and looked around.

The house looked empty and quiet.

"Hello?" I called out. "Mother?"

There was a loud crash in the back bedroom.

I followed the sound, walking through the narrow hallway. My wet boots squeaking on the floorboards, trailing long puddles of water behind me.

Mother's bedroom door was closed.

"Hello?" I rapped my fist on her door. "Mother, are you in there?"

There was no answer.

I knocked again. "Mother?"

"I'm busy," Mother said, muffled behind the door. "Go away, please."

I thought for a moment.

Something was wrong.

I turned the metal knob and pushed the door open.

She was naked.

So was *he*.

Mother screamed.

I stood motionless looking at them.

The lanky boy, with coal black hair, was behind my mother, shirtless. He slid on his jeans and boots as fast as he could move.

"Quinn!" she pressed her hands into my chest. "Don't hurt him! Please!"

I ignored her. My teeth clenched together, and I heard one of my molars crack. I charged forward and grabbed Scrubs by his throat. Both of them screamed at me, but I couldn't hear their shouting. I could only see their mouths wrench open.

She threw her fists at me, trying to beat me off him. Then Scrubs lurched his arms out and joined the fight. He socked me in the mouth. My head flew back from the blow, but I felt no pain.

I felt nothing.

I tossed Scrubs out of her room and he slammed against the wall of the hallway. I shoved his body through the narrow hall like a sack of grain. He banged into the hollow walls and the framed photographs fell from their nails, crashing to the floor.

I tugged him through the front door by his belt, then slung him into the railing on the porch. I lunged forward at him with every bit of strength I had. Scrubs fell backward, over the railing, arcing through the air. He thumped onto the wet mud.

He lay there for a moment, covered in red dirt, the rain pounding on him. Then, Scrubs leapt to his feet and shook his wet hair. He stood in a wide legged stance, then yelled something at me.

I couldn't hear what he shouted.

Neither did I care.

He shook his fist in the air, with a gaping mouth. Then, like a linebacker he dropped his shoulder low, and charged me. His shoulder smashed into my ribs, knocking me off my feet. I fell backward onto the ground, and the wind shot from my lungs. Scrubs crawled on top of me, pinning me down with his knees. I tried to push back at him, but he landed two heavy blows to my face. I swung my fists again, waving them in the air at him, but I made no contact.

He was walloping me.

Hard.

The rain smacked us as we struggled. Fat drops of water fell from the sky, lubricating his blows to my face.

He thrashed at my nose, and I heard my bones break like pieces of glass behind my skin. I attempted to shield myself from his fists, but it was to no avail. Scrubs threw his clenched hands into my cheeks until I tasted my own blood on my tongue.

He was a better fighter than I was–meaner.

He sprang to his feet and began kicking.

He kicked me in the head with his thick boot.

My thin temple made a cracking noise. I felt my neck pop, my vision bounced sideways with each kick.

He kicked again, and I felt my ribs snap.

He kicked again. My knee exploded.

Again. And again.

And again.

Until I lay limp like a rag doll.

I lifted up my eyes, looking through a blurry red haze. Crimson-colored shapes danced across my vision, but I couldn't make them out. I could see Sonnet hanging off his back, like a toddler on a piggy back ride. It reminded me of the rides I used to give Emma Claire when she was younger. I'd take Emma running through the woods like that. She'd holler like an Indian while I ran as fast as I could.

Sonnet's arms squeezed Scrubs' neck, her tiny fists flapped at him. I tried to call out to her, but I couldn't make my voice work.

He threw her off of his body, and she landed in the mud. Not about to give up, Sonnet leapt back to her feet. She began throwing bits of gravel at him with everything she had within her.

One rock after another.

He shielded himself from the gravel, but a small stone popped him on the forehead, drawing his blood.

Sonnet was aiming to kill him dead.

However she could.

And there was no telling what that woman could do when she decided to do something.

I tried again to scream, but nothing came out of my mouth.

I could only lie there, watching them.

Breathing.

My world faded to black.

13.

I have a curious way of remembering information. My mind keeps no recorded timeline, no calendar of events. I kept my sepia-toned memories in a big box. I store them somewhere in the closet of my mind, unorganized, and unlabeled. It's the only organizational system I knew: one big mess.

I waded through an endless pool of faded recollections, in no particular succession. They fired at me from the edges of my mind, at random.

Like gunshots.

Deep within my memory, I saw Emma Claire losing her front teeth. She stood on the back porch, her gums covered in rich blood. That silly grin on her face was half happy, half angry.

A typical face for her.

I saw Mother digging in her garden. She scooped sweet potatoes out of the soil and tossed them into a wicker basket. Then, I looked behind me and I saw myself, docking the skiff on the shore, singlehanded. I observed myself from outside myself. A strange experience. I looked at my lanky body and long legs. My skin looked old and worn, the corners of my eyes lined and creased with the years. My ears were as big as ever.

God, I was old.

After that, I floated through the north Floridian forest, like a bird. I drifted high above the trees, over our unfinished house, the one I was building. The fresh yellow pine planks and rusty nails could be seen from way up in the sky. Not a bad looking hunk of lumber, if I did say so myself.

Flooding my memory were images of her, looking as if she'd

crawled out of a fine painting. Her body covered by her long auburn hair, draping down to her ankles. Like a religious character from the Bible.

After her, I saw my daddy, sitting peaceful in tall grass, relaxed. He chewed on a piece of cane like he did each November. His gaunt frame wore the faded denim clothes of an oysterman. The boots he wore looked like big leather boats. His big hands looked like baseball mitts.

Oh, how he hated baseball.

What a waste of time he thought it was.

Too bad for him.

In the distance, I saw Mullet riding a red horse, wearing a ten-gallon hat. The horse rocked back onto its rear legs and charged its front hooves into the air. Mullet looked down from his horse and spoke to me in a sober tone, like a cowboy in the movies.

His voice was deep and stern.

"Come back to us, Old Timer," Mullet said. "Come back home to us right now, you here me?"

I had the urge to open my eyes. But when I tried, I found that my eyelids were too crusted shut. It was as if someone had painted over them with rabbit glue.

I tried again, and this time my eyes broke free.

The first thing I saw was Mullet.

He wore a ten-gallon hat, just like in my dream.

When the light made my head ache. Like something was pushing against my face from behind. I blinked once, the colors were so bright that they hurt to look at.

"Oh Jeezus," Mother said, looking into my eyes.

"There you are," Mullet said. "About time you joined us, Old Timer."

Mother yelled, "He's awake. Someone, come quick!"

"Quinn," Sonnet's voice said above me.

I closed my eyes again.

It felt better that way.

"Can you hear us?" Sonnet asked. "Quinn, honey?"

"Sure he can hear us," Mullet said.

Sonnet touched my cheek. "Quinn? Let us know that you hear us."

I opened my eyes again and turned my head toward the sound of Sonnet's voice. The shooting pain in my neck felt like a dull knife.

"Oh, God, he can hear us." Sonnet laid her hands on my chest, and wept. "You can hear us. You're alive, thank God."

"Look," Mother said. "He's trying to say something."

I struggled my mouth open. My jaw hurt like hell.

"W-W-Where–" My voice scraped against my throat.

"Go ahead, try again," Sonnet said.

It was like she was teaching me to read all over again.

"Where the–"

Mullet grinned. "Spit it out, you can do it."

"W-W-Where the hell did Mullet get that cowboy hat?" I said.

The words came out like gravel.

"Ha!" Mullet clapped his hands and laughed, "There he is. There's my pal!"

"Oh my God," Sonnet said, drying her face. "You can talk."

"This damn hat?" said Mullet. "It's your hat now, Old Timer. Consider it your prize."

"B-B-But I don't want it."

"Then I'm giving it to Freckles."

I squinted at him. "Aww, t-t-to hell with y-y-ou."

I tried to swallow, but my throat was sour with bile. My tongue stuck to the roof of my mouth. I drew in a lungful of air, my ribs creaked like an old accordion.

Mother stroked my face with her hands. That hurt too. I looked up into her familiar eyes, the same eyes I'd seen since infancy.

It was then I remembered.

Remembered why I hurt so bad.

"Oh, Quinn," Mother said.

I tried to smile at her, but the muscles in my face refused to cooperate. I looked over to Sonnet. But Sonnet was not looking at me. She was looking at my mother with piss and vinegar in her eyes.

"Honey, do you hurt?" Sonnet asked. "How do you feel?"

I smiled, and my cheekbones felt like they might shatter.

I coughed. "B-B-Best I've felt in years."

~

The entire left side of my body was dark with stains, black and purple ones. Pools of dark blood bloomed beneath my skin. Some of them shaped like black crescents.

Impressions from the toe of a boot.

I held onto Emma Claire's shoulders for balance. We limped along the white tiled corridor, shuffling one foot in front of the other. Each step hurt worse than the last.

I gritted my teeth and moaned under my breath.

"Good," Emma Claire said. "You can do it."

I smiled at her, and she winced back at me.

I must've looked like a black and blue monster.

"I need to sit down, right now," I grunted.

"Right now?"

"Yes, my legs feel like two cheese straws."

"What's that mean?"

"It means I need to sit."

"Okay, let's sit down right here."

We sat on one of the benches in the long hallway, and I panted with exhaustion. My ribs ached, and my lungs hurt. The flat metal bench was ice cold on the backs of my bare thighs.

"Is this better?" Emma Claire asked.

"Much."

"How do you feel?"

"Like I got into a fight with a man wearing boots."

"Oh, Quinn, be serious for once."

I ignored that comment.

I had earned a joke or two.

A man in a white lab coat walked past us, puffing on a cigarette. He looked important as he strutted through the corridor. The misty smoke filled the hallway with a sweet smell. It lingered there above my head.

I turned to Emma Claire, who was staring down at the floor.

"How have you been?" I asked her.

"Me?"

"Yes, this is me being serious."

Emma shrugged. "I guess I'm doing fine. But it's you I'm worried about."

"Don't worry about me, just take a look at me, I'm great."

She did not laugh.

I lifted my heavy arm and put it on her leg. I tried to pat her thigh, but it took too much energy, so I just rested it there.

"I don't feel like joking," she said. "Scrubs almost killed you."

"Yeah, but you ought to see what he looks like."

"I have seen him, he barely has a scratch."

"Some heal quicker than others."

"Be serious. This is serious, Quinn."

I adjusted my sore haunches on the bench and grimaced. The doctors told me they couldn't find my tailbone in the X-rays. They had no idea where exactly it went off to. I was convinced that it traveled up to my brain, fulfilling the insult that Bobby Harris hurled at me whenever I'd beat him in poker. If he'd called me a bonehead once, he'd said it a million times.

Emma dried her eyes. "This is all my fault Quinn, it's all because of me. Me."

"None of that is your fault, Emma. In fact, none of this even concerned you at all, it was between me and Scrubs."

"And Mother."

I didn't respond to that.

"Oh, I wish you would've killed him. I wish you would've ripped his head off."

"Imagine how I feel."

She observed the bruises on my face. "Oh, Quinn, I'll never forgive myself."

The smell of the man's cigarette smoke still wafted in the corridor. I could taste it on my tongue and feel it in my temples.

"What have I done?" she said, wiping her face. "I've ruined your life."

"Oh, hush now, you didn't do anything wrong, and I'm going to pull through just fine."

"How can you say that?"

"Easy, I just did."

She let out a pained laugh. "If you could only see yourself, you look like hell."

"I do?"

"Unquestionably."

So that's how you used that word.

She looked down at her lap again. "Four days, Quinn. Four days you looked like you belonged in a coffin, all you could do was breathe. We all thought he killed you. We thought you were dead. You should've seen yourself, it was horrible."

I shifted my weight and tried to cross my legs. My leg felt like it was going to snap like a twig. I grabbed my knee and leaned forward. I groaned in a hoarse voice. I started coughing and then laughed though I don't know why. When I did that, there was a flapping sound in my lungs. It sounded like someone had shoved a piece of tissue paper down in my windpipe.

"Quinn, what can I do? Speak to me."

"Easy, Emma. I'll be fine. I just forgot that I can't cross my legs."

Her face was serious as a fever.

"But now that you mention it," I said. "There is something you can do for me."

"Sure, Quinn. Anything. Just say the word."

"I'm in desperate need of an unquestionable pack of smokes."

She rolled her eyes. "That's not how you use the word."

~

The hospital was a towering place, monumental, large enough to be a city of its own. The white walls and shiny surfaces looked clean. Like they'd never been touched. Almost like artifacts from a church. There were three beds in my room, but they were vacant. I was fortunate enough to have the room all to myself.

I looked up from my book and smiled at Sonnet sitting beside my bed. She never left me. That woman. Sonnet stayed in the hospital with me night and day. She hadn't been home since they checked me in several weeks earlier. We lived in that room and did our best bathing ourselves with spit baths.

We both smelled like the backside of a filthy Billy Goat.

"And oh, my soul, where you stand," I read aloud, staccato and slow.

Sonnet bobbed her head in rhythm.

"S-S-Surr…." I struggled with the long word on the page.

"Surrounded," she filled in the blank for me.

I squinted at the paragraph, sitting erect in my bed, reading aloud in my tired voice. Sonnet sat at my bedside.

She knew the poem backward and forward.

Poetry was a something she'd imposed upon me since our first years of marriage. To help me practice reading. Almost every evening she pistol-whipped me with a book until I spat out poetry.

Or swear words.

Sometimes both.

"Surrounded," I continued. "Surrounded, in measureless oceans of space."

"Wow, that was impressive," she said. "Those are long words."

"I remember them from last time."

"Well at least you remember them."

I ran my finger along the words and kept reading.

Sonnet leaned back in her chair and adjusted Mullet's ten-gallon hat on her small head. She closed her eyes again and listened to me read. She wanted to soak in the meaning of the mangled lyrics that plopped out of my mouth.

Not an easy task.

She was a faithful lover of poetry, art, and song. Often she tried to share these joys with me, but they were like pearls given to pigs.

Of all the arts, poetry was her favorite. Sonnet did not permit me to read anything but poetry. It was the most complete form of art, she thought. And she refused to allow me anything else. Not even if I were in the hospital, covered in bandages.

I didn't understand half of what she made me read.

I bumbled the words on the page like a blind butcher.

"Case—," I stammered.

"Ceaseless," she corrected me.

"Cassseless."

"No, Cease-less."

"That's what I said."

"No it wasn't."

"Well, it's what I meant to say."

She smiled and finished reciting the verse, "Ceaseless musing, venturing throwing. Seeking."

"Show-off." I laid the book in my lap and watched her fly.

Her words sounded like long flowing things.

"'Seeking the spheres to connect them; 'Til the bridge you will need be formed, 'til the ductile anchor hold, 'til the gossamer thread you fling, catch somewhere–'"

"Oh, my soul," I finished.

"That's right." She smiled again. "Oh, my soul."

She pushed the brim of her ten-gallon hat up and looked at my bruised face.

"That's one of my favorite poems," she said.

I stabbed my cigarette into the ashtray beside the bed.

"You act like I don't already know that. We've read it nearly a hundred times."

"Don't you like it?"

"Sure, but I've never really understood it."

"It's not that hard to understand."

"Speak for yourself Ceaseless-Musing-Venturing-Woman."

She straightened her dress and stood up.

"Well, it's a poem about a spider," she said. "A spider who is trying to figure life out."

I gave her a smile, like I understood.

I did not.

The only spiders I knew of were grass spiders. They were odd creatures. They finished every web they weaved with a tight zig-zag pattern. It was their signature. They made their webs behind our shed, and underneath our porch steps. And they did it without any fear of us. They were unlike the other spiders; grass spiders never hid from us. It was almost as if they wanted to us to see them.

"A spider," I said. "That's inspiring."

She used her hands when she spoke. "It's a simple, but smart way to talk about the struggle of life. He's saying that our lives are small, insignificant, that we're all like tiny spiders."

"Uplifting."

"Isn't it?"

"Unquestionably."

She crawled onto the bed beside me. She placed the ten-gallon hat over my bandaged head. The big hat felt heavy on my bruised cranium.

"The spider is reaching out," she said. "Out into the big world, trying to find something."

"Trying to find what?"

"Whatever it is that we're all looking for."

"I didn't know I was looking for anything."

"We all are."

"I didn't know it was even lost."

"We're all looking for something that's greater than ourselves. The spider, like us all, is yearning to shoot his string out. Shooting at that thing he's looking for. Hoping he'll finally connect with it."

"You're too smart." I touched her nose with the tip of my finger.

"No, the spider is the same as you and me. We all look for ways to connect the dots. We want to explain what's happening to us. But the truth is, there are no explanations."

"There aren't?"

"Nope. Sometimes, we're just tiny spiders in a big pointless world. We crawl on a web, one we don't understand. We're all trying to figure out what things mean. But the cold truth is, there's no meaning. No great explanation."

I shifted my sore rear in the bed.

I had no idea what the hell she was talking about.

"Well, I don't like spiders," I said.

"It's not about spiders."

"I thought you said it was."

"Well, it is, but it's not."

"I wish you could hear yourself, you don't make a lick of sense."

Just then, Mother's dark figure appeared, standing against the light of the doorway. She was carrying a big brown basket in her arms, and a bouquet. Mother was freshly-bathed and dressed, unlike Sonnet and me.

She knocked on the door jamb.

Sonnet sat up straight in the bed, looking at her.

"Hey, there," I said to Mother. "You startled us."

Sonnet watched Mother with grave eyes.

"Mind if I come in?" Mother asked.

"Sure." I removed the silly hat from my head and tossed it aside.

Mother did not move.

I realized that Mother wasn't asking me.

"May I?" Mother asked Sonnet.

Sonnet did not answer her, but sprang to her feet, and picked up the book from my lap. She clipped out of the room without even looking back at Mother.

Like a spider.

~

"I brought you these." Mother removed several packs of cigarettes from her basket. "One-Elevens, just like you like."

I picked up one of the packets and looked at the Indian chief on the label. His feathered headdress would've gone well with the new cowboy hat I'd acquired. I closed my eyes and imagined myself in an Indian headdress, Sonnet in the ten-gallon hat.

We were regular cowpokes.

"You didn't have to go to any trouble," I said.

"Please, it wasn't any trouble. I also brought you peanut butter, a tin of biscuits, and several oranges too. I know how you love oranges. Oh, and there's a box of tea in there, and some coffee. I didn't know if they let you have coffee here."

"I don't think we have a way to make coffee."

"Oh my, I didn't even think of that."

Mother was stiff and awkward. Care-taking was not something she did well. She set the basket aside and plopped her hands in her lap.

We were both silent.

"Geez, this place is huge," she finally said. "I mean, really big."

She spoke like we were meeting for the first time.

"It's huge," I answered.

Mother was wearing one of her nicest green dresses. The nicest one she owned in fact, the one with white flowers on it. She was lean as ever, and her profile was more angular than I remembered it.

Despite Mother's worn face, she was lovely. Forty had been kinder to her than it had been to most women. She had a kind of charm that transcended her outward appearance. In that moment, I understood the appeal she had on men.

It was a carefree kind of allure.

"How's Emma Claire?" I asked.

Mother shook her head. "God, how should I know?"

I imagined the terrible fights they'd likely had.

Emma Claire could be downright violent.

"Well, then how're you doing?" I asked. "Are you doing okay?"

She waved me off with her hand.

"Oh, no you don't. Don't do that to me, Quinn. Do not do that to me, not here, not now."

I was quiet.

She stood up. "Don't do that holier-than-Thou thing that you do. It makes me feel like shit. Do you hear me? Like shit."

I opened my mouth to speak, but thought it better to remain quiet.

"I don't need you worrying about me." Mother folded her arms across her chest and rubbed her shoulders. "I don't need that, not right now."

"Okay, why don't we change the subject?"

I was no fool. Mother wasn't about to let that happen.

She closed her eyes, and a small tear rolled down her cheek.

"Quinn, you don't think I know I deserve to rot in hell? It's me who belongs in that bed, not you."

She stood up and walked to the window, leaning her forehead against it. Her breath fogged up the glass. "I've ruined everyone's lives."

I sighed.

And it hurt my ribs to sigh.

I tried not to remember what she'd done with Emma Claire's boyfriend. But it was impossible to erase such images from my memory. I didn't want to remember her lean naked body, or her pale-colored breasts. But those vivid scenes lodged into my head forever.

By a pair of boots.

"Lord, you're a long way up," she said, looking down.

"Four floors high."

"Wow, I don't think I've ever been so high up."

"Me neither."

I fumbled the yellow carton of cigarettes open. Then I tossed the package of cigarettes to Mother.

"Mother, can I be honest with you?"

She looked at me.

Mother wasn't sure about sentences that started like that.

"Mother, I'm concerned. I'm afraid that you and Emma Claire are going to destroy each other if you stay in the same house. I mean really hurt one another. It worries me."

"Me? Well, I'd never hurt anyone." She lit both of our cigarettes, then clicked the lighter shut.

Mother knew I wasn't talking about her.

I felt the smoke soothe my ribs. "I know that. But Emma Claire's not thinking clearly, and you know what kind of temper she has."

"Yeah." Mother closed her eyes.

"You and Emma Claire need some distance between you. A lot of distance. I mean it."

"So what are you saying? I should leave town?" she asked.

"Lord no, don't be silly, I don't mean you. You don't need to go anywhere."

"What do you suggest?"

"Emma Claire can stay at Sonnet's parents' house long as she needs. Until things settle down. I've already spoken with them about it."

"I see." Mother pulled the smoke inward and held her breath for a moment. "With you and Sonnet? That house is about to pop as it is."

I wanted to say something heartwarming. Something about family, something cheerful and folksy, but it felt inappropriate.

"Well, hell." Mother said. "I guess it doesn't matter anyhow, Emma Claire is through with me forever. And I don't blame her."

The smoke drifted out of Mother's mouth as she spoke.

"I wouldn't blame Emma for anything." Mother pinched the bridge of her nose and sighed. "All we've ever done is fight. Since the day she was born. Fight, fight, fight. And after what happened to you, I've seen enough fighting to last a lifetime."

Mother had a knack for making understatements.

~

The little cafe was loud with chatter. The woman carrying our tray of food was a plump, older lady with a broad face. She had platinum blonde hair. It was not like any blonde I'd seen before; it was drier, more wiry. Sonnet told me that it was color from a bottle, I was not aware such things existed.

The woman weaved through a crowd of men in military uniforms, holding a tray high up in the air. The group of oily-haired men sat wrong-ways in their chairs. They shouted in happy voices, puffing on cigarettes, bubbling with laughter.

"Here we are." The woman set steaming mugs on the table and slid an enormous plate toward me, covered in white pepper gravy. She eyed the white bandages underneath my cowboy hat. "What happened to you, sweetie?"

"Oh, it's nothing." I touched my head. "I fell off my tricycle."

"Must've been a tall tricycle."

"Very tall, and it only had one wheel."

When the woman left our table, we stared at the food with wonder.

"You know, Old Timer." Mullet jabbed his plate with a fork.

"Lollipop and Billy were just asking about you the other day, asked how you were recovering. All the other fellas out on the oyster beds have asked too."

I doubted that very seriously.

Lollipop didn't care for me at all.

I didn't care a thing for him either.

But it was sweet of Mullet to lie like that.

"I told the fellas that you were doing just fine up here in Tally," Mullet said. "Told them that you were being pampered, like royalty."

"Oh, please," Sonnet laughed. "We were never treated like royalty. Not once. I can't wait to get home and take a real bath. I feel all greasy."

"I did notice y'all were smelling gamey." Mullet took a bite. "Hell, it's been two weeks since you bathed. You two've sprouted moss in your belly buttons by now."

"Don't be vulgar, Mullet," Sonnet said. "We're eating."

The spit baths Sonnet gave me in the hospital were humiliating. But she was gentle. She'd washed my shattered purple cheekbones, as if they were her own cheeks. She called them whore's baths; I had to ask her how on earth she came by such a term.

Sonnet had taken charge in the hospital. She'd bossed the nurses around, using swear words when needed. I liked to watch her swear and cuss. She was better at it than I was. She demanded the nurses teach her how to change my bandages. And they did.

They were terrified of her.

One of the black nurses had taken a liking to Sonnet. Which wasn't hard to do. The nurse taught Sonnet how to apply the bandages to my bloody head, step by step. Sonnet was a quick learner. Eventually she was able to wrap my head with her eyes shut. The nurse sent us home with an entire box of bandages, first aid, and supplies. The woman also gave Sonnet a few jars of scuppernong jam.

It was good jam.

"God, I'm ready to be in our own bed," I said.

"Me too," said Sonnet. "But I don't even want to think about how jam packed it is at Momma and Daddy's house. Especially with Emma Claire there now. It's going to be mad."

"Well, not to change the subject." Mullet pointed his fork at my hat. "But you look good in your new hat, Old Timer. It suits you."

"Naw," I said. "I look like an idiot. Sonnet's making me wear it."

"Well, I think he looks like he could be in pictures." Sonnet adjusted the hat. "And it looks a sight better than all those bandages stuck to his messy hair."

I touched the hat. "Where'd you even get this thing Mullet?"

"Won it."

"So now you play for people's clothing?" Sonnet's voice dripped with Baptist piety. "For their hats?"

Mullet wiped his beard. "It's a lot better than working for money."

"Let the tools remain in the workshop," I said. "Let the money remain unearned." I took a bow. "Walt Whitman."

Sonnet smiled at me, and her freckles nearly leapt off of her face.

"Well, dammit." Mullet set his fork down and pushed his plate away. "Freckles, you've screwed him up with all that ridiculous poetry."

~

We rode home along the twisting, turning dirt roads. They carved a dusty maze through the patch-worked farmland between our town and Tallahassee.

The lanky sap-green trees, and wide open blossoming fields looked like illustrated postcards. Rotting fence posts, stuck up from the edges of the roads. They were overgrown with saw greenbrier, and tall golden grass. The gnarled wood posts looked like old Indians pointing us homeward.

I sat limp in the passenger seat next to Sonnet. My face throbbed like a ripe tomato, pulsing with each beat of my heart. The landscape change with each mile. And I was about to fall asleep. The droning noise of the truck was hypnotic. Eventually, the engine won, lulling me into slumber. But I didn't dream.

I was too tired to do that.

When I awoke, we were already in the driveway of Sonnet's home, and the sun was beginning to set. The sight of her parents' house made me glad, it thawed me from the inside out. Two weeks spent in a world of white walls, and mercury lights left me missing home. I needed to see something faded, something moldy, something well-loved by our native humidity.

Emma Claire sat on the front porch, watching us in the driveway. Sonnet's little brothers, Blair and Crick, swarmed around Emma. They buzzed back and forth like honeybees, trying to impress her. Blair waved his wooden handgun into the air like a killer while Crick ran in circles.

Their red hair looked like dollops of copper.

"Put your arm around my shoulder," Sonnet said. "That's it."

I extended my sore legs and eased my weight onto my knees slow and gentle. Mullet had given me a cane while I was in the hospital that had the shape of a fish carved onto the handle. The fish's varnished scales were engraved scallops on wood.

Sonnet called the cane my fish-stick.

Mullet told me that he'd carved the cane himself, long ago, out of an old piece of oak. I had my doubts about that. The initials carved on the handle of the cane were GW. There was no way to know for certain where it came from. He was bad to tell fibs. Either Mullet had carved it, or some poor old bastard was missing a cowboy hat and a walking stick.

"Use your fish-stick," Sonnet said, guiding me forward. "Almost there. Almost to the porch."

I hobbled up the little path to the front door like a ninety-year-old. Like a man missing his tailbone. I leaned my weight onto my cane, limping with uneven steps.

"Hey, look at Quinn's hat!" Crick shouted. "He looks like an honest-to-God cowboy."

I smiled at them, removed my ten-gallon hat, and threw it at the boys. It zipped through the air like a boomerang. Before the hat landed on the ground, Crick had already given Blair a bloody lip over it.

"Give that hat back," Sonnet shouted. "That's not yours, it belongs to Quinn."

They did not heed her.

Emma Claire met me at the porch. She stood to her feet and hugged me. I grimaced in pain. My shoulders were not exactly ready to be squeezed.

"Hey, kid," I said. "What're you doing here all alone? Where's Rena and Brother's car?"

"I'm just babysitting." Emma Claire shrugged. "Don't ask me."

"Hey." I turned to Sonnet. "Where're Brother and Rena?"

"Gone."

"Where? It's a weeknight."

She swatted my rear. "They're out. Now quit asking so many damn questions. Let's get you inside and bathe your stank-ass."

And bathe my stank-ass she would.

~

It was humbling, having Sonnet wash me like a hound dog who'd been sprayed by a skunk. The truth was, I felt like a wounded animal that needed to be finished off and buried in the backyard.

She patted my body with the rag, like she was blotting someone with a sunburn. I watched her as she did it; she was quiet and thorough. I raised my arm, she dabbed the thin skin that covered my busted ribs. She touched the rag on the wounds as soft as she was able. I held my other arm in the air and let her clean that side too.

She smiled at me now and then.

To let me know she didn't mind.

There are many personalities in the world. Takers, pleasers, lovers, and persistent losers. They all have their own place in life. I suppose, the world needs them. Without them, it wouldn't work right.

I realized then, Sonnet was a giver.

She helped me change into my cotton clothes. It felt nice to be in a clean pair of clothes that didn't smell like a hospital. The smell of the hospital's strong chemicals and strange soap had made my nose dry. The stiff gowns were uncomfortable, riding up into the folds of my body.

Sonnet sat me down on the edge of the bed. She wrapped the thick gauze bandages around my scuffed head, around my mop of hair. Just like the black nurse had taught her to do. Then, Sonnet placed the brown ten-gallon hat over my bandaged head like a crown.

A crown for a fool.

"I hate this hat," I said. "It looks ridiculous."

"Well I like it; you look refined."

"Refined?"

"Like powdered sugar."

"What's that mean?"

"Never you mind."

I looked at my reflection in the mirror. The deep pockets beneath my eyes were sagging like saddle bags. Some of the bruises on my face had faded away, but the big ones on my cheeks were still there. They were light brown now. My jaws were puffy and swollen, and my face was pale.

"God," I said. "I look like something a cow digested."

"Hush, you look so much better than you did."

I believed her.

I took the hat off and leaned back onto my soft pillow.

"Hey, what are you doing?" she asked. "You can't sleep now, we have somewhere to be."

I covered my eyes with my hands. "Can't you go without me? I don't feel like going anywhere tonight. I feel like I've been clubbed with a baseball bat."

"No dummy, you're coming with me."

I begged and pleaded, but I should've known that resistance was futile. Sonnet had a way of making me do whatever the hell she wanted.

And that was that.

~

Emma Claire rode in the bed of Mullet's truck with Crick and Blair. They fought for her attention like male kittens. They slapped each other and flexed their ten-year-old muscles like strongmen in the circus. Emma Claire wore a smile on her face, watching their hormones whirl around her.

I sat in the cab with Sonnet while Mullet drove down the road. My eyelids kept falling, threatening to send me off to Dreamworld. I resisted. I looked up at Lady Eve, painted on the interior of Mullet's truck cab. The image of the sinful woman looked down at me, with that same look she always had.

Bewildered.

I could sympathize with her.

I draped my arm out of the open truck window as we darted down the road. The summer air was infectious. I breathed it in like it was the first time I'd ever tasted it. My cracked ribs expanded in freedom, and I didn't mind the pain. The air was thick, and it tasted good on my tongue. I looked out the window at the squatty wood buildings that rocketed past us. They were battered from our coastal air, like real buildings ought to be.

Everything was ugly. Good ugly.

I was home.

No one said much of anything during the truck ride, they just let me be. Mullet chewed his mouthful of chaw, spitting into a cup now and then. Beside him, Sonnet wore a suppressed grin, resting her hand on mine. They were both quiet as clams.

I sat up straight in my seat. "What the hell's going on, you two? Why are you being so quiet? I'm in no mood for games. I feel like my head isn't even attached to my body."

But no one answered me.

Maybe my head wasn't attached.

"Did you hear me, you two? I'm tired, I don't feel like playing. Where are we going?"

Sonnet patted my hand.

We neared the dirt road where I grew up, and I felt a twinge of anxiety, a raw pang in my stomach. Memories of my walloping flooded my mind. Like gory photographs. The sound of that boy's boot against my temples was one that I wanted to forget. Along with the smirk on that snot's face when he knew he had me licked.

"Just relax," Sonnet said.

"Listen to Freckles, Old Timer."

"You two are beginning to worry me," I said.

Mullet drove past Mother's mailbox and turned into the next driveway. I looked out the window at a brand new green mailbox with my name on it. "Q. Applewhite," painted in white paint.

And then I saw it.

A lily-white house in the distance, at the end of the road, positioned on the edge of the bay. Its gracious wrap around porch, and green shutters were magnificent.

It was a glorified shack, but Jesus-Lord was it pretty.

My jaw went slack.

Sonnet's parents were on the porch with a bunch of other smiling faces I recognized. People from our town, and from Sonnet's church. The familiar folks on the porch all waved at us. I could see their bright teeth glaring in the distance.

"Well looky here," Mullet muttered. "Now just what is all this about?"

I looked over at him; he was grinning like a fool.

When we parked, Sonnet helped me out of the truck, and the people on the porch applauded me. I leaned onto my fish cane and waved back at them. We both waved at each other for a few minutes.

I didn't know what else to do.

When I saw the house up close, it liked to yank the breath from my lungs. The finished home was the most marvelous pile of pine I'd ever seen. We walked along the perimeter of the house. I ran my hands along the white painted clapboards. The green shingled roof poked upward at the sky, and the shutters splayed outward in a welcome. I touched the glass-paned windows on the porch. I flipped on the porch light and watched it glow orange.

My eyes hazed over with tears.

"You like it, Old Timer?"

"Oh, Mullet." My voice broke. "It's perfect."

Sonnet put her arms around me and squeezed me hard enough to break my ribs all over again. But it felt good to be squeezed. I held her, and smelled her fragrant hair, my face buried in her soft, freckly shoulder.

"Welcome home, cowboy," she said.

14.

"Every time I see you, I see how you have grown, Quinlan. You are tall and long-boned. A full man," old McRyan said. "It is good. Yes, it is good."

McRyan turned his head and looked out at the bay with his wrinkly eyes. He watched a heron high step through the shallow water.

"See?" he said. "Even the white heron knows it is so."

I smiled at him.

He was as crazy as a baby coon.

No one knew exactly how crazy the white-haired Indian was. He rarely said enough to give himself away. He usually said only enough to make people wonder about him.

McRyan claimed to be one of the extinct Apalachee, but Mullet said McRyan was likely a Creek Indian from up north. He'd probably changed his name to something Irish-sounding, like lots of them did. There was no way to know for certain what McRyan's real story was; he had no family in our town.

McRyan crawled down from his seat atop the carriage and grunted with the effort. His legs moved slow, and he walked with a permanent bend at the waist.

"You are changing much, growing older and sturdy. Like the rivers and the bays."

"Sturdy?" I looked at my cane.

"Yes. You have a third leg now. Three is better than two."

Funny man.

McRyan limped to the back of his carriage and reached into a wood crate. He removed a jar of amber-colored honey and handed it to me. I took the jar from his old, leathery hands. The honeycomb inside the jar peeked back at me from behind the dark honey.

"I haven't had your honey in a while," I said, leaning onto my cane.

"It is healing honey." He nodded to my cane. "Honey is good medicine. The best that there is."

"Is that a money back guarantee?"

"I did not hear you, Quinlan, what was that?"

"Never mind."

McRyan looked out at the forest. He hitched his thumbs in his suspenders. "I remember when this land belonged to my ancestors," he said. "During the days of the wild boar. The days of the Spanish. My mother was born right over there." He pointed his craggy finger to the pine trees behind Mother's house. "Mmm hmm, you have heard now, that it is so."

"Is that right?" I looked toward the trees in the distance, then dug the folded wad of money from my pocket. "And how much do I owe you for the honey today, Mister McRyan?"

"Oh no." He held up his hands. "I do not sell, I come only to trade, as I have done with your father, and as I have done with you in the past."

I knew he'd say that.

I still liked to offer him money just the same.

"Moonshine again?" I asked.

"If it is not any trouble, yes."

I smiled. "No trouble at all, I got plenty of shine. Wait here while I go fetch it."

He removed his hat, revealing his white hair. "I will wait for you."

I knew he'd say that, too.

I limped up our porch steps, leaning onto my cane, thinking about crazy, old McRyan. He'd been stopping by our house since I was a little boy. I wondered where on Earth he lived, or if his mother was anything like mine. It's funny how you can know people for a long time, but still know little about them. I wondered what he looked like as a young man; maybe strong like a warrior. Throughout his supposed two-century-long life, I'm sure his appearance had changed a little.

Emma Claire had changed, too. In fact, she changed a little more each day, her long bones kept getting thicker. She became heavier inside though her outside didn't seem to change much. She was still as lean and pretty as anything. She was just a bit taller.

She hardly saw Mother anymore. Occasionally, Emma would need something from Mother's house. She'd walk through the woods to Mother's, pop in, and then dart out as quick as a lizard. The two of them did not talk.

Never.

Emma would not even speak of Mother during conversation. Nor would she acknowledge Mother's name when it was spoken. It was as if Mother had been wiped from her memory.

Blotted out like a stain.

I tugged the string above my head, the pantry lightbulb lit the little room. I stood on my tip toes and rifled through the top shelves. I removed two jelly jars of moonshine hidden in the back then clicked the light off. I held one jar beneath my arm, hobbling with the cane, and moonshine in my hand.

I'd grown to love the taste of shine, the older I got. I remember hating the taste of it when I was a child, but I reckon tastes change as you get older. I much preferred shine to whiskey. God, I couldn't stand whiskey. I hated gin even worse. Gin tasted like sugar and turpentine to me. If forced to choose between the two, gin and whiskey, I'd choose kerosene.

When I walked through the den, I caught a glimpse of Emma Claire in her bedroom. She was lying on her bed, reading. Like she always did.

Emma Claire lived with us. In the new house. Most days, she stayed in her bedroom, which was on the other side of our home. She came out from time to time, to get something to eat, or to visit with Sonnet and me. But most of the time she was content to stay in her little hole. She'd stretch out on her bed, deep in her magazines, playing her radio. She seemed well adapted to her new life in our home.

But she wasn't the same girl.

She was harder now.

I tapped my cane on her door; she looked up and smiled at me.

"What's up?" I asked.

"Oh nothing, just reading."

"Don't read too much, it'll make your eyes go bad."

I sounded like a cracker if ever there was one.

I gimped down the porch steps and handed the jars of moonshine to McRyan. His weathered face lit up. The lines and wrinkles on his cheeks moved upward with his smile. His teeth, crooked and brown, looked like stained ivory.

If he wouldn't have been so old, he might've been ugly.

"I did not expect to receive two jars, Quinlan," he said. "This is a most pleasant gift." He walked to the rear of his carriage and lifted a canvas tarp. He dug again through his wooden crates. Beneath the bundles of leafy greens were four dead squirrels and two coons. "Please accept the squirrels and raccoons for the extra jar you have traded me."

"No, there's no need, Mister McRyan, it's just moonshine."

"I do not wish to make an unfair trade, Quinlan, it is not our way."

"No, Mister McRyan, don't worry about it."

"Please, Quinlan."

Well.

They were nice-looking coons.

"Okay, thank you, Mister McRyan." I reached and plucked the furry carcasses from the crate by the tails. "I suppose I'll have to make some coon stew tonight, now."

"And please take this as well." McRyan handed me a dark colored root vegetable that was about the size of my fist. "It is for the woman who carries a child in her belly."

I looked at him with furrowed eyebrows.

"Child?"

"Your Mother."

Stupefied, I wondered if McRyan was an Indian sage like he claimed he was. We had told no one in town about Mother's condition.

"How on earth could you know such a thing, Mister McRyan?" I asked.

He gazed toward Mother's clapboard house in the distance. There, on the porch stood Mother. She rubbed her big stomach, smoking a cigarette, watching us.

"My eyes are old," said McRyan. "But I can see her. She is a beautiful woman, her."

That's what most men thought.

I chuckled for a moment, safe in the knowledge that McRyan was still as crazy as a bare-assed ape. It was evident, Mother was very pregnant. She was getting plumper than any of us had ever seen her. Her neck was thicker, and her face more rounded. She'd begun walking with her spine bent backward, like she was growing a great anchor in her tummy. Still as lazy as ever, Mother spent her days reclining, with her feet propped up on a pillow.

Nothing new in that.

"Well, thank you, sir." I took the root vegetable from him. "I'll be sure to give it to her."

"See that you do." McRyan climbed onto his carriage and thwacked his horse with the reigns. His horse snorted and shook its head. McRyan paused and looked outward at the pines.

"This will all change again," he said. "And then it will change again as it has a century of times before." He waved his hand at the forest. "You will know it is so. You already know it is so."

"Yessir." I smiled at the sweet old lunatic.

McRyan tipped his hat to me. His rickety carriage bobbed down the driveway, and then out of sight.

I looked back at Mother who was standing on her porch. Sonnet stood next to her, waving her white arm at me.

I waved back to them.

It was a curious relationship, Sonnet and Mother. At first, Sonnet disliked my mother with a purple-puckered passion. Sonnet wasn't someone who was quick to forgive. And God knows Mother wasn't someone who was easy to wink at.

But soon, Sonnet's sympathy trumped her bitterness. She began to feel for Mother, living alone in that house, carrying a baby in her womb, without a soul in the world to care for her.

Such things were wrong.

No.

Such things were worse than wrong.

They were indecent.

Sonnet swallowed her distaste for my mother and began attending to her like a Hebrew slave. She spent more time at Mother's than she did at our own house. And she was a better Baptist for it.

She cooked Mother's rice and beans, her collards, her grits, and dusted Mother's furniture. She picked the weeds out of Mother's flower beds, mopped her dusty floorboards, and Sonnet complained about it every damned step of the way.

I didn't say she was a perfect Baptist.

Sonnet treated Mother like a four-year-old, scolding her at times, and Mother found it amusing. Well, it was amusing. Somehow, in spite of the odd circumstances, the two of them had forged a queer friendship. It puzzled me. It was a kinship that had no foundation other than Sonnet's tender heart.

People with tender hearts will befuddle you when given the chance.

I clomped into the kitchen, set the jar of dark honey on the counter, twisted the lid open, and dipped my pinky in it. It tasted like flowers and peaches. There aren't many things in life better than honey. Except fishing, and maybe morning cigarettes.

And making love.

A few things, but not many.

The phone rang in the hall like an angry bell. I walked to the hall, leaning on my cane, and I took the honey with me.

"Applewhite's residence."

I loved saying that.

"Hey," Sonnet's voice said. "Can you bring the salt over to your mother's?"

"Sure."

"Right now I mean, I need it for your Mother's butter beans, and the butter too, your mother's out of butter."

The phone company had installed phones in our two houses a few months earlier. One in Mother's and one in ours. The expensive phones changed everything in our lives. No longer did we hike over to Mother's to see if she needed anything.

"Quinn, are you still there?"

"Yes."

"I also need two onions, bring those too."

Phones. They were convenient, but I didn't care for them. I still wasn't accustomed to using them. They were awkward things, not designed for people with only one good ear. Sonnet and Mother did not share my problem. They talked every ten minutes on the thing, chatting about their daily routines. They peppered in healthy doses of gossip for good measure.

They loved hot-off-the-press gossip.

"Is that all?" I asked. "Butter, salt, and onions?"

"Yep, that's all I need."

I knew better than to believe her.

"Whoa, whoa, wait," said Sonnet. "Since you're on your way over here, bring the sugar. She's almost out of that, too."

"I can only carry so much with my one hand," I said, looking at the fish cane. "Remember?"

"Well I'm not asking for anything heavy."

Not yet she wasn't.

In the daytime, the phone in our hall would ring two short times signaling that Sonnet's friends, Mariah and Betty, were on the party-line. Sonnet would break her neck rushing to the little phone in the hallway. She'd leave the dishes soaking in the sink, and the bed torn apart unmade.

The phone was her idol. But I'd never have said it to her. Sonnet would've beat me into orange pulp if I'd suggested she was breaking the second commandment.

Or was it the first?

Thanks to the telephone, Sonnet knew every bit of gossip that went on in our town, even the meaningless stories no one cared about. She'd relate these tales to me almost every evening, with an animated and wild-eyed face. I think she liked retelling gossip stories more than she liked hearing about them.

Though I'm not entirely sure about that.

That April, Sonnet filled me in on every stitch of gossip between Saint Joe and Perry. She told me of Samuel Brown's affair with the hussy in Carrabelle. She told me about Susan Polle's new husband, who was richer than Jesus. About how he'd turned Susan into a spoiled wretch. Sonnet told me of Mister Slidell, who'd drowned himself while fishing in the bay one night, drunk as a whistle. Slidell always was bad to drink, it came as no surprise.

Sonnet also heard things about our family. Things about Emma Claire, about Mother. A lot about Mother. But Sonnet didn't ever tell me about such things.

"Okay," I spoke into the mouthpiece. "Butter, onions, salt, and sugar. That's it?"

There was silence on the other end of the line.

"Hold on, Quinn," Sonnet's tinny voice said. "Your mother's adding a few more things to the list."

These women were going to be the death of me.

"Okay, Quinn, get a pencil, there's more."

"How much more?"

"Are you writing it down?"

"No, I'll remember it."

"I think it's better if you write it down."

"Okay," I lied. "I have a pencil, go ahead."

"Here's the final list. We need butter, onions, salt, sugar, two eggs, flour, and some baking powder. Not baking soda, mind you, the baking powder," she drew out her vowels when she said it. "Also some garlic, vinegar, a few towels, one jar of scuppernong jelly, and bring a couple packs of cigarettes too."

I closed my eyes. "Is that it?"

"Yes." She paused for a moment. "No, hang on. Your mother is adding more to the list."

~

Mother sat on the bed with her hands on her stomach, rubbing them back and forth, like she was warming herself up from the cold. The damp heat in the room was enough to melt our faces off. It was a wet heat that you could feel all over your body. It crawled down your armpits, and into your pants, dripping down your ankles.

If I didn't love the humidity so much, I would've hated it.

"Which lightbulb needs changing?" I asked Mother.

"That one up there." Mother pointed to the light.

I opened the step ladder up into a pyramid, noticing that Mother's house was as spotless as it had ever been before. Sonnet was a ruthless housekeeper. No grain of dust went unpunished. Even the walls looked scrubbed clean.

"How's Emma Claire?" Mother asked.

I shrugged my shoulders. "She's about the same I guess. She doesn't say much."

The pregnancy had softened Mother, made her voice quieter.

"Does she still hate me?" Mother asked. "She has a right to hate me."

"Mother, I don't want to hear you talk that way."

"Well, it's true. She probably hates me, and this baby, too. But, I don't blame her, it's her right."

I unscrewed the lightbulb and tossed it onto Mother's bed.

"Quinn, would you have wanted me to get rid of the baby?"

I screwed the new lightbulb into the socket, and it popped with a quick flash.

"Dammit," I said.

"Oh, I'll get another one." Mother stirred in her bed, sitting up straight.

"No, no, I'll get it," I said. "Sit back down. You're pregnant."

"Well, you're no spring chicken, yourself."

"Me? I'm as good as ever."

I stepped down the ladder, my knee joints throbbing under the pressure. Regardless of my knees, ladders made me nervous. Mister Chadwick fell down a ladder one year earlier, and he was never the same afterward. After his accident, he wasn't even able to utter his own name, let alone change lightbulbs.

Mother handed me a fresh lightbulb. "Quinn, I want this baby to be loved."

"I know you do."

"Will you love it?"

"Of course I will."

Mother smiled.

"And you can bet your ass Sonnet will love it too."

We both laughed a little at that.

Then she tightened her face. "Do you think Emma Claire will ever come around to loving it?"

I did not answer, but let out a big lungful of air. There was absolutely no way to know for certain about that. Emma Claire was a mystery. To all of us.

"You're so quiet," Mother said. "What goes on in that mind of yours?"

"Nothing, really." I tapped my head with my cane. "Pretty empty up here, to tell you the truth."

"Well, you've always been quiet." She touched her belly and rubbed it. "I remember the day you were born, you were quiet then, too." Mother let out a giggle. "God, I was just a child back then, when I had you. Younger than Emma Claire is now. Can you imagine that?"

Yes I could.

"Oh," she said. "I was so excited to meet you. I named you Quinn before I even knew you were a boy. Long before."

"But, what if I'd been a girl?"

"Then I would have called you Mildred."

Thank the Lord I was a boy.

She looked out the window. "I couldn't sleep for months. I'd lay awake in bed next to my brothers, excited, before anyone else knew I was pregnant, I'd talk to you underneath my breath. I'd tell you about all my dreams, all the places I wanted to go."

Conversations like that must've taken half the night.

I sat down on the edge of her bed and looked at her, resting my chin on my cane. I wasn't about to interrupt her.

"You know," she said. "When I had you, it was the tallest moment in my life. I felt like I was a hundred-feet tall, like the Liberty Statue, like nothing could ever kill me. And you didn't make a noise, you never even cried."

"I didn't cry at all?"

"Not a lick," she laughed. "You looked like a stretched out bull frog with them long legs you got."

I tried not to smile, but it was true, I did bare a resemblance to a bullfrog. If bullfrogs ever sprouted pairs of ears, we'd be twins.

"How are your legs doing?" she asked.

I patted my thighs. "Getting better. Just weak, is all."

"That's good. Do you think you'll ever walk without that cane?"

"Oh sure, just need more time to heal."

She thought for a moment, she wasn't thinking about my legs. Neither was I.

"I'm not a very deserving person," she said. "God knows. But I don't want this baby growing up with the whole world hating it. How can I make sure that people don't hate this baby?"

I had no idea if such a thing was possible.

People in our town could be cruel.

"I just can't ruin another life, like I've ruined Emma Claire's." She paused. "Like I have yours. I've made a mess of everything. You both have every right to hate me."

I reached my brown hand out and laid it on her warm stomach.

I didn't hate anyone.

In fact, sometimes I felt as if I were the only person in the universe who understood my mother.

"Well?" she asked. "Say something. What do you think about all this?"

I thought for a moment, then smiled. "We're going to have a baby Applewhite loose in the house. That's what I think."

She gave me a weak grin.

A pregnant grin.

She knew I was right.

You can never have too many Applewhites running around.

~

The wind was as warm as hot syrup. The breeze whizzed past the trees on the shore, weaving through their limbs like it had somewhere to be. It whistled through the wheat-colored marshlands of pale grass, sweet smelling.

I rode along the water in my little white skiff, hugging the shore. I bought the new skiff from Captain Bilsham for seven dollars, though it wasn't really new. Bilsham had used it for years as a shore dinghy for his bigger boat.

Bilsham was a strange old man who sold fish in town sometimes and lived aboard a long sailboat. People said that he came from old money, and had gone batty when his wife left him for the traveling Methodist preacher, years ago. To me, Bilsham always smelled funny, like an amalgamation of skunk and cigars. I wasn't sure he ever bathed on that old boat.

Few people knew him. He wasn't a particularly sociable person; he could be downright mean sometimes. He moored himself behind our house during the spring months, making himself our neighbor. Whether we liked it or not. Then, he'd up and disappear for the rest of the year, sailing off to God-knows-where.

He didn't stay in any one place for long.

His little shore dinghy was a fine craft, about eight feet. The white paint I'd put on her made her look brand new to the untrained eye. I was proud, drifting along.

The skiff was the newest thing I'd ever owned. I was a cracker, and crackers rarely bought new things; it was a wasteful thing to do.

Secondhand things were just as good.

It's how we are.

I even bought my boots secondhand, from Mister Emmet, along with Emma Claire's saddle shoes. Mister Emmet took in everyone's old shoes and boots, put new soles on them, and then resold them for cheap. There was no telling who'd owned my boots before Mister Emmet got his hands on them. Maybe somebody rich.

God, I hope not.

I clutched my fishing rod in my left hand and dug a little blood-colored smoking pipe out of my trouser pocket. Daddy's pipe. It was one of the few things of his that I had remaining. All his belongings, trinkets, and clothes, had somehow gotten lost in the shuffle of life. I'd even lost his pocket knife somehow.

I never forgave myself for that.

I bit the pipe, resting it in the corner of my smile. I let the mouthpiece settle on my back teeth. It felt big and awkward in my mouth. I lit it with my lighter, and puffed on it, sending a wreath of violet smoke into the air. I took a long draw from it, breathing in the taste of the tobacco. When I did that, the hot smoke set my throat on fire, filling my chest with ash. I spit the pipe out, and doubled over, hacking soot from my lungs.

Thank God no one was around to see me.

The pipe fell into the bottom of the wood boat, still smoking like a campfire. I scooped a handful of river water in my hand, dousing it.

I was a bumbling moron.

I resolved to give up smoking for good.

Even cigarettes.

It's simpler than it sounds. Quitting smoking is easy.

I'd done it hundreds of times.

I looked at the blood-colored pipe and tried to remember Daddy's face. It was in that moment I realized nothing could revive my father's memory. Not even his pipe. He continued to disintegrate, and would soon fade from my memory completely. Like he'd never existed at all. Like a man who'd never even lived. It made me a little sad to think such a thing.

Just thinking about such things made me want a cigarette.

I stood in front of the kitchen counter, easing my weight onto the cane. Cooking with a walking stick was a one-handed ordeal. I dipped the hunks of fish into a bath of eggs and milk, then pressed them into a bowl of white flour. The black iron pan on the stove heating up over the flame. Hot grease in the pan made a popping noise that rang like a bell.

Sonnet and Mother marched up the porch steps, through the back of the kitchen, the screen door slapped behind them. Mother was wearing a wide-brimmed hat, the kind of hat ladies wear on Sundays, or to tea parties.

Or to funerals.

"Oh, boy," Sonnet said, smelling the food in the air. "What'd you catch today?"

"Thirty-one little pinfish," I said.

Mother laughed. "Must've been a bad day on the water if you're frying up baitfish for supper."

"It's not polite to make fun of the crippled," I said.

"You mean your ear or your legs?" Sonnet said.

My wife was hilarious.

"Well, I love pinfish," Sonnet said. "We ate them all the time growing up."

"I love 'em, too," I said. "I'd just love them a whole lot more if they were twelve inches longer."

Mother deflated into a chair and removed her large hat, fanning herself with it. She was breathless from pregnant exhaustion.

"So where were you two all day?" I asked.

"We went to the pictures," Sonnet said. "Your mother's never seen a picture show. Can you believe that?"

"I've seen a silent one," Mother interjected. "But it was so long ago, I barely remember it."

Sonnet plucked an apron from the pantry doorknob. She picked out two round white onions from a bowl, then lobbed off the ends with her knife. She could chop vegetables faster than a dog in heat.

"Oh, it was marvelous," Mother said. "I've always wanted to see Clark Gable in person. I've only ever read about him."

"Your mother's in love," Sonnet added.

"Who's Clark Gable?" I asked.

"An actor your mother likes."

"He's not just some actor," Mother corrected her. "He's the berries."

"Is it good to be the berries?" I asked.

"How would I know?" said Sonnet. "Your mother also ate all the damn peanuts. She didn't leave me nary a one."

Mother gave a mischievous grin.

I laid a hunk of fish into the hot grease. "I wondered where y'all took the truck off to. I was beginning to worry that y'all might've driven yourselves into the bay."

Sonnet punched my shoulder. "I'm not that bad of a driver."

Sonnet was a terrible driver. But I decided not to argue with a woman who was holding a knife.

"Well," Mother said. "She's a better driver than I am. I'm grateful to her. The picture show was everything I thought it would be. I owe her one."

One what?

Mother owed everyone something.

"You're welcome, Lyla," Sonnet said. "I'll add it to a long list of favors that you owe me." With that, Sonnet curtsied right there in the kitchen.

Mother smiled at her and saluted.

The two of them were absurd.

"You know," Mother explained. "The movie house wasn't even built when your daddy was alive, but your daddy would've never taken me anyway; he would've thought it a waste of money."

Everything was a waste of money to Dale Applewhite.

Even groceries.

"Carl never took me, either," Mother added. "Not ever. That good-for-nothing bastard."

"Oh, let's not talk about that fool," Sonnet said. "My daddy can't stand Mister Carl Plight, hates him ever since Carl cheated at cards when they were boys. Daddy hate's a cheat."

That was an understatement.

I'm surprised her daddy didn't slit old Carl's throat with a toothbrush.

"Hey, you two," Mother said. "Is there anything I can do to help with dinner you two?"

"You?" Sonnet laughed. "Since when do you help with anything?"

Sonnet made a pertinent point.

She turned to look at Mother. "Just hush now, try to relax. Sit right there and be lazy. When the baby's born, there's going to be plenty that you can do to help out."

"I feel like I've been so worthless lately," Mother said.

"Well." Sonnet raised an eyebrow. "I wish I could disagree with you."

Sonnet peeled away the skin from the onion and sliced it into fat rings. Then she wiped her teary eyes with the backs of her hands, sniffing her nose. Onions made Sonnet cry. Every single time.

"You know," Mother said. "I've heard that if you chew bubble gum while you're cutting onions, you won't cry at all."

Sonnet sniffed. "I've heard that too. Don't know if I believe it."

Mother began digging in her purse. "I think I have some gum."

Just then, Emma Claire's shape appeared in the doorway behind Mother. She clutched an armload of books in her arms. Her sharp eyes darted back and forth, watching us.

"Well," Emma Claire remarked. "I've heard that if you lick a piece of cold steel, it takes your tears away."

The room went silent for a moment.

"I've never heard that," Sonnet said.

"Hi, Emma Claire," Mother's chair creaked, she turned to look at Emma.

"I've also heard," Emma Claire said. "If you eat a mess of bay leaves while you're pregnant that your baby will die. You might consider that, Mother."

Sonnet slapped the knife onto the wood block and glared at Emma.

"Emma Claire," Sonnet said firmly, her pale complexion as red as an apple. "I'll not hear such talk in my own damn house. You'll get out of here with such disgusting language."

But Emma Claire was not sorry.

"Shoo, go on now." Sonnet waved her hands at Emma Claire. "Pay no attention to her, Lyla, she's only jealous we didn't invite her to the movies."

"Yes." Mother looked down at the table. "I'm sure that's it."

~

Emma Claire sat on the other side of the boat with a culling iron in her hands. She smacked the oysters with it, knocking the growths from their shells. The tapping sound reverberated over the cool water like a miniature Indian drum.

I scissored the huge tongs together looking out at the shore of the bay. A squirrel darted along one of the trees, running up the limbs. Someone's granddaddy in a previous life, no doubt. Someone's daddy. Maybe even an Apalachee boy, one of the same who'd inhabited this place long ago. I wondered for a moment if old McRyan was one of them, an ancient spirit lingering on, from an eroded world.

Then I chuckled to myself. That man was as crazy as a duck

looking for thunder.

"Where's Mullet today?" Emma Claire asked. "Why am I out here doing his stupid, boring job?"

"You're not doing his job," I said. "I'm the one who culls."

"Well, it's a boring job."

"Don't forget stupid."

She stared at me with a concerned look. "Hey, are you sure you're able lift those heavy tongs? I can do it if you need to take the weight off your knees."

"Naw, I'm fine," I grunted. "It's good for me to do it. Also, you're slow enough with that culling iron. If I were to let you work these tongs, we'd be out here until Jesus comes back."

She didn't laugh.

Emma Claire never laughed much anymore.

Her interest in things she once loved had waned. She cared little about the open water anymore. She was only helping me out of obligation.

I was a cripple.

"You know," I said. "This work isn't boring, or stupid, if you let your mind wander. It can be fun."

"But what if I don't know how to do that?" she asked. "What if one, such as myself, is a rather gregarious, loquacious?"

"Well, that's just unquestionable."

She rolled her eyes. "That's not how you use that word."

Damn. I was so close.

Emma Claire had changed. Inside and out. She was cooler than she used to be. Only one week earlier, Emma Claire had kicked one of the feral cats living beneath the porch, kicked it in the ribs. It shocked us. We didn't know what had come over her. The poor cat tried to wrap itself around Emma Claire's leg, it nearly made her stumble. Emma reacted by kicking it almost three feet into the air. The red cat's chest was damaged from the blow, and it broke my ever-loving heart.

Kicking is the worst form of violence that there is.

That's a fact.

After the incident, the cat laid there on the corner of our porch wheezing, curled up. Sonnet left a saucer of shredded fish and soft butter out for the cat, but it turned his nose up at the food. We were almost certain that it would die.

In contrast to Emma Claire, Sonnet loved the feral cats. She fed them every morning and evening without fail. And even though she claimed that she hated doing it, I knew better.

Sonnet was as soft as buttered grits inside.

It wasn't long before the cats adopted Sonnet as their new mother; they followed her wherever she went. She would stoop down and unwrap them from her white legs, talking to them in a high-pitched whisper. I suspected that hiding deep inside Sonnet was a frustrated momma waiting to be released.

"I need to tell you something." Emma Claire tossed an oyster into the water, and it made a splash. "Something important."

"Go ahead," I said. "Let me have it."

"I'm leaving."

I turned to look at her. "Leaving?"

"From here."

The tall girl sitting across from me did not smile. She just sat there. Her square shoulders folded down into her narrow waist. She was a female version of Daddy.

"Leaving?" I cocked my good ear toward her. "Where?"

"I've gotten a scholarship." She tapped the oyster with the iron. "They've let me enroll for the summer."

I shoved the tongs into the water, feeling for a bed of oysters below.

"College? Where?"

"The college is in Georgia," she said. "It's far. Really far."

Just the way she wanted it.

I lifted the tongs out of the water and spilled the oysters on the deck of the boat. Then I sat down on my haunches. My tailbone was still sore. Doctors told me it would take maybe a year to heal.

I suspected they were lying.

"I see," I said to Emma. "So you're gone already."

Emma Claire looked out across the water and set her culling iron down. She was silent, watching the wind move along the water, forming a million gray-green scallops on the surface.

"Yeah. But I'll miss you," she said.

I swallowed the lump in my throat. "I'll miss you, too."

"I don't want to leave, you know."

Liar.

I looked down at the deck of the boat. "I don't blame you, Emma."

"I'll miss this place."

Another lie.

I tossed a tiny oyster into the water. There was a paleness enveloping the world, and it wasn't the blanket of clouds. It was a change in the atmosphere. It seemed like the sun had never shined before, and would never shine again.

A pelican flew by us like a little airplane. He flew in a wide arcing motion, making grand circles above the water, before settling on top of an old branch. He looked like an Apalachee bird, if ever there was one. The Apalachee could talk to the animals. That's what I heard.

Old man McRyan spoke to the birds. I'd seen him do it before.

He talked to dead coons, and piles of cow droppings, too.

"Look on the bright side," she said. "I can always call you on the telephone."

"Or you could write me letters."

Emma Claire's dark eyes were as brown as creek water.

"Oh yes," she said. "I forget, you can read now, not quite as good as me, but yes, I'll write you every day if you want."

I smiled. She could be such a little brat when she wanted to me.

I loved that little brat.

~

The next month came and went in the blink of an eye. Like a warm rainstorm in the afternoons, the kind that only last for an hour or so. Those small storms rush up fast. They're tiny storm clouds; you can see blue skies on both sides of them.

There was food. Lots of food. Emma Claire ate well during her last weeks with us; I cooked all her favorite dishes. It was one of the ways I showed love. Biscuits and creamed corn. I prepared cheese grits by the barrel. I also made of coon stew, fried squirrel, and sweet potato casserole.

And of course, her favorite.

Blue crab.

By the boatload.

Those last few weeks I caught more blue crab than some men catch in a lifetime. I laid all five of my traps out in the bay and checked them twice a day. Mullet caught one of the Chaplain boys trying to steal crabs from one of my traps. Mullet was furious. When the Chaplains woke up the next morning, they found a dozen freshly-drilled holes in their boat.

Mullet didn't care to comment on the matter.

On the day of Emma Claire's graduation ceremony, Sonnet, Mother, Mullet, and I all attended. We showed up looking like a team of crackers wearing our Sunday best. I felt goofy dressed in Daddy's old clothes, bound up in a necktie. And I'm pretty sure I looked like it, too.

We all watched Emma Claire waltz through the gymnasium like a heron, graceful, self-assured. She was the tallest graduate in the senior class, a good three inches taller than the other girls.

Her square hat made her look even taller.

The hat looked ridiculous.

On the dreary morning Emma Claire boarded the bus to leave us. She was carrying my old tote sack. It was the sack that Mother made me for me when I was a boy. My initials had almost faded from the bag, but they were still legible.

The other girls on the bus carried leather suitcases, trimmed in bright stripes, with gold clasps. Their styled hair, and shiny saddle shoes, were different from Emma Claire's simple attire. They waved to their parents with energetic movements, giggling with one another like crickets. In their eyes, you could see that they were happier about the world than Emma Claire was.

They smiled more than she did.

A lot more.

Still, they weren't half as smart as she was. They were dull-witted girls; I could tell by the way they laughed. They were interested in other things. Boys, probably.

I stood on the sidewalk, slumped sideways on my cane, waving goodbye to the bus, watching it disappear down the street. It faded out of sight. I'd be lying if I said I didn't cry.

And just like that, the blue crab dinners stopped.

She was gone.

When I went home, I found our house felt like a tomb without Emma Claire's radio in the back room. Often I'd lie in bed with my eyes open, remembering her childish face. I remembered how Emma Claire used to flail her baby arms about when she slept as a toddler.

I remembered how she'd pounce through the back yard as a child, kicking pinecones into the bay. How she once loved her feral cats, before the darkness took hold of her.

I thought about how Emma Claire used to fish better than any boy ever could, how fearless she was, gutting them without hesitation. My memories of her were like faded photos, like enamel after years of abuse. Without her, our house felt bigger, like there was more air inside it. Like someone had left a window open.

I didn't want to eat any more blue crab for a while.

It didn't taste as good anymore.

At supper time, Sonnet, Mother, and I sat around the table, eating and talking to each other, trying not to look at the one empty seat.

~

Sonnet sat by the window in our bedroom, brushing her auburn hair with long, downward strokes. She looked into the vanity mirror at herself while she pulled the hairbrush.

The vanity dresser had been her grandmother's long ago. It was handmade by her grandfather, one of Sonnet's prized possessions. Built entirely out of red oak, it was as ugly as a stump full of spiders. I have no idea why she liked the horrid thing. Though I would've never made such a remark to Sonnet. Not even if someone threatened to cut off my ears with a spoon.

I pretended to like the dresser.

"'They are immortal,' I read aloud to her. "'All those stars both silvery and golden shall shine out again.'"

She glanced at me in her mirror. I lay on the bed, and held the little leather bound book underneath the lamp, using my finger to guide me along each verse.

Exactly the way Sonnet had taught me to.

"'They are great stars,'" I read. "'And the little ones shall shine out again, they endure.' I set the book down on my chest, and folded my hands behind my head. I looked at the ceiling. "I don't see how this poem has anything to do with the beach."

"It's symbolic."

"Is that a French thing?"

"No it's an allegorical."

"I've never tasted one of those before."

"You turtle-head." she stood up and inspected her figure in the mirror. "This poem is an easy one to understand."

"Speak for yourself, Frenchy."

"It's about how sadness won't triumph over happiness."

I thought for a moment. "You mean like good over evil?"

"Or hate over love."

I stared at the ceiling, observing the pale flatness of it. It was a lot like the cryptic poem, flat and meaningless.

"I don't know if I believe that or not," I said.

"You don't believe that love wins over hate?"

I shrugged. I wasn't so sure.

"But it's right there. The poet proves it, right in the poem."

"I don't think a poem can prove anything."

"If the poem's true, it proves everything."

"How do we know it's true?"

"Because it's Walt Whitman."

As if that meant anything to me.

"Don't you see?" she said. "He's pulling back the curtain of mystery, showing us the laws of nature, itself."

"I don't like laws."

Sonnet stood there with her head tilted at me. She put her hands on her graceful hips. I could see the rise and fall of her shape through her nightgown. Suddenly, I didn't care about the poem anymore.

"They aren't those kind of laws," she said.

I closed the book. "Like when they made alcohol illegal. Now there was a stupid law. Or illegal gambling, that's a dumb law, too.

"The poet's laying it out plainly," she said. "He's saying the nightly sky keeps changing, like everything else. He's telling us that the bad clouds will pull back and give way to clear skies, and in the same way, love triumphs over hate."

I nodded like I was still listening, but I was still thinking about her nightgown.

She smacked my thigh. "Don't you believe that?"

"I don't know. Maybe."

"How can you be so despondent?"

"I can't answer that."

"Why not?"

"Because I don't know what 'despondent' means."

I looked at Sonnet sitting on the edge of the bed. She was as innocent as rain water. She lived in a world where good was real, and where right was always the winner.

I sighed a big breath. "I believe that everything changes. That much I believe is true. I just don't know if I can believe that it's always for the better."

She turned and looked at me. "Well, you could believe it. If you weren't such a damn stick in the mud."

"Is that what despondent means?"

"Unquestionably."

Jesus, she was good.

The little wood phone in the hall vibrated, piercing through the evening like a tambourine. Sonnet rose from the bed and went to answer it.

"Hello?" I heard her say.

Then she fell silent.

"Okay," Sonnet said in a serious voice. "Stay right there and don't move." Sonnet slammed the phone down onto the cradle and then tossed my cane onto the bed.

The cane smacked me in the face.

"Hey, what gives?" I moaned.

"Your mother's having the baby."

15.

The sun cut through the windows of Mother's bedroom, filling it up with warmth. The beams of light shot through the dusty air and made the room look like a cloudy glass of water.

Mother lay on her bed, asleep while Sonnet stood near the window, rocking the baby in her arms. Sonnet hummed a melody too faint for me to hear, but it wasn't meant for me to hear anyway.

It was private.

Mother had a summer baby. And Sonnet's mother said summer babies were healthier than autumn babies, or winter babies. I suppose that's because of all the sunshine. She said babies born during such a season were free from the hateful grays of winter.

Mother named him Beau, which was short for beautiful; it was a name that Mother liked the sound of. Though I'm not sure why.

I hated the name.

Instead, we nicknamed him Pin because he was as small as a pinfish. He was nearly as feisty as one, too. Pin. It was a good, strong, cracker-name if ever there was one.

Pin was a gangly creature with knobby knees, and monkey elbows. The little patch of hair on his head was the blackest mess of fur I'd ever seen on a baby. He reached his lanky arms out, hands grasping, like he was going to grab the world by the throat and throw it into the bay if he ever caught it.

I hope he caught it one day.

I was still trying.

Mother's hand draped limp over her face as she slept. She was weak from birthing; she'd been in bed for almost two weeks. Sometimes I'd peek past her bedroom door open while she slept and watch her. Even though she was sick, she didn't wear the face of a woman punished. Mother looked satisfied. It was a look I'd never seen on her face before.

Not ever.

The doctor said Mother had a serious infection. He told us she would likely recover, but that Mother would be bad-tired for a while, that she'd sleep the days away. For several weeks on end, maybe.

He was right. It didn't matter how loud we spoke, or how heavy our steps were in the house, Mother slept through it all. Sonnet would help Mother out of bed to do her necessaries. Mother would shuffle down the hallway to use the bathroom like a ghost. The whole business would take fifteen minutes to complete. Then, Mother would lie in her bed, panting like an exhausted dog from the grand effort.

Pin became Sonnet's child during those first few weeks. He latched onto her like a catfish. It made her happy. Sonnet was never without little Pin in her arms, he fit right in the nook of her bosom, like he'd been tailored to her. She'd wander around the house with Pin in her clutches, talking to him in her whispering voice, or singing to him.

She never sang to me.

That was my fault, though. She'd tried singing once. When she did, I made a grave mistake. I laughed so hard at her shaky voice, that she gave me a black eye as compensation. No fooling. Sonnet socked me right in the face. I insisted that her behavior was a slight overreaction on her part.

She disagreed.

She never sang to me again.

But she would sing to Pin. And she would do it without a drop of hesitation. She loved Pin like her own. Sometimes, I'd find the two of them in the kitchen late at night. She'd rock him back and forth in the dark, resting in her clutches like a little bag of corn flour. They looked like they were having a deep conversation, one that didn't concern me. Because it didn't. She'd smile at Pin, and he'd return the favor by wrinkling up his button nose.

When Emma Claire called our house, I did not tell her about Pin, and she did not ask about him. I couldn't blame her, I guess. I knew she didn't want to know about the baby, or about the joy we all felt.

We were happier than we'd been in years.

Emma Claire was a world apart from us, all the way up in Cuthbert, Georgia, which might as well have been Sweden. So far away. It was as though Emma had resigned from our family altogether.

I watched Sonnet hold Pin near to her face, and bounce him up and down, singing to him in her silly voice. I recognized the song; she sang it in a whisper.

I dared not utter a word about that shaky voice of hers.

She looked at Pin with nothing but love. The black sin that brought Pin into our world had already vanished with the morning dew, and we remembered it no more. Mother's iniquity left no monument unto itself. It was long forgotten. All that remained was a beautiful white baby floating in its wake.

Everything in our sky had changed. The dark clouds of sadness had lifted from our lives. Like the poet said: the veil had lifted, and the stars shined again. And the stars had been up there all along, waiting behind the clouds. Waiting for the right moment.

Fickle little fellas.

That season came like the morning fog that hovers over the forest floor, broken up by the pegboard of tall pine trees. The kind of fog that drifts through the air like a floating bed linen and then vanishes as soon as the sun reaches out to touch it.

And so went the summer.

~

It was a wooden room, with more books than I'd ever seen in one place before. I've often wondered what someone does with that many books. It would've taken me three lifetimes to read through them all. The carved cases stretched from floor to ceiling, shooting upward like towers. The thick volumes were bigger than Sonnet's family Bible.

Sonnet's mother would read from that damned Bible in the evenings. And she'd read it aloud. I think Miss Rena enjoyed torturing us by doing that. She'd recite verse after verse, in the King's-English, boring us to half to death. I pleaded with God strike Rena mute sometimes. Whenever Rena would pause to clear her throat, I'd wonder if God had made good on my request.

He never did.

"I ain't never seen so many books in all my life," Mullet said, stroking his beard. "What a waste."

"Look." I pointed my cane upward. "Wonder who that is."

A white porcelain bust atop the shelf peered down at us with a knowing look. Flat eyes without pupils.

"Must be Moses," Mullet said. "Or Jesus, or Abraham."

"Actually, it's Brutus," the silver-haired man said, entering the office.

"I don't know that Bible character," Mullet said. "But he looks rowdy if you ask me."

"Oh yes, very rowdy. He was the life of the party in his day."

Some party.

He looked boring as hell to me.

"I'm sorry to have kept you gentlemen waiting." The man extended his hand to me.

"We were just admiring your books," said Mullet.

Mullet could be a sarcastic devil.

"Yes well, I haven't read most of them; I only have them around to impress people who wait in my office. It's important to make an impression with clients."

The man walked behind his desk and gestured for us to sit down.

"Please, gentlemen, sit," he said.

We did not sit.

The man ignored us and sat down behind his wooden desk. He removed a thick cigar from a gold leafed box, bit off the tip, and spit it into the garbage can.

"Cigar?" he offered.

"No thanks," I said. "We didn't come to visit, I'm here as a courtesy."

"Courtesy?" he raised his eyebrows.

"Yessir."

"To what do I owe this privilege?"

"Well, I'm sure, by now, you've heard people talking.…"

He thought for a moment. "No, I haven't. I don't think."

The words felt heavy in my throat, like the cement used to anchor buoys in the bay.

I held my hat in my hands. "Well sir, there's a lot of gossip going around about my mother."

"Gossip?" The man clicked his lighter open. "What gossip? And please, do sit down, you're worrying me standing like that."

We gave in and sat down in the uncomfortable wooden chairs. My tailbone cursed me for sitting on such a hard surface.

"I'm talking about my mother," I continued. "Lyla Applewhite."

The man shook his head, shrugging his shoulders.

He was a good pretender.

Better than I was.

I sighed. "Well, I suppose, if you don't know." I paused. "You see sir, your son, Scrubs, and my mother …."

The sliver haired man set his cigar down and leaned forward. "Are you about to tell me that story was true?"

I nodded.

The man leaned back into his chair. "Well then, that explains why you have a cane."

"Yessir." I hung my head.

I was awfully young to be using a cane.

He stared at me. "So it's all true? All of it? You had a spirited altercation over the incident?"

That was one way to put it.

"Yessir," I mumbled. "But you see, that's not why I'm here. That is, a few weeks ago my Mother had the baby and sh–"

"Baby?" The man shot forward.

"Yessir, a little boy."

"A little boy? My God. What are you implying?"

"A baby boy sir, that's what I'm saying."

He tapped the ash from his cigar. "Son, am I hearing you right?"

Either he was harder of hearing than I was, or I was stuttering.

The man stared at us, the muscles on his face tight. He stood up and folded his arms across his chest. Mullet looked over to me, we both shifted uneasy in our chairs.

"You must be plumb-crazy," the man finally said.

"Sir?" I tilted my good ear toward him.

"This is absurd. You don't think I know what this is about? You two are just after money."

Now I was the one who was hard of hearing.

Which I was.

"Look, son," the man said. "I'm sorry about your condition. About the fight. But you're barking up the wrong pine. I don't believe anything about a damned baby."

The man hitched his thumbs in his pockets and stared at me.

Rich people love to put crackers in their place.

It makes them feel rich.

"You slithering bastard." Mullet leapt to his feet. "Believe whatever the hell you want. We ain't asking you for nary a goddamn thing."

Mullet stepped closer to the silver-haired man. He was a foot shorter than the man. And twice as scrappy.

Mullet leaned his head in. "I know Quinn don't want me saying nothing we'll regret later, but I'm not scared of opening my mouth a little."

Mullet was never afraid to do that.

"Your boy almost murdered Quinn, here; he might carry that cane for the rest of his life." Mullet took a step forward. "In this here town, we cripple dirty fighters like your boy. You hear me?"

The man stepped back.

"You might not've ever heard about that law before," Mullet glanced toward the man's bookcase. "It ain't in those damn books you got over there, but it's a real law just the same. Ask any fisherman. He'll tell you as much."

"That's enough, Mullet," I interrupted, standing from my chair. "We're not here to make trouble, or to ask for any money, I only wanted you to know about the baby. It was a courtesy visit."

Mullet and I walked toward the door.

"Wait," the man called out. He drooped his head down, pinching the bridge of his nose. "Don't go. Please, gentlemen, just wait a moment. Please."

We turned to look him.

"I'm sorry," he said. "For how I've behaved. I haven't been myself lately."

Mullet was not about to forgive him.

"You see," the man said. "I thought you two already knew."

He looked at us for a response.

We gave none.

He sighed. "I thought you knew about my son."

Mullet and I exchanged looks.

The man ducked his head and began to sob right there. He wandered over to a black leather sofa and collapsed in it.

"My boy was killed," the man said. "Two weeks ago."

We were silent.

The man dried his cheek. "In action. His whole battalion. Gone."

The room grew heavy. I remembered Scrubs' brown boot slamming into my head. The way Sonnet threw pieces of gravel at him. They were things I wanted to forget.

"I had no idea," I said, removing my hat. "I'm sorry."

No sooner had I gotten the words out of my mouth than Mullet slapped my shoulder.

"Put your goddamn hat on, Quinn," Mullet said. "Serves the boy goddamn-right."

"Huh?" the man said.

"You heard me right, you rich, old buzzard," Mullet said. "That boy deserved to die for what he done. I ain't sorry. And neither is Quinn."

And then we left.

~

Sonnet stood in the kitchen with Pin in her arms, looking out the window over the sink. The two of them peered out the clear panes of glass at the gray clouds over the bay. She rocked Pin from side to side, balancing him against her shoulder, swaying to a rhythm that only she could hear. Pin's tiny legs dangled below him like pink sausages wrapped in knitted booties.

My bare feet creaked on the floorboards. I stood in the doorway eavesdropping on their conversation.

Sonnet turned to look at me and grinned.

"Hey, Uncle Quinn," she whispered.

I crept near to them. "How's my little fella?"

I grazed my finger on Pin's face, his white skin was soft to the touch. Like tender fat.

I love baby skin.

"Wave hello to Quinn," Sonnet said. "Wave hello to Brother Quinn."

She waved his little hand up and down at me.

But Pin wasn't about to be told what to do. He broke free from her grasp, reached out and gripped my thumb. He put it into his mouth, latching his gums on me like a calf does.

"I taste like oysters." I pulled my finger from his mouth, then wiped it on my shirt. "Old, stinky oysters."

I leaned forward and kissed Pin's cheek. He grinned like someone had goosed him. I nuzzled my cold nose onto his, looking into his big eyes. The little strands of his coal black hair peeked beneath his cap, like weeds in Mother's flowerbed.

"Tell Uncle Quinn what we had for lunch," Sonnet said.

Pin didn't even try.

He just looked at me with those surprised eyes.

Sonnet said, "We had peas, mashed green beans, and mashed carrots."

"Wow," I said. "Sounds like old Pin is eating better than the rest of us put together, all them fresh vegetables."

Pin flashed a brief smile, it was the same kind of toothless smile an old man has.

I hobbled over to the sink and held my hands underneath the faucet of warm water. The salty muck from the bay had stained my fingers with a foul odor impossible to wash away. I'd been a fisherman too long; the stench of the sea had worked its way into my body. Into my blood.

You can't wash things like that away.

Sonnet came behind me. She pecked a kiss onto the back of my sweaty neck and patted my back.

"Quinn," she said.

I dried my hands with a dishrag. "What is it?"

"The doctor came by today," she said, still rocking Pin side to side.

I tilted my good ear toward Sonnet. "Doctor?"

"Yes, he came by this morning." Sonnet tightened her lips. "Quinn, honey, it's not good."

~

I knocked on the door before walking into Mother's room.

The bedroom was dark, and the curtains were shut. Mother's face poked out of the covers. She lay on the bed, swathed in sheets, with a white face. Her jaw quivering. Pieces of her hair matted to her wet forehead like wild, twisted curls of gold.

I could feel her body heat from where I stood.

"Come in," she said.

I walked past the bed and flung the curtains open to let daylight into the dank room. It was something my daddy would've done. Daddy believed sunlight had the power to heal anything from scrapes to malaria. It had been his usual prescription for all sickness, ample exposure to the sun. It was a ridiculous notion, but it was bred into me, and you can't remove things like that from your mind.

"Jeezus, I need a cigarette," Mother said.

I reached into my shirt pocket to get her one.

"No, no." She waved me away. "I can't have any. Doctor said no cigarettes. But I'm craving one, real bad. I can taste it."

I knew the feeling.

She looked at my cane. "How's your knee?"

"Oh, fine." I slid the pack of cigarettes back into my pocket and sat down onto the edge of the bed. "Don't worry about me, I'll be just fine."

Her usual nervous energy was nowhere. Mother was as calm as bathwater.

"Doctor Wilks says I'm not doing well."

I put my hand on top of her hand and felt the hotness of it beneath my own. It liked to turn my stomach inside out.

"It's this infection," she said. "Can't get my fever to go down."

I didn't answer.

"He says it's getting worse," she whispered.

Worse.

It made my blood stop.

The woman in bed looked nothing like the girl who pitched a

baseball against the shed in our backyard. I remembered the songs she used to sing to herself while she sewed dresses in the den, drinking sugary tea. Sweet enough to make your jaw hurt. The woman in my memory was healthy, supple, and humming with life. This sick lady, draped in blankets, was too thin and drawn to be my mother.

"What can I do?" I asked.

"Nothing to be done," she coughed. "Maybe pray."

It was her attempt at a joke.

And it made me smile.

She knew we didn't pray, and she knew we didn't go to church. We never used the name God in a serious way. In that moment, I felt sorry for not being a churchgoer. Religion might've made our lives better, somehow, if we'd have only tried it. I wondered if churchgoers died happy. Maybe they did. With little smiles smeared on their blessed faces while the pastor read from the Psalms.

Hell with it.

I'd rather go to hell than die like that.

"Quinn," she said. "I'm so sorry."

A crystal tear rolled down her cheek. "Don't be sorry, Mother."

She patted my leg. "God, I'm so scared."

I'll bet she was.

Tears swelled in my eyes, making the world look watery and unstable. The warm droplets fell onto my shirt.

She flashed me another pained smile at me. "Christ, I want a cigarette so bad." She coughed again.

And I wanted nothing more than to give her one.

Instead, I just wiped my eyes with my sleeve.

Mother let her tired eyes fold shut, and her mouth fall open, slack-jawed. Her tiny neck stretched thin enough so that I could see the blue veins beneath her skin. She breathed slowly, and I could smell her awful breath. I pressed my face against her chest, listening to her heart thud against her delicate ribs.

I wondered how long it would keep doing that.

I used the cane to help myself stand up from the bed, she lay there, covered with a heap of sheets. The blankets mounded six inches high on top of her, to keep her warm.

She looked like a doe resting in the woods.

I let her sleep.

~

The loose, rickety truck groaned and snapped with each bump in the road. Daddy's truck was old, worn, not at all highway-worthy. It felt like it might fall apart at any given moment. Like it might shatter into a pile of a million bolts and springs right there on the shoulder of the road. But it was my vehicle.

I was lucky to have it.

Most crackers didn't even have electricity.

The landscape continued to change outside my windows like a kaleidoscope of lime greens. I leaned forward, and looked out the windshield at the blank sky, growing dark. Evening settled in on the world like a nesting dog. On the seat next to me was a folded paper map, marked with a red pencil. Red pencil-drawn lines shooting northward to Cuthbert.

Which is somewhere near Timbuktu.

Sonnet had outlined a path on the map for me to follow in case I got lost. But the map was more of a precaution, the route to Cuthbert was an easy one. All I had to do was look for the colorful road signs along the highway pasted with the number twenty-seven and follow them.

Easy enough that even a cracker could do it.

I looked over at the basket on the passenger seat. Sonnet had packed for me a thermos of coffee, some dried biscuits, a hunk of cheese, and five oranges.

And one jelly jar of moonshine.

In case I got lost.

As the miles piled up behind me, the black and white memories in my mind did too. I thought of Mother, and how different she was than the mothers of my youth. They all seemed like hags compared to mine. Their drab dresses, and thick stockings. My mother was hardly more than a teenager in those years. Still beautiful and crisp.

The other mothers resented her for it.

Mother hated them for resenting her.

They resented her for that too.

I had not been able to reach Emma Claire by phone before I'd left our town. No one at Emma's boarding house seemed to know where she was that day. The dreadful old woman on the other end of the line, Mrs. Fieldings, was suspicious when I called. I suppose she didn't much like males. Especially if they were calling on the phone. I told Mrs. Fieldings I was Emma Claire's father, that eased her suspicions a little.

But not completely.

The sun was dipping below the tree line, and the world became dark. The trees rocketed past me like black streaks pointing upward. Cuthbert was a long way north of Tallahassee, and I'd never traveled farther than that before. Not in my entire life. It was no wonder I had such poor geographical knowledge, I'd never crossed the state line. Not a single time. I'd never needed to travel past Tallahassee.

My friend, Rolly once visited his aunt in Atlanta, and he liked to have a heart attack from the experience. He said wandering around such a tall city, where there's no water in sight, almost suffocated him. He told me there were thousands of people, both white and black. They were all clumped together in one place walking in zig zag patterns downtown. Like they were the busiest people in the world

To make matters worse, they all talked fast.

Rolly talked as slow as a turtle eating peanut butter.

I wouldn't have lasted a minute in a place like that.

Cuthbert was a small city, but still, the idea of being in a foreign place terrified me. The further I drove from our town, the more unsettled I felt. I needed a sip of shine, is what I needed.

My wife must've known that.

And a sip is what I took.

I pulled the truck over on the side of the road, near a pasture, and limped out of the truck a hurry. I wobbled with the cane through the tall grass, to an old oak tree. There, I relieved my full bladder like a lathered horse.

Coffee and moonshine will do that to you.

I looked up at the sky. It was a deep violet color, scattered with bright white stars that clung to the night like fireflies in a jar. After relieving myself, I crawled back into my truck and threw the cane onto the dashboard. I nipped once more at the jar of shine before carrying on.

I sped down the highway like a fighter plane, following the markers on the road. They were hard to see in the dark. My one headlight lit the highway before me, and I cursed myself for not having replaced the busted lamp before I'd left.

I was in a hurry.

I'd left in such a blitz, I didn't even bother to check my radiator, or kick my tires. I would've forgotten my hat, too, if Sonnet wouldn't have brought it to me. The ten-gallon hat I'd once thought so atrocious, had grown on me. I wore it all the time. It'd become my trademark.

The kids in town all called me Hopalong Cassidy.

Hoppy for short.

In the distance, a little metal sign on the side of the road drew closer to me. It was faded and dented. I leaned forward and squinted my eyes through the darkness.

"Welcome to Cuthbert, Georgia," it read.

I smiled.

Long ago, I wouldn't have even been able to read that damn sign.

~

Mrs. Fieldings wore her hair in a tight gray bun snug behind her head. She refused to let me enter the boarding house. She was adamant about not letting anyone past the door who was not wearing a skirt or dress. So I sat on the little porch steps, spinning my cane in my hands, waiting for Emma Claire. My clothes had absorbed the Georgian humidity. I was a soggy mess. The thick sweat clung to my forehead like gravy.

There was no breeze to speak of.

Only flies.

I glanced behind me. The old woman watched me from behind the glass window, making sure I stayed in my designated spot on the porch.

I smiled and waved at her.

She did not smile back.

Women.

I watched the horseflies swarm around the bright porch light above me like restless little devils. A fly landed on the porch that was as big as an elephant's tooth. I would've killed him if I'd been back home. But I was only a visitor; the fly didn't belong to me.

The screeching noise of a vehicle pierced the silence. I could hear the engine's deep rumbling in my good ear. I turned to see a fine-looking red car pull alongside the sidewalk, polished so bright I could see my reflection in the panel.

A brown haired young man scurried out of the driver's seat, wearing tan saddle shoes and a bow tie. He jogged around the front of the car and opened up the passenger door of the vehicle. Emma Claire stepped out like a royal queen, dressed in a pink gown I'd never seen before. She walked like a lady. Her legs were long, and her shoulders were broad like Daddy's had once been.

She was his twin.

The boy hooked his arm around Emma Claire's. They walked side by side, clicking their shoes on the pavement. They held their heads erect, like a couple of young roosters.

She was marvelous.

"Quinn?" she said. "Is that you?"

I staggered to my feet, brushing off my dungarees.

She hurried toward me, galloping like a gazelle. We embraced. I held her closer than ever before and squeezed her.

Lord, how I'd missed that girl.

"What in God's name are you doing here?" Emma Claire released me.

The boy in the tweed jacket cleared his throat.

"Oh, I'm sorry," Emma Claire said. "How rude of me. Quinn, this is Spencer. Spencer, this is my brother Quinn."

Spencer leaned in and thrust his hand outward.

The boy had a firm handshake, and a few freckles on his face.

I trusted people with freckles.

"Glad to meet you, Spencer," I said. "I'm Quinn, Emma Claire's moderately ugly brother."

He did not laugh.

"Pleased to meet you, sir," he said.

He called me sir.

A good sign.

Emma Claire was finished with formalities. "Tell me what's up, Quinn. Why are you here like this?"

"Well, I tried to call, but no one knew where you were." I rubbed the back of my neck. "It's about Mother."

Emma Claire's face became hard.

"The truth is, Emma Claire, she's not well."

"What do you mean?"

"What I mean is, she's been sick."

"What?"

I shook my head. "Really sick."

"What does that mean?"

"It means we don't know how long she has." I shifted onto my cane. "We don't think she has much time. Doctor says it's bad."

Emma Claire brought her hand up over her mouth. "Oh Jesus-Jeremiah."

She sounded like a cracker when she said it.

Her big brown eyes glassed over. "I had no idea; I didn't know she was sick."

"Well, we didn't want to tell you, since you're so busy up here in Cuthbert, with school and all."

"Is this from the baby?"

I didn't know how to answer such a question. It felt strange to call Pin a baby, I'd grown to know him as just Pin.

Emma Claire thought for a moment. Then, she wiped the tears from her eyes. Her make-up made her look much older than she was.

She smoothed her hair, and finally said, "I'll run upstairs and get my things, and I'll be fast."

I believed her too.

Emma Claire never did anything slow.

~

Sonnet and I played with Pin on the front porch of Mother's house, bouncing him up and down. The pollen from the pine trees fell in huge yellow sheets blanketing everything in gold. The yellow pollen dusted the surfaces our whole world. The hood of my old truck, and every upturned leaf on the ground lay covered in it. It was a pale dust that clung to all things.

Even water.

Pollen is what happens when the pines make love.

And they do it without a hint of shame.

Some people were allergic to pollen. Deathly allergic. In fact, some folks were so allergic to the pollen that they had to stay inside all summer because of it. Suzie Connors used to stay trapped inside during the dog days and miss out on the fun. Poor Suzie. But her absence suited me just fine.

Suzie always was a little tattle-butt.

I was not allergic to pollen. Not at all. No one in my family was. We could've snorted a pile of the stuff and be just fine. Once, one of the Chaplain boys tried that very thing. He was a drunk as duck at the time. The pollen made him cough like dog for a whole day afterward.

Emma Claire was in Mother's back bedroom for several hours. When I'd peeked my head into the room to check on them, Emma Claire was sitting next to Mother's bed. She held her knees against her chest, talking in a soft voice. I didn't know what they talked about, whether it was good or bad. It wasn't any of my business.

They had a score to settle that dated back a long time.

Sonnet pinched Pin's white cheek, he erupted in a giggle.

"You think it'll rain?" Sonnet asked.

I glanced upward. The sky looked like rain, but I knew it was a false alarm. Real rain clouds didn't look quite so jittery. Real storm clouds looked fierce.

"Naw," I said. "Think it'll blow over."

"How do you know?"

"Easy. See those birds right there?"

"Yes."

"They wouldn't be there if it was going to rain."

She squinted her eyes at me, to see if I was lying or not, she knew how I liked to tease her.

"Really?" she asked.

"Hand to God."

She relaxed her face. "Well, that's interesting, I never knew that."

There's no way she could've known it.

Because I was teasing.

Sonnet handed Pin to me. I set him on my lap, bouncing him on my aching knee. His head bobbed from side to side like a rag doll. I remembered bouncing Emma Claire in the same way long ago. She loved to open her baby mouth and make noises of all kinds. Humming happy infant sounds. As a baby, Emma Claire loved the sound of her own voice more than anything.

I suppose not much had changed.

"What do you think they're talking about in there?" Sonnet asked.

I shrugged. "Lord knows. I hope good things."

Sonnet swiped her finger in the yellow dust on the porch. "I reckon they have a hundred years' worth of grievances to hash out."

"Reckon so."

"You know, Emma Claire seems so different now." Sonnet inspected the tip of her yellow finger. "She's changed, gotten older."

Emma Claire did seem older.

Tougher.

"Quinn," she asked. "Have I gotten older-looking?"

"You? Never."

She leaned back. "I feel older."

"Join the club, sister." I patted my bum knee.

She smiled. "Will you still love me when I'm old? When I'm gray?"

"Honey, I'll still love you when we're dead."

She liked that answer.

I looked down at Pin in my lap, his eyes had that same wildness Mother had, that same zip of electricity behind them. It was the same look that Emma Claire had long ago before she'd been overtaken by sadness.

Before she got older.

The screen door slapped shut, and Emma Claire's bare feet thumped on the porch behind us. She leaned against the post, and wiped her raw pink nose, sniffing. It wasn't the pollen that had her all stuffed up. She looked out at the forest and said nothing.

Her eyes were worn bloodshot.

"How's she doing?" Sonnet asked.

Emma Claire let out a breath that was strong enough to blow over a sailboat. "She seems weak. And she really, really wants a cigarette."

I handed Pin to Sonnet and stood onto my shaky legs.

"Where are you going?" Sonnet asked.

My eyes were getting bloodshot too.

"Dammit," I said. "I'm going to give that woman a cigarette."

16.

We all watched Pin leap up from his seat at the supper table and run to the front door with heavy feet. He galloped it the clumsy way that four-year-olds do. He moved so fast that it looked like he might fall face first onto the floor. But he somehow managed to keep himself upright.

Clever little man.

"Get back here, Pin." Sonnet snapped her fingers. "Finish your supper."

Pin turned to look at her.

"You do as I say," Sonnet said.

Pin did not move. He touched the knob of the front door and rested his hand there. He was taking his life into his own hands.

Sonnet came unglued.

"Did you hear what I said? Don't you dare, or I'll tan your little white ass with a wood spoon."

She would, too.

I'd seen it at least a million times.

Pin had a bad case of the touches. That's what Sonnet called them. She said that Pin had to touch everything he could get his grubby hands on. Once, Pin pitched a fit because he wanted to touch the red money box on top of the icebox. He would not rest until he could lay his white hands on it. So, Sonnet brought the box down for him to look at, and removed the lid for him.

Pin's eyes got as big as baseballs.

The box was filled with silver coins. Not a copper penny in the bunch. Sonnet's Daddy told her long ago that if she filled the tin box up with nickels and dimes, she'd have over one thousand and seven dollars. I'm not sure how they came by such a number. But that's what they said.

Throughout Sonnet's life, she found herself unable to leave the red box well enough alone.

The box was never in any danger of filling up.

Sonnet snapped her fingers again at Pin.

"She's not here yet, Pin, now I said get back here and finish your supper, or so help me…."

I always shuddered at what came after those words.

Something terrible, I'm sure.

Pin let go of the doorknob and walked back to the supper table with his head down.

"When's she coming?" Pin asked.

"Soon enough," Mrs. Rena interjected. "Now eat your supper like your momma said, Pin."

Rena was an expert with babies and toddlers. And Pin could sense Rena's confidence in matters of childrearing. Mrs. Rena knew what to do in every toddler-related circumstance, no matter what the situation was. She knew how to treat sick babies with pickle juice, and how to rub fresh pine sap on their chests when they had colds.

"Do you want any more milk, Pin?" Rena asked, holding the jug.

"Yep," he said.

"Yes what?"

"Yes, ma'am."

"Try again."

"Yes, please, ma'am."

Rena smiled, and Pin got his milk.

Mrs. Rena taught Sonnet many things. Like how to make cloth diapers out of old hominy sacks, or how to boil vegetables in sugar water so that Pin would eat them. And Sonnet heeded her mother. She boiled our carrots and peas in so much sugar, Pin couldn't get enough of them.

Neither could I.

Pin was a quiet boy, and I never heard him cry much. Sonnet said it was rare for him break down and sob like many children do. He was a sunny child, and curious as hell.

Sometimes Pin would ride on the oyster skiff with me during the days. He would watch the birds high step in the shallow marshes of the bay like slow soldiers. Most of the time Pin was as silent as a turtle on the water. But now and then he would get so overcome with giddiness that he would shout at the birds at the top of his lungs. Then he'd mope when they flew away.

I explained to him that birds didn't like to be shouted at.

He started whispering to the birds from then on.

"Would you look at that," Brother said to Pin. "Little Pin's eating a

Pinfish. Pin's eating a pin. I must be seeing double." Brother blinked his eyes. "Am I seeing double? I think I am."

Pin smiled at Brother, and the whole table smiled with him.

"It's me, Gandy," Pin said, raising his hands high up in the air.

Pin called Sonnet's father Gandy because it was the closest he could get to the word *granddaddy*. Brother liked the nickname, and often referred to himself as Gandy out in public.

It was Brother's honorary title.

We would never call him Brother again.

The other fellas in town all knew Brother was proud as a government mule regarding Pin; they'd roll their eyes whenever Brother started talking about Pin. But they never goaded Brother about such things, not to his face. It would've been indecent to do such a thing.

Brother carried Pin in his arms wherever he went.

He reached across the table and poked Pin in the shoulder.

"That's right," Brother said. "You're a little old pinfish."

Pin giggled. "I am not, Gandy."

"You are so."

"Am not."

"You are so."

"Y'all two hush," Rena said.

If Rena wouldn't have stopped their playful argument, it might've gone on until Pin was eighteen years old.

I watched Brother with Pin and remembered how my own daddy sat in the very chair that Brother occupied. Daddy was never as playful as Brother. Daddy was calm, eating his supper, quiet as a rock. Then, Daddy would pack his pipe with dark tobacco, and let the smoke waft around his head in big blue swirls. Sometimes he'd blow big O-rings into the air.

That was about as playful as he ever got.

After Mother died, we moved into Mother's old house and made our home there. The house I grew up in. I loved being there. It felt right. Sonnet's family moved into the white clapboard house across the way, the one Brother helped me build. It was the first time in Brother's life he didn't pay a dime to live somewhere. That man had paid rent every four weeks, without fail, since he was a boy living in Perry.

If anyone deserved a break from such things, it was Brother.

"Where are Crick and Blair tonight?" I asked.

"Good Lord," Brother said. "There ain't no telling with them two. Probably tearing up the roads, sniffing every female between here and Saint Joe."

"Reginald." Rena swatted Brother's shoulder. "You hush that kind of talk in front of Pin, hush it right now."

I tried not to let Rena see me laugh.

She did.

And she gave me the stink-eye for it.

At night, Sonnet and I slept in Mother's old room. Pin took over my old room at the end of the hall. Sometimes, when he was sleeping in my old bed he looked a little like Emma Claire did when she used to sleep there. Sprawled out like dead wood, sleeping harder that I could myself.

Sleeping as hard as mother once slept.

The whole house reminded me of Mother, and I could smell her scent in every room. It was as though she were waiting behind the open doors, lurking to surprise me.

Like she used to do when I was a boy.

Earlier that day, underneath a loose floorboard in Mother's closet, I'd found a shoebox covered in thick dust. Inside the box were magazine clippings of black and white movie stars. A whole pile of cutout photos of glamorous women in big dresses and dashing young shirtless men. I found a post card with a picture of Ireland on it, and a red colored photograph of the Grand Canyon.

That woman was nothing if not a dreamer.

And she never visited any of the places she wanted to.

Also in the shoebox was a curious collection of love notes written by a man named Percy, who I'd never heard of. The sloppy cursive letters revealed he was smitten with my young mother. They read like the voices of melodramatic children, whining. Percy wrote that he'd rather die than not be in my mother's arms. And in another letter, Percy threatened to kill himself if Mother didn't run away with him to Columbus.

I wondered where Percy was, what he was like.

He must've been different than my daddy.

When I finished pilfering through her box, I placed the lid on it, and tucked it back beneath the floorboard. I had no intentions of ever moving it.

Not ever.

Hidden in the house were many things belonging to Mother. I found Mother's old coffee mug in the back of the cabinet, filled with money. I found a dusty pulp magazine fallen behind her dresser. She loved romance stories. I found a little box of chocolates that had melted beneath her bed, half eaten. I also found a pack of Chesterfields buried in the back of a drawer in the kitchen, wrapped up in an old dish towel. I smoked one. Then I wrapped the package of cigarettes up in the rag and hid it again.

They would always be hers.

There was a knock at the door, and we all looked up from our plates. Pin leapt off his seat again and ran to the front of the house like his pants were on fire.

"She's here!" Pin shouted in a voice loud enough to wake the fish.

I rose from the table and shuffled to the front door, clicking my cane on the wood floor. Pin led the way for me. I could see her through the front window, standing there on the porch in the darkness. That familiar long, dark hair.

Two big cow eyes blinking back at me.

I opened the door, and Pin shot toward her like a bullet. She squatted down and swept him up into her arms, swinging him in a circle.

"Emma Kare," Pin shouted.

~

Emma Claire wore a long white gown that came all the way down to the floor. It was a beautiful dress that our mother would've killed to have–if she'd been alive.

The nicest dresses my mother ever owned were the ones that she made herself from bolts of discounted fabric. They were pretty dresses, and she was proud of them. But they weren't gowns. She never had a reason to wear such a thing.

Much to Mother's disappointment.

I rested my chin on my cane, looking at a framed picture of Jesus on the wall of the dressing room. He was sitting in a field with several sheep gathered around him, wearing a queer look on his face. I didn't much care for Jesus. He never did much for me. Out of all the Bible characters, I was sure I liked Lady Eve the best.

She was misunderstood.

"Do you like your suit?" Emma Claire asked.

"Oh, it's just dandy."

"Really?"

"Unquestionably."

"Stop it. It was an expensive suit."

"The suit's fine," I said straightening my tie. "Appropriate for a church. Or for a funeral."

"Quit being daft, I think you look good in it."

I looked like a circus goat.

The truth was, I felt uncomfortable in churches. I didn't hate them. But they felt confining to me. The white paneling of the chapel only closed out the towering pines and serene water outside. The interior of the church, no matter how holy, was no match for the forest, or the river. I was inclined to agree with the ancient Indians. The forest was chapel enough for me.

Emma Claire straightened my jacket collar, making sure it was just so. The necktie was cutting off the circulation to my face.

"I don't mean any disrespect, Emma," I said. "But I've got to ask it."

"Ask what?"

"Ask you if you're you sure about this. You don't have to go through with it you know."

"With what?"

"Everything, the wedding."

She smiled at me. "I'm very sure about it, you can stop worrying now."

Not a chance.

"Spencer seems like a good man," I said. "Don't misunderstand me, but I just want you to be smart about this. You don't have to do anything you're not ready to do."

"What I want is for you not to worry about me today. Just for one day, can you do that?"

"I'm not worrying, I'm only doing what brothers do."

She shook her head. "No, you're doing what pessimists do."

"You mean the jokers who invaded Russia?"

"I'm surprised you even know about that."

I was smarter than the average cracker.

Emma Claire leaned forward and embraced me. I couldn't tell who she reminded me of in that moment.

Mother or Daddy.

She wouldn't have known which parent she took after anyway. Emma Claire told me once that she was unable to remember anything about Daddy, not even the way he looked. That meant she had no idea how much she resembled him, or how much she acted like him. But she was his twin. In fact, most everything she did reminded me of him.

Emma Claire leaned forward. "I'll be fine," Emma said into my good ear so that I could hear her.

I did not answer her.

Neither was I sure she was right.

God, how she looked like my daddy.

The only images Emma knew of Daddy were from the strip of carnival photographs Mother had in her dresser. It was a skinny strip of black and white photos that showed a young man's serious face staring at the camera. He was as skinny as a reed. His big serious eyes looked like they might've popped right off of his face.

"Spencer's a good man," Emma Claire assured me.

"I'm sure he is."

"He is."

"I believe you."

"No you don't."

I was a terrible liar.

Emma Claire sat down on the wood bench, crossing her legs. Her bouquet was one that Sonnet had made for her. I had no idea how Sonnet learned to make bouquets.

"Spencer kind of reminds me of you," Emma Claire said.

"Well, that's generous of you," I said. "But I'm a cracker, and that's a far cry from being a doctor."

"You're not a cracker."

"I hate to break it to you Emma, but we both are."

"We are not."

"I promise I won't tell Spencer."

"I'm not a cracker."

She said it like she meant it.

"Emma Claire, I'm sure he's figured it out by now."

I sat down next to her and exhaled. My suit was about to choke me to death, and I was overdue for a cigarette. I hated suits. I didn't even wear one to my own wedding. The only time I ever cared to wear a suit was at my funeral.

"Oh, Quinn." she stood up and walked over to stained glass window.

I shook my head. "What is it?"

"Mother and me."

"Huh?"

"We were both horrible. Selfish."

I shifted in my seat. "Hush, now, it's your wedding day Emma Claire."

But she wasn't finished.

"Sometimes, I'm not sure who was worse, Mother or me." She touched the stained glass, running her fingers along the lines between the colors. "You know, I hated her."

I leaned against the wall. "I know."

It was no secret.

"I hated her for a long time. Long before she–" Emma grew silent. "Well, you know, before she did what she did."

I knew what Emma was talking about.

Very well.

"Do you hate her still?" I asked.

"No, I miss her." Emma Claire's eyes became heavy with tears. "If you can believe that. Now that she's dead, I realize how much I loved her."

It was the first time I'd ever heard Emma Claire speak in such a way about her own mother. It made my heart heavy.

"I miss her, too," I said.

Emma Claire dabbed her eyelids with a lacy handkerchief. Her profile was like a long-necked bird against the bright glass window of the dressing room.

There came a light rapping from the wood door of the room.

"You two ready?" Rena asked, poking in her head. "Because it's time."

Emma Claire walked over to me, and I stood up with the help of my cane. She hooked her arm around mine and squeezed it. I looked at her, there by my side. I remembered the girl who wandered through the backyard in stained clothes. The girl with a trail of feral cats following behind her. The child with skinned up knees. I couldn't tell whether my sadness was the happy kind, or if my happiness was the sad kind.

Maybe a little of both.

Emma straightened her veil in the mirror. "Yes, we're ready."

She drew in a breath through pursed lips, and it made me smile to see her so damned nervous.

"What about you?" she asked me. "How're you, Quinn?"

I adjusted my weight onto the cane and looked at my ugly face in the mirror. My ears were large and pink, and my nose looked like the fat snout of a pig.

"Well." I exhaled a big breath. "I am of old and young."

She furrowed her eyebrows. "Huh?"

"I am of the foolish as much as the wise," I said. "'Regardless of the others, ever regardful of the others, maternal as well as paternal, a child as well as a man.'"

"What are you talking about?"

"Walt Whitman."

The piano in the church began to play the pounding familiar melody that accompanies love and tuxedos. I could hear the people in the congregation stand to their feet like a herd of cattle. The thick chapel doors swung open. A hundred smiling faces glared back at us.

"You and that stupid poetry." Emma Claire rolled her eyes. "I have no idea what in the hell you just said."

~

Emma Claire's new in-laws owned a sprawling home positioned right on the Gulf, out past Carrabelle. It was the biggest thing I'd ever seen. It almost made me dizzy to look at. Their massive home was a wooden marvel. It reached toward the sky with a gabled roofline, cedar shingles, and tall paned windows.

It must've taken a century to build.

Spencer's father had hired a brass band from Tallahassee to play for the dinner guests. The band arranged themselves on a small stage that faced the Gulf. They played fast paced colored-jazz for a slew of eager dancers in nice clothes.

Strings of glowing lights draped over the flat pinewood dance floor. They lit up yellow and orange, like big fireflies on a telephone wire. Sonnet wanted to dance, but I was a cripple, and neither of us knew how we would've managed such a thing.

So we didn't.

The truth was, Sonnet only knew how to buck dance anyhow. Buck dancing wasn't done on dance floors, but around campfires, with corn liquor. Sometimes, Sonnet would hike up her skirt and buck dance in the kitchen, just to remind herself she could still do it. Pin would clap his hands watching her, and I'd laugh while she pounded her heels on the floorboards.

She was the prettiest cracker you ever saw.

I took a sip of my whiskey and winced at the flavor.

It tasted like sweetened outhouse water.

I watched Emma Claire out on the floor with her arms wrapped around Spencer. She knew how to dance. I wasn't sure how she'd learned. Her feet moved with the rhythms of the music like pistons in a straight engine, deliberate and smooth. She and Spencer weaved beneath the lights, all the other dancers all grinned at them.

It was her night.

She deserved the grins.

The dinner guests clapped their hands at the end of each song, and the horn players took grand bows on the stage. They looked like happy musicians. I often wondered what it would be like to play an instrument. I'd always wanted to learn to play the trumpet. It looked like a fun instrument to play.

I once saw a visiting soldier play the trumpet down at Norma's. His face turned as red as a strawberry, and his cheeks looked like they might pop. He played jazz, and it sounded like he was having a real time. But crackers didn't play the trumpet. The banjo, or the fiddle maybe. Never the trumpet.

You couldn't sing along with a trumpet.

I was never one to toot my own horn, anyhow.

I set my glass down and wandered from the crowd. I stabbed my cane on the sand, walking and out toward the restless Gulf. The gray, weathered pier that jutted out into the waves looked like it went on for miles into the night. The wind whipped around me. It made me cold. I looked at the water, spreading itself outward like a dark, wooly blanket. The incoming tide beat upon itself, crashing with white foamy slaps onto the sand.

Mother.

I wondered where her soul had gone off to, or if she'd revisited earth as an animal, like Daddy suggested. It was a foolish notion, but I'd grown to embrace it through the years. It was one of the last things of my daddy's that I owned.

His beliefs.

I felt a dull thudding on the wooden planks of the pier behind me. I turned to see Sonnet walking toward me, carrying two glasses in her hands, and her shoes tucked beneath her arms. I recognized her wide-skirted green dress as one of Mother's old ones.

The green one with white flowers.

The fabric swayed back and forth against Sonnet's shins like a lime flag in the night breeze. I'd seen that dress a hundred times before. Maybe two hundred times. I remembered Mother wearing it long ago. I remembered when Mother first made the dress.

God, how she loved to make dresses.

Sonnet handed me a drink. Her lips moved, but I could not hear her, the wind was too strong. That, and I was getting more deaf every day.

I took the cold glass and sipped from it.

It tasted God-awful. Like bitter licorice and lemons.

"It's horrible, isn't it?" she said.

"Terrible," I said. "I thought fancy liquor was supposed to taste good. This tastes awful. I'd rather have some shine."

She took a sip. "I reckon it's all a matter of what you're used to drinking."

I took another drink. Its warmth traveled down my throat.

"What are you doing out here by yourself?" she asked.

I shrugged. "Thinking, I guess."

I looked again at the water. I thought about Pin, about how he sometimes romped in the backyard. That boy wandered. He'd play near the bay, on the soft ground, marching like a soldier. How the cats loved to creep behind him in a line. It reminded me of a younger version of

Emma Claire. Though Pin didn't look like Emma. No.

Pin looked like Mother.

A little more every day.

Sonnet and I would gang up on Pin and tickle the life out of him while he lay on his bed. He'd laugh until he almost choked to death. He sounded just like Mother. Then, Sonnet would sweep him up in her arms, tuck his head into the hollow of her shoulder, and sing a made up song to him.

I suspected Pin felt the same about Sonnet's singing voice as I did. I needed to warn him about her. I decided that I would tell him the story about my black eye.

For his own protection.

"You miss her?" Sonnet asked, laying her hand on my shoulder.

I loosened my tie and took another sip. "I do."

"Yeah." she nodded. "I do too."

"Especially tonight. She should've been here."

"I know."

"She would've loved it."

Sonnet gave a half smile.

It was true. I missed Mother. I missed all the trouble she made for me. I missed her sassy attitude, even her selfishness. Mother was a woman who launched out too soon. Like a young girl dangling on the rope swing by the creek, jumping into the water too early.

That was never a smart thing to do.

I speak from experience.

My mother had surrendered her youth early on and exchanged it for my well-worn father. She'd become stunted. She never grew up, not all the way. The fifteen-year-old girl made a mess of our lives, and hers. Though, I don't believe she meant to, I believe she did the best she was able to do with herself.

And with us.

Whether it was true or not, I believed.

And I believed it because I wanted to.

That's the way things work sometimes.

You believe what you want to, so that you can make it through. And you do make it through. Somehow.

Sonnet leaned her head into my chest. "I miss her spirit. It was one of a kind."

I exhaled in agreement.

My mother's spirit was one of a kind.

Few could see my mother, who she really was. The men in town only saw her small waist and round hips, their wives saw her scandalous beauty. My father saw her irrational youth, and he loved her for it. Emma Claire saw her bleak failures, and she hated her for them. But beneath the exterior of my mother, just a few layers below her sticky selfishness, I knew her essence. And I knew her. She was beauty and sadness. All wrapped up into one person.

My mother was good and bad.

Beautiful to a fault, and fidgety as a flea.

Both righteous and selfish.

Hot and cold.

She was Lyla.

ABOUT THE AUTHOR

Sean Dietrich is a columnist, humorist, and novelist, known for his commentary on life in the American South. His columns have appeared in *South Magazine,* the *Bitter Southerner, Thom Magazine, Tallahassee Democrat,* and he has authored six books and three novels.

An avid sailor and fisherman, when he's not writing, he spends much of his time aboard his sailboat *(The S.S. Squirrel),* along with his coonhound, Ellie Mae.

Made in United States
Orlando, FL
06 February 2023

29597140R00133